Cause for Scandal
by Anna DePalo

ᛒ ᚷ ᛈ ᚲ

From the Diary of Maeve Elliott

Ever since birth, my twin granddaughters, Summer and Scarlet, have been total opposites. Scarlet is a whirlwind, a blur of colour and energy with a wild side. And then there's sensible Summer, who has never given me a sleepless night. Until now.

The tabloid photo caused quite a stir. After all, we least expected it from her. She knows well the demands that come with being an Elliott. But life, as Summer and I know, doesn't always go according to plan.

Her Zeke is charming and sweet and – I'm not too old to notice – very handsome. Beyond that, he and Summer are nothing alike. But that's what my parents said about me and Patrick – fifty-seven years ago. No, Summer is changing, searching…and for the first time I see a sparkle in her Irish-green eyes. Could it be love?

The Forbidden Twin
by Susan Crosby

ꙨꞋꝏꙐꞋ

From the Diary of Maeve Elliott

Since she was a wee child, my granddaughter Scarlet has been surrounded by whirling wind. The spirit, as we say, runs high in that one. But even someone as wild as the Irish coast has her soft side. I see it in her.

I also see wistfulness. Perhaps it comes from her missing the other half of herself – her twin, Summer. While Summer has found her love and is trailing him around the world, Scarlet has been left alone for the first time in her life. She needs to find a husband who will treasure her.

I pray the man Scarlet chooses will be up to the test – and up to standard. After all, there's nothing more important than family...

Cause for Scandal
ANNA DePALO

The Forbidden Twin
SUSAN CROSBY

MILLS & BOON®

Desire™

*First published in Great Britain 2007
Harlequin Mills & Boon Limited,
Eton House, 18-24 Paradise Road, Richmond, Surrey TW9 1SR*

The publisher acknowledges the copyright holders of the
individual works as follows:

Cause for Scandal © Harlequin Books S.A. 2006
The Forbidden Twin © Harlequin Books S.A. 2006

*Special thanks and acknowledgement are given to Anna DePalo
and Susan Crosby for their contribution to THE ELLIOTTS series.*

ISBN: 978 0 263 85011 6

51-0307

*Printed and bound in Spain
by Litografía Rosés S.A., Barcelona*

CAUSE FOR SCANDAL
by
Anna DePalo

For Amy Liu and Gloria Miller,
two friends that I couldn't do without.

ANNA DePALO

A lifelong book lover, Anna discovered that she was a writer at heart when she realised that not everyone travels around with a full cast of characters in their head. She has lived in Italy and England, learned to speak French, graduated from Harvard, earned graduate degrees in political science and law, forgotten how to speak French and married her own dashing hero.

Anna has been an intellectual-property lawyer in New York City. She loves travelling, reading, writing, old movies, chocolate and Italian (which she hasn't forgotten how to speak, thanks to her extended Italian family). Readers are invited to surf to www.desireauthors.com and can also visit her at www.annadepalo.com.

THE ELLIOTS

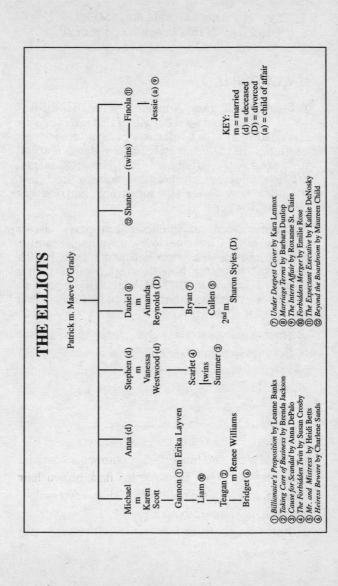

Patrick m. Maeve O'Grady

Michael
m
Karen
Scott

Anna (d)

Gannon ① m Erika Layyen

Liam ⑩

Teagan ②
m Renee Williams

Bridget ⑥

Stephen (d)
m
Vanessa
Westwood (d)

Scarlet ④
⎱ twins
Summer ③

Daniel ⑧
m
Amanda
Reynolds (D)

Bryan ⑦

Cullen ⑤

2nd m
Sharon Styles (D)

② Shane ── (twins)

Finola ⑪

Jessie (a) ⑨

KEY:
m = married
(d) = deceased
(D) = divorced
(a) = child of affair

① *Billionaire's Proposition* by Leanne Banks
② *Taking Care of Business* by Brenda Jackson
③ *Cause for Scandal* by Anna DePalo
④ *The Forbidden Twin* by Susan Crosby
⑤ *Mr. and Mistress* by Heidi Betts
⑥ *Heiress Beware* by Charlene Sands
⑦ *Under Deepest Cover* by Kara Lennox
⑧ *Marriage Terms* by Barbara Dunlop
⑨ *The Intern Affair* by Roxanne St. Claire
⑩ *Forbidden Merger* by Emilie Rose
⑪ *The Expectant Executive* by Kathie DeNosky
⑫ *Beyond the Boardroom* by Maureen Child

One

She needed this interview. Her career depended on it. Her *plan* depended on it. And, as far as she could see, all that stood in her way were a few burly security guards, her lack of a backstage pass and close to twenty thousand shrieking Zeke Woodlow fans.

Summer looked at Zeke on stage. Even from her seat twelve rows back, his charisma was palpable. His blue jeans and black T-shirt outlined a lean and muscular physique. He wore his dark-brown hair longish, touching the collar of his shirt, and tousled, emphasizing his bad-boy image.

It was his gorgeous face, however, that really got

his fans going. Summer itched to capture that arresting face with her camera.

Just then Zeke seemed to look right at her, and Summer held her breath. The connection lasted just an instant, but she felt his intensity down to the tips of her toes.

She only expelled a breath when he looked away.

No doubt about it. Zeke Woodlow's sex appeal was potent.

Not that he was her type, of course.

She looked down at the round, two-carat, brilliant-cut diamond engagement ring on her hand.

Not at all.

As she was again jostled by fans, she bit back a sigh of impatience and looked around.

Madison Square Garden. One of New York City's premier venues. Host to political conventions, site for countless sporting events and witness to history. Frank Sinatra, Elvis Presley, The Rolling Stones, Elton John, Bruce Springsteen...and now Zeke Woodlow—Grammy winner, rock sensation and current "it" boy of the music world, whose latest CD, *Falling For You,* had gone diamond, selling over ten million copies.

Summer had all the vital information on Zeke. She knew that he'd grown up in New York but now lived in a Beverly Hills mansion, that he'd become famous for his sexy lyrics and that he'd helped start

Musicians for a Cure, which had led to his headlining a Madison Square Garden concert series to benefit cancer research.

But, while she had all the facts, she didn't have access, and unfortunately she had her heart set on getting an interview with Zeke for *The Buzz*. She'd been thinking for months about how to win a promotion at work. Her paternal grandfather, Patrick Elliott, believed even relatives had to work their way up within the family publishing empire.

So, when she'd come home one day and spotted an advertisement for Musicians for a Cure among her mail, she knew she'd found her ticket to moving up from lowly copy editor to trusted reporter. An interview with Zeke Woodlow would be just right for *The Buzz*, which was locked in a fierce battle not only with its closest rival in format, *Entertainment Weekly*, but also with other Elliott magazines. Patrick Elliott had declared that the head of whichever magazine in the family empire was the most profitable by the end of the year would become the new CEO of EPH—Elliott Publication Holdings—when he stepped down.

Now, clutching her notepad and pen, she shifted from one foot to the other. She'd come to the concert straight from work and she felt uncomfortable. Her toes in her chunky-heeled boots had been stepped on more times than she could count. Her pinstriped pants were perfect for the office but were too warm and out of place among a sea of jeans. Her turtleneck felt similarly tight and hot in the heat generated by thousands of swaying, dancing, jiggling bodies.

Around her, the audience seemed to move like a wave, swaying toward the stage and back, caressing the outer perimeter of Zeke Woodlow's spotlight.

Because she was just a copy editor, she knew Zeke's publicist would have laughed in her face if she'd asked for an exclusive interview. But she hoped if she got close to Zeke himself, she could convince him to talk to her. After all, she was ambitious, articulate and musically aware, and she worked for *The Buzz*—even if her position didn't qualify her for a backstage press pass.

When Zeke finished the song he was singing, the crowd went wild. He joked with the audience, his sexy voice filling the arena and dancing across her skin like an intimate caress.

"More?" he asked, his voice deep and smooth as silk, teasing the crowd.

The audience hooted and hollered in response.

"I can't hear you," he said, cupping his hand to his ear.

The crowd roared.

"All right!" Zeke motioned to the band behind him, then slung the strap of an electric guitar over his shoulder. The music struck up, and Zeke started crooning one of his biggest hits, a ballad called "Beautiful in My Arms."

As he sang about making love beneath waving palm trees, with the humid night air pressing around, Summer felt herself being seduced right along with the rest of the crowd, lulled into a magical moment. Only when the song faded away was the spell broken, and, even then, it took a few seconds before she shook herself and told herself to stop being ridiculous.

She had to remember she was here for one purpose and one purpose only, and it wasn't to become another of Zeke Woodlow's ardent admirers.

Thirty minutes later, when the concert had ended and the crowd was making for the exits, she pushed through the throng, intent on getting backstage. Unfortunately, her progress was halted by a tall and tough-looking security guard.

"Excuse me," she said, "I'd like to get backstage."

The guard peered down at her, his eyes catching on her ring for an instant, his arms folded. "Right. You and a few thousand other people."

"I'm a member of the press," she said. She invested her voice with the same tone that she'd heard hundreds of times from the headmistress of the private girls' school that she'd attended along with her identical twin, Scarlet.

"Let's see your backstage pass."

"I don't have one. You see—"

But Mr. Hefty-and-Imperturbable had already

started shaking his head. "No pass, no access. It's that simple."

She wanted to say, "Can we talk about this?" But since she doubted that would work, she fished in her handbag for a business card. She held one up. "See? I'm a staff member—" she didn't bother identifying *which* staff member "—at *The Buzz*. You've heard of *The Buzz*, haven't you?"

Mr. Hefty just glanced from the business card to her, not bothering to take the card from her. "Like I said, only authorized persons are permitted backstage."

Argh. She should have been prepared for this.

"Fine," she said in exasperation, trying one last gambit, "but don't blame me when heads roll because Zeke Woodlow lost his chance at an interview with one of the leading entertainment magazines in the country."

The guard merely quirked a brow.

Turning on her heel, she marched away with her head held high. At school, Ms. Donaldson would have been proud.

All right, she thought, so she wasn't going to get to interview Zeke in his dressing room. She knew he had to leave the Garden sometime, though, and when he did, she'd be waiting for him. She hadn't spent close to three hours getting shoved and poked by his fans for nothing. She *needed* this interview.

An hour later, however, she felt as if she'd been huddling in the chilly, damp March night forever, and she started to ask herself how much she needed this interview. She was tired, hungry and wanted to go home.

She started fishing around in her purse for a breath mint—anything edible, frankly—until a commotion caused her to look up and notice that Zeke had emerged.

Unfortunately, he was surrounded by handlers and security personnel. Despite that, she ran forward, knowing she had only a few moments before he ducked into the limousine that had pulled up. "Zeke! Mr. Woodlow!"

Just then, the space around Zeke became frenetic. Paparazzi flashbulbs went off, and some girls started screaming and jumping up and down.

Her forward progress came to a halt as she collided with a brick wall—or, more precisely, she realized as she looked up, the blue-clad form of one of New York's finest. She took an involuntary step back as the police officer—one of several near the limo, she now noticed—blocked her way.

"Step back," he ordered.

Looking over the officer's shoulder, she noticed Zeke duck into the car, and her shoulders slumped.

Four hours, twenty-seven minutes and twenty-plus songs. And now, finally, defeat.

She felt like wailing in frustration. As if on cue, a raindrop hit her cheek, then another. She looked up, grimaced and then made a beeline for the taxi stand on Seventh Avenue. Once it started raining in earnest, she knew there wouldn't be an empty cab in sight.

Twenty-five minutes later, she reached the Upper West Side townhouse owned by her grandparents and used by them as a secondary residence.

When she got to the top floor, where she and Scarlet had living quarters, her sister padded out of her room to greet her. "Well, how'd it go?" asked Scarlet, who was dressed in red silk pajamas.

Taking in her sister's sleepwear, she thought again that she and Scarlet couldn't be more different, despite being identical twins. Scarlet was known as flamboyant and wild and crazy, while she was thought of as sensible and methodical.

"Horribly," she responded, plopping down on the couch and unzipping her boots. She wiggled her toes in relief. "I don't know what ever made me think I could land this interview with Zeke. I couldn't even get near him! The guy has better security than the pope and the president combined."

She summarized the events of the evening for Scarlet, then shrugged. "It was a crazy plan to begin with, but now I need another career-making scheme. Any ideas?"

"That's it?" Scarlet asked disbelievingly. "Just like that—" she snapped her fingers "—you're giving up on Zeke?"

"Not just like that," she said, snapping her fingers

right back. "Haven't you been listening to anything I've said?"

"Isn't there one more concert scheduled for tomorrow night? You've still got a shot at getting the interview."

"Scar, hello?" She was used to administering a dose of reality to counter her sister's exuberance. "There isn't going to be an interview."

Scarlet rested her hands on her hips. "Well, not with you dressed like *that* there isn't."

She looked down at her clothes. "What's wrong with the way I'm dressed?"

"You're dressed like a nun." Gesturing with one hand, Scarlet added, "You're practically covered from head to toe."

"It's cold outside," she said defensively. "Besides, are you seriously suggesting I'd get anywhere by showing some cleavage?"

"Well, it can't hurt."

"Right, and I suppose it would help if I borrowed a few things from your closet," she said dryly.

Her sister's eyes lit up. "Now there's an idea."

Scarlet's love of fashion was well known. She often sketched designs and sometimes made her own clothes, and Summer admired her for it, though her own taste in clothes was more sedate.

"Forget it."

"It's perfect! Why didn't I think of it before?"

"What?"

"The way to get past Zeke Woodlow's security. Dress up as a rock groupie. They're always allowing attractive women backstage."

"Why?"

Scarlet sighed in exasperation. "Summer, sometimes I swear you were born with the mindset of a fifty-year-old. Why do you think? Sometimes it's sex, sometimes it's fawning attention and sometimes it's just positive publicity, because the women will later gush to reporters about talking to a rock star."

"Oh, please! You want me to dress like an airhead? I'm looking to inspire respect as a reporter, not lust as a bimbette."

Scarlet spun on her heel. "Come on! Tomorrow night you're going to be dressed to seduce. The serious part can come *after* you get your stiletto in the door. You're going to a rock concert, not doing an interview at the United Nations."

Summer sighed, but she got up and trudged after her twin. She could easily imagine what Scarlet had in mind—and *that* was the problem.

As one stiletto-heeled foot hit the pavement, Summer steeled herself for what lay ahead. She looked up at the Garden as she emerged from the cab and chanted Scarlet's advice from earlier.

Release your inner goddess.... Release your inner goddess....

She kept up the chant as she walked toward the entrance to the Garden.

At five o'clock, she'd left her desk at work and taken the elevator at EPH's headquarters down to *Charisma*'s offices, where her sister was employed. Scarlet had helped her dress in the clothes that they'd pulled from the closet last night, then had applied her makeup and styled her hair.

Summer didn't have to wonder how she looked. She'd stared at her image in the full-length mirror at *Charisma*'s offices long enough.

Dramatic. Sexy. In short, a different person. Her lips twisted wryly. A different person who happened to look a lot like Scarlet herself. Not surprisingly, of course, since she was dressed in Scarlet's clothes, and Scarlet—whether by design or subconsciously—appeared to think that *sexy* meant a lot like the look she herself wore when hitting the town hard.

Summer touched her hair. It was down and loose, its curls cascading past her shoulders.

Beneath her short, belted pea coat, she wore a black suede skirt that ended above the knee and black boots that ended right below. If Scarlet was to be believed, knees were sexy.

Her deep-red top plunged low, revealing tantalizing cleavage, and her face was made-up. Normally she favored a natural look, using matte lipstick with just a hint of color. But tonight, her lips were a dark red and had a lovely sheen due to the smattering of gold dust in her lipstick.

Apparently, gold of twenty-three karats or higher was edible. Who'd have known? Certainly not her. But as assistant fashion editor at *Charisma*—EPH's answer to *Vogue*—Scarlet was in a position to know.

As she walked into the Garden, Summer looked down at her ringless hand. There was no telltale pale band on her skin to give her away.

Her sister had insisted that she leave her engagement ring at home. When she'd protested, Scarlet had taken her hand and tugged at the ring herself.

"Don't be ridiculous, Summer," her sister had said. "How do you expect to impersonate a rock groupie?"

"What's the ring got to do with it?" she'd shot back, trying to pull her hand from Scarlet's grasp.

"Haven't we been over this? Groupies are allowed backstage because they're young, sexy and *single*. Are you going to go to all this trouble just to be done in by a ring?"

In the end, she'd let Scarlet take the ring. But the whole thing still didn't sit well with her. It felt as if she were being disloyal to John.

That feeling was ridiculous, of course. Tonight wasn't a date. She just happened to be trying to lure a rock star to do an interview by using some sex appeal. What the heck was wrong with that?

In fact, she had almost convinced herself. Almost.

She thought about John again. He'd be returning from his business trip soon—which was a good thing, since they had a wedding to plan.

She was a meticulous planner and list keeper, and getting engaged at twenty-five put her right on target as far as the five-year plan that she'd drawn up for herself.

It read like this: twenty-five, become engaged and rise to full reporter status at *The Buzz*; twenty-six, get married; twenty-eight, make name for self as hotshot entertainment reporter; thirty, rise to management position at *The Buzz* and become pregnant.

So far, so good. It helped, of course, that John had his own five-year plan. It was one of the things that had helped her pick him from the field of men that she used to date and that she had eventually winnowed down to The One.

Like her, John was serious and ambitious. At twenty-nine, he was already a partner at his advertising firm and had an impressive clientele that required him to fly around the country on business.

He was her perfect complement, and by this time next year she'd be Mrs. John Harlan. After nine months of dating, John had popped the question to her over a romantic dinner on Valentine's Day.

The perfection of the proposal had been the last proof she'd needed that she was making the right decision: she'd been thinking that Valentine's Day would be the right time to get engaged, but the comportment-school grad in her had been too polite to drop hints. But then John had gone ahead and proposed.

So what if, late at night, alone in bed, she experienced the occasional twinge of unease? Weren't all brides supposed to be nervous?

Turning her attention to the concert as it finally started, she soon found herself swept up in the dreamy mood that she'd fallen into the night before.

If she'd been tempted to dismiss last night's concert as a fluke, this time there could be no denying Zeke Woodlow's power as a performer and, more importantly, his ability to affect her.

Occasionally, she stopped to write in a small notebook, searching for the right adjectives to describe his performance and his electric effect on the audience.

When Zeke got to "Beautiful in My Arms," she again felt magically transported and as if he were singing just for her. It was almost like the feeling she'd experienced in one other situation—when she'd let herself do something totally out of character….

She jerked her mind back from the direction of her thoughts. No sense thinking about that now. It was her little secret. Tonight was about getting a job done.

This time with some luck—and insider tips from a coworker at *The Buzz*—she managed to sneak out of the arena at the end of the concert and locate the hallway that led to the performers' dressing rooms.

She had her coat unbuttoned—as Scarlet had said, "Show them the goods"—and a small suede handbag dangled from one hand.

She steeled herself as she approached the first burly security detail standing guard. *You can do this.*

She flashed him a breezy smile, noticing his eyes did a quick dart up and down as she approached. His face relaxed a fraction, male appreciation replacing cold stoniness.

Well, well. Scarlet was right.

Feeling suddenly empowered, she kept her smile in place and flicked him a coy look. "I'm here to see Zeke. He said to look him up when he was in New York."

"Did he?"

She nodded, standing close. "I spoke to Marty—" she'd made sure she knew the name of Zeke's manager, since, if you were going to lie through your teeth, there was no sense in being wrong "—and he said to come right up after the concert."

"You know Marty?"

"Only for the last five cities. I've seen Zeke play in L.A., Chicago, Boston…." She trailed off, then added significantly, "We've always had a great time."

Mr. Burly nodded over his shoulder. "Third door on the left."

That was it? She felt like crying with relief. Instead, she smiled and said, "Thanks."

She thought she could get used to life as an auburn-haired bombshell. She felt liberated, almost reckless.

In front of Zeke's door, she took a steadying breath and knocked.

"Come in," said a male voice through the door.

Turning the doorknob, she stepped inside the softly lit dressing room.

From the other side of the room, his voice reached her. "I've been waiting for you."

His voice went through her like a heady shot of vodka. Deep, sexy, rich and vibrant, it was even more potent up close and personal than it was on stage.

His back stayed turned to her as he picked up a cell phone from a nearby table and pushed some buttons. "I'll be ready to leave for the hotel in about ten minutes. Is that okay with you, Marty?"

She could see he was still dressed in the black jeans and T-shirt that he'd worn on stage. His tight rear end was nicely defined beneath the denim, and the cotton of his shirt stretched across his muscular back and shoulders.

She cleared her throat. "I'm not Marty."

He swung around and stopped, staring at her.

His face was striking. Good-looking, yes, but also

compelling. And then there were the eyes. Oh, Lord, his eyes. They were as blue and fathomless as the ocean. She'd have said his face tended to harshness if it were not for them. Despite his reputation in the press for being somewhat surly, he had sweet eyes.

With the part of her brain that still functioned, she noticed he remained motionless. Was it just her imagination or was he as dumbstruck as she was?

"Yeah," he drawled finally, "I can see you're definitely not Marty. So who are you?"

Two

The notes of the song drifted through Zeke's mind again. It was the same song that sounded in his head whenever he dreamed of *her*. It would linger tantalizingly at the edges of his memory when he awoke, but dissipate into nothingness before he could grasp it, write it down and make it his own.

This time, though, the notes of the song sounded more clearly. It was as if the woman standing in front of him were calling them forth. She even looked like the woman in the photograph—the woman of his dreams. She was slender but curvaceous, and had long, auburn hair, though a shade or two lighter than the woman in the picture. And, he'd recognize those astonishing green eyes anywhere.

The major difference was that the woman in the anonymous photograph that he'd purchased at a street fair was dressed as a Greek goddess, while this one was certainly twenty-first century and doubtless a rock groupie at that. He didn't know who the photographer or the subject of the photograph was, but he did have one hint: the photo was called "Daphne at Play," according to the handwritten inscription across the bottom of its white matte frame.

Awareness stirred within him, and his muscles tightened. Whatever it was about this woman, she called to him. In his dreams, he'd imagined her hair splayed across his bed, her arms and legs wrapped around him, drawing him in.

Feeling himself grow hot, he asked brusquely, "You didn't answer my question. What's your name?"

Her eyes darted away before returning to his. "C-Caitlin."

He released the breath that he hadn't known he was holding. So, she wasn't Daphne. Still, he couldn't resist asking, "Have you done any modeling?"

Her brows drew together. "No."

"Well, you should consider it." Definitely not Daphne.

She raised her brows. "Really?"

"Really." He gave her a slow, appreciative smile

as he walked toward her. "You've got the body and face for it. And your eyes are unusual…captivating." He'd often wondered if the pale green eyes of the woman in his photograph had been real or a trick of lighting or computer technology.

"I could say the same thing about you."

He laughed. She was bewitching. He realized she must be one of those rock groupies that Marty sometimes sent backstage after a concert. Girls clamored for access to rock stars like him, and Marty thought it was good PR for him to appear accessible to some extent.

If Caitlin was the key to unlocking his creativity— and, hell, even if she wasn't—he knew he had to get to know her better. He'd never experienced such a profound connection with someone so fast. She was nearly the living embodiment of his fantasies.

He gestured to a couch. "Have a seat." He looked around. "Do you want a drink?"

"Th-thanks."

He quirked a brow. Made her nervous, did he? "To the seat or the drink?"

He watched in fascination as a telltale flush rose from the tops of her breasts to her face. "Yes to both," she said as walked over and sat on the couch, dropping her coat and handbag beside her.

"Beer okay?"

"Yes, thank you."

Turning away to pull two beers from a small fridge and pop the caps off, he puzzled over her reaction. Usually, women were all too ready to throw themselves at him in situations like this. Caitlin, however, was the picture of reserved politeness.

Surprisingly, he found he was turned on by it. He gave himself a mental shake. He needed to get a grip. Her resemblance to Daphne was muddying his mind.

He handed her a beer as he sat down next to her. She looked as if she wasn't sure what to do with it for a second, then, after watching him take a swig, delicately tipped the bottle to her lips and took a sip.

He felt that sip straight down to his groin and shifted. The room felt as if it were getting hotter and smaller by the second.

Still not looking at him, she quickly took another swallow of beer, causing even more foam to appear near the top of the bottle.

He smiled. "Didn't anyone ever teach you how to drink from a beer bottle?"

"I'm doing it wrong?"

He touched his bottle to hers. "Yeah," he said with mock gravity. "Look at the foam that's forming."

She tilted her bottle to the side for a better look. "Oh."

"Watch," he commanded. "Don't create any suction. Part your lips just a little and don't cover the whole opening." He brought the bottle to his lips and drank deeply. He prayed the cold beer would help cool him down.

She raised the bottle to her lips and imitated him.

"That's right," he said.

When she lowered the bottle, she looked at him, and he knew he wanted to kiss her. Her lips were pouty and red but still had an innocence to them.

In fact, though she was dressed provocatively, something didn't seem to fit. He could have sworn she was more pearls and cashmere than leather and spandex.

"Tell me about you," he said.

"What would you like to know?"

Everything. "Did you like the concert?"

"Yes. I liked hearing you sing 'Beautiful in My Arms.'"

"Did you?" He eyed her. It was the song he'd written on the day he'd purchased "Daphne at Play."

"What do you like about it?"

She shifted, her gaze falling away from his. "It's just…nice."

"Just…nice?"

"Magical. It makes me think about—"

"Making love?" he joked.

Her gaze jerked to his. "No."

He sobered. "I'm kidding. You know all the stuff that's in there about making love under the palm trees?" At her nod, he said, "It seems to make a lot of people think about sex."

When she broke into a smile, he sank fast.

"No," she said slowly, "it makes me think about holding tight to one special person—the person you want to cling to on the darkest days."

Lord, she surprised him. Most people stopped at the sex part, but then most people weren't straight out of his fantasies.

"Do you usually let strange women into your dressing room?" she asked suddenly, then looked horrified the minute the words had left her mouth.

He fought a smile. "Sometimes," he admitted. "My manager seems to think my being accessible to fans to some extent is good for PR."

"Is that why you're here now?"

He shrugged. "It's part of the job. I flirt and play nice. Usually the women will turn around afterward and gush about meeting Zeke Woodlow. It keeps a nice, positive buzz going out there among the public and the press."

She nodded.

He couldn't believe he was being this honest with her, but she had the type of face—classically beautiful and innocent—that spoke to him. He just found it easy to tell her things. Marty, he knew, would be wincing right now.

"Which part of your job do you like the most?" she asked.

"The songwriting."

Her eyes widened a fraction. "Not the performing?"

"No," he said curtly. She had a knack for homing in on sensitive subjects, he'd give her that.

Clearing his throat, he nodded at her beer. "Drink up."

She took another sip.

He took another swig himself before offering a small explanation. "The concerts are just icing on the cake."

"Isn't it a little unusual for singers to write their own songs these days?"

"Rare," he concurred.

She looked around. "What about the parties? Don't you have an after-party to go to right now?"

"Yeah, but I prefer hiding out in here with you."

Her head swung back toward him. "Oh."

It was true, he realized. She radiated an aura of sweetness and purity that was all too rare in his world. "Sometimes I skip the parties, especially when I've got a busy schedule the next day."

"What do you do when there aren't any parties?"

There was always a party somewhere for someone like him, he wanted to say. Instead, he admitted, "Finagle an invitation from some staff member to a family dinner."

Her answering smile lit up her face.

They stared at each other until her smile slowly faded.

He felt the urge to kiss her rise again.

He started to lift his hand to her face when a knock sounded at the door.

Damn.

"Who is it?" he demanded.

One of the tech guys for the band stuck his head around the door. "Car's here. Marty wanted me to let you know. He's already left for the hotel."

He stood. "Right. Ten minutes."

With a quick look from him to Caitlin and back, the tech guy said, "Great" and then shut the door.

Zeke reached for Caitlin's beer while she stood up. Their fingers brushed as he took the bottle from her, sending a bolt of awareness shooting through him. From the look in her eyes, she felt it, too.

"Do you want to leave with me?" he asked.

Tell him, tell him. Tell him that you're here to get an interview.

Instead, Summer heard herself say, "Okay."

He looked satisfied. "Great."

When she'd walked into the room, some instinct that it was too early to blurt her true purpose had made her give him her middle name—Caitlin—when he'd asked. After that, it had been a quick and easy slide to the point of no return. He obviously thought she was a fan, and the more time passed, the harder it got for her to correct his misinterpretation.

Since she'd walked into the dressing room, she'd

been hit with an awareness of him that was powerful and overwhelming. At first, she'd been nervous and jittery, then they'd slid into the type of personal conversation that happened between people who'd known each other forever and a day.

But the strange thing was, she *did* feel as if she knew him. Maybe that feeling was due to all the research that she'd done on him, or maybe it was due to going to his concerts.

Nevertheless, looking at him now—at his blue, blue eyes, chiseled features, broad shoulders and muscled physique—she couldn't stop her heart from thudding or the shivers that chased over her skin.

She might feel as if she'd known him forever and a day, but her body still clamored for a carnal knowledge that was more than the illusion of remembrances.

Zeke picked up her coat and bag from the sofa. After giving her the handbag, he held her coat for her.

The gesture both surprised and pleased her. Who'd have thought a rock sensation like him would have manners worthy of Ms. Donaldson's comportment school class?

Turning, she slid her arms into the coat sleeves. When he released his hold on the collar, his hand brushed her neck, and heat zipped through her. He had an intoxicating effect on her, and she found that she didn't want it to stop.

Turning back to him, she gave him a bright smile.

"Ready?" he asked, reaching over to pull a leather jacket off a hook.

She nodded. At some point—soon, very soon—she knew she'd have to tell him that she was a reporter looking for an interview. In the meantime, though, she could buy herself some time to find the right opening for that revelation.

Zeke led the way down a corridor and to an area behind the concert stage. Bodyguards and handlers soon joined them, one of them opening a door that led outside, where she was hit by a blast of March cold air.

Looking around, she realized they were still in an enclosed area, though the driveway sloped down to the street. "Where are we?" she asked.

He must have noticed her shivering, because he asked, "Cold?" He put an arm around her as a limo pulled up.

She shivered again, though not just from the cold.

As he glanced down at her, the corners of his lips tilted upward. "To answer your question, this is the 'secret' exit out of here. The driveway leads down to a parking area for loading and unloading equipment. Both the driveway and the parking area have limited public access."

"It's not the way you left last night," she blurted, then felt her face turn hot with embarrassment.

He grinned. "Watching, were you?"

"Maybe." Standing pressed against him, she was

acutely aware of the heat emanating from him. Traitorously, her body wanted only to snuggle closer.

"Last night, I left through the suites and clubs entrance. I went up to some of the private boxes after the concert in order to thank some of the big donors to the event." He winked. "It pays off in future fundraising efforts."

"Oh." In her naiveté, she'd just assumed most stars left through the lofty-sounding suites and clubs entrance. Now she realized that catching sight of his departure last night had been pure luck.

"Of course," he said, "it had the added benefit of throwing off some of the fans and paparazzi." He nodded at the limo that had pulled up in front of them. "Once the car hits the street outside, don't be surprised if there are photographers trying to hold up high-powered lenses to the tinted car windows."

"Sounds awful." Not only did it sound awful, she knew it *was* awful. Though her life was nothing like Zeke's, as a member of the wealthy and powerful Elliott clan, she'd had some experience with photographers snapping unexpected pictures of her.

A guard with a walkie-talkie in his hand reached over and opened one of the passenger doors to the limo for them.

"In you go," Zeke said.

Once they were inside and the car was moving, she asked, "Where are we going?"

"The Waldorf-Astoria," he said. "I always stay there when I'm in town."

Oh. She just prayed she didn't run into an acquaintance of her grandparents or one of the other Elliotts. Dressed as she was and in the company of reputed bad-boy rocker Zeke Woodlow, she'd definitely raise some eyebrows.

As soon as the limo cleared the guard's security post and hit the street, flashbulbs started to go off—just as Zeke had predicted. Fortunately, the stoplight at the corner was green, so the limo was able to make a clean getaway before anyone could press a camera against the car window. Summer fervently hoped no one had gotten a photo of her.

The Waldorf-Astoria was a different matter. When they arrived at its front entrance, security guards and handlers got out first from a car that had preceded the limo to the hotel.

She was soon thankful for the extra protection. As she and Zeke alighted from their car and hurried to the front door of the hotel, several security guards held back photographers and squealing fans.

Summer kept her head down and tried to shield her face with the raised collar of her coat and with the hand that she kept cupped over her eyes. She didn't want to be too obvious about avoiding photographers because she didn't want to make Zeke suspicious. On the other hand, she didn't even want to think about the repercussions of their photo landing on Page Six of the *New York Post* in the morning.

Once they were inside, she followed Zeke as he made his way to the elevator bank.

He glanced down at her in amusement. "Camera shy?"

"Do they always know where you're staying?" she asked in exasperation.

He shrugged. "They always do. Of course, in New York, I'm always at the Waldorf, so there's not much guess work."

"And do the handlers never leave you?"

He tossed her a sly grin. "You're about to find out," he said as he stepped into the elevator behind her, punched a button and watched the doors slide shut.

In the confined space, she was again very aware of him—of his all-male aura and blatant sex appeal. "Where are we going?" she asked, trying to keep her tone even.

"My suite," he said as the doors to the elevator opened again.

Tell him. Tell him. It really was past time that she came clean about what she was doing here. They were about to go back to his hotel room!

And yet, the words wouldn't come. She was caught up in the strange excitement that seemed to exist between them.

They walked past another security guard—one

whose job evidently was to ensure that no uninvited
guests made their way to Zeke's door—and then they
were inside Zeke's suite.

Classical music wafted through the space. Following him down a long corridor, she stopped at the
entrance to a huge parlor graced by a large chande-
lier. A dining room table large enough to sit twelve
sat along one end of the room, while a fireplace and
couches and chairs clustered at another.

The decor was tasteful and not at all tacky and
lavish—the latter, she admitted, was sort of what
she'd been expecting of a rock sensation's hotel ac-
commodations.

"Now, you know why I always stay at the Waldorf," he said with a quick grin, dropping his jacket
onto a nearby chair.

"Mmm," she said as he took her coat and bag from
her.

She was used to understated luxury. She'd grown
up surrounded by it. She just hadn't expected it from
his quarter, but since he had no reason to assume
she'd be anything but very impressed, she refrained
from saying something committal.

He stood inches from her, and they stared at
each other.

"If you'd like to use the bathroom to freshen up,"
he said, breaking the tension, "it's down the hall and
to the right."

"Th-thanks."

Her voice sounded breathless to her own ears. She needed time to think, time to figure out what to do.

When she continued not to make a move, he stepped aside for her.

She felt heat rise to her face. "I—I'll be right back."

She cursed the fact that she kept stumbling over her words. Could she seem any more devoid of poise?

Behind her, she heard him say, "I'm going to change shirts."

"Sure." She tried to sound nonchalant, but she felt his every step behind her.

She stopped in the narrow hallway, before the open door to the bathroom, and turned back toward him, nearly colliding with him in the process.

He reached out to steady her, and they both froze, his hands on her upper arms.

His eyes, she noted again hazily, were the most incredible blue that she'd ever seen.

"I've wanted to do this," he said thickly.

"What?" she breathed.

"This." He bent his head and kissed her.

The kiss was electric, and she felt it clear down to her toes.

When he broke away, he said, "This is going to sound crazy, but I feel as if I know you. As if I knew you before tonight, I mean."

"Not crazy. I feel the same way," she confessed.

How could she explain? It *was* crazy. Yet, she felt as if she'd known him—had been waiting for this moment—her entire life.

He bent his head again, and she waited for the already familiar scent and flavor of him.

The kiss this time was a slow and erotic dance, and she found herself leaning back against the wall for support.

She shuddered as he took the kiss deeper, and she opened to him, sliding her hands up his chest and to his shoulders to draw him closer. Pressed against him, she felt every inch of his lean, muscular form, from his firm thighs to the hard plane of his chest.

His lips moved from hers to trail kisses along her jawline to the sensitive spot below her ear. When his lips traced the delicate shell of her ear, a moan escaped her.

She felt a stab of pure lust. She'd never had the teenage crushes that other girls had had on movie stars and celebrities. She'd been too sensible for that type of thing. Now, though, confronted by a real rock star, her resistance crumbled like a house of sand.

His hands ran down her sides, over her hips and then to her back, molding her to him.

"We have to stop," she murmured.

"Right," he said, intent on kissing her neck.

She turned her head to the side to give him better access. "This is wrong."

"But it feels so right."

She couldn't argue with that logic.

"I've been seeing you in my dreams," he said.

"Sounds lovely."

He laughed against her throat. "It has been." He raised his head and looked into her eyes. "But the real thing is better."

He cupped her face and delivered a searing kiss.

When he finally lifted his head, they were both breathing hard. "Trust me?"

She nodded.

He bent and, sliding an arm behind her knees, lifted her as if she weighed no more than a feather.

She pulled his head down for another scorching kiss, then he headed for the room at the end of the hall.

The everyday, sensible Summer Elliott would have panicked by now. *This* Summer Elliott, however, could only feel an overwhelming sense of anticipation.

Release your inner goddess…. Release your inner goddess….

Yes. It wasn't just that her clothes were different tonight. Her inhibitions had also evaporated faster than water in the desert.

Listening to Zeke sing one slow-burn love song

after another, then being in his presence—hearing that sexy voice, looking into his blue eyes, feeling his arousing touch—her defenses were at a low ebb.

He carried her into a room that was expensively decorated and set her down at the foot of a king-size bed.

His fingers went to the hem of her sweater. "You don't mind if I get rid of this, do you? I have this need to touch you."

The sensible Summer Elliott was alarmed, but the uninhibited Summer just said, "Please."

The top came off, and he tossed it aside, his eyes widening with appreciation as he took in her wine-colored demi bra.

"Beautiful," he muttered.

She shivered in response to his blatant appreciation. She was thankful now that she'd let Scarlet coax her into wearing her sexiest underwear—underwear that, not coincidentally, she'd been talked into buying by her sister on their most recent shopping trip together.

She'd thought she'd have little use for the satin bra and matching panties. In fact, she remembered arguing with Scarlet last night and saying, "I don't see why I need to wear sexy underwear to the concert. After all, it's not as if anyone is going to see it."

Scarlet had sighed impatiently. "It's all part of dressing the role. If you dress sexier, you'll feel and act sexier."

Now Zeke caressed her with his fingertips, tracing

circles on her shoulders before feathering downward over her arms and then the tops of her breasts.

If he'd been anything but gentle, she'd have turned and fled. Instead, she felt herself melting under his tenderness.

He lowered the strap of her bra and his hand came up to cup the exposed breast, the pad of his thumb flicking over the nipple and making it hard and distended. The look on his face was dark, intense and clouded with desire.

A low whimper escaped from her. Her knees felt like jelly, while all her most sensitive spots were charged with awareness. When he pulled her against him and took her nipple in his mouth, she sagged against him, running her fingers through his hair.

With one hand, he unhooked her bra and pulled it off. His mouth moved to her other breast, and his hands roamed, busy with divesting her of her skirt. Dimly, she heard her skirt rustle to the ground, even as she concentrated on the pleasurable sensations of his mouth at her breast.

When he finally pulled back, his gaze swept over her and widened. She was dressed only in her panties, thigh-high hose and long boots.

"Wow." Yanking his shirt over his head, he added jokingly, "Guess I'll have to level the playing field."

She drank him in as he undressed. He was gorgeous, his chest flat and muscled, his body lean and strong.

When they came together again, it was all questing hands and torrid kisses.

She felt his erection press against her, and rubbed against it.

He raised his head and groaned. "I want you."

"Yes."

"You're a fantasy come to life."

"I'll bet," she teased, looking down at herself. "Stiletto boots and hose?"

"Oh, yeah." His eyes glinted. "Sit back and I'll help you off with them."

Obediently, she sat on the bed behind her and raised her leg.

Slowly, his eyes never leaving hers, he lowered the zipper of one boot and tossed it aside. He rolled down her stocking, tossed it aside as well, and then pressed a hot kiss to the inside of her ankle.

She'd never been more aroused in her life. Mesmerized, she watched him do the same to her other leg.

Afterward, he kicked off his shoes and undid his jeans, pulling the latter off along with his underwear, so that he stood before her naked and aroused.

"You're gorgeous," she said.

He quirked a brow, amusement crossing his face. "Same to you." He glanced around, then walked over to a carry-on bag on a nearby chair. After some rustling, he pulled something out and turned back to the bed. "For a second, I thought I didn't have any."

She glanced at the small packet in his hand. Protection. Suddenly, the enormity of what she was about to do hit her, and she gulped. "I guess this is as good a moment as any to tell you—"

"Yes?"

"I've never done this before."

Three

Summer watched as Zeke stopped, looking stunned. "Never?"

She shook her head, uncertain of his reaction. "Never."

She could swear she heard him murmur, "I thought so."

"What?"

"Nothing." He looked bemused. "It looks like it's a set of firsts." He paused. "I've never gone to bed with a virgin."

"Oh." She digested that information for a second. "Not even in high school?"

"Nope." Then he teased, "Making some assumptions, aren't we?"

She felt herself blush with embarrassment.

He held her gaze. "We don't have to if you're not ready."

Here it was, she thought. Her last chance to back out. Strangely, though, she realized it was the last thing she wanted. "I still want to," she whispered. "I still want you."

He nodded, and his shoulders relaxed. "Believe me, you couldn't want me any more than I want you right now."

Turning, he walked to the adjacent bathroom.

"What are you doing?" she asked.

"Getting some lubrication," he said over his shoulder. "We're going to need it."

She sat up on the bed.

He came back, set a tube down on the night table and ripped open the foil packet that he'd retrieved earlier.

"Let me," she said, gazing at him. "Teach me."

He swallowed—hard.

"Please," she said, reaching out a hand.

He took her hand and guided her, letting her roll the protection onto him. His eyes closed with pleasure.

She continued to stroke him even with the protection on, and he showed her what to do.

"Ah," he breathed, opening his eyes, which were cloudy with desire. "I'm about to come out of my skin."

She held her arms out to him, and he came down beside her on the bed, gathering her into his embrace. He began to kiss her, starting with her lips, then moving to her neck and shoulders and lower.

She felt languorous, wanton and sexy, and one by one, her muscles relaxed. This was better than a Swedish massage, she thought, and they hadn't even reached climax yet.

He kneaded her flesh while his lips touched here and there, making her come alive.

She shifted restlessly under the gentle onslaught. Finally, when she thought she couldn't stand any more, he opened the tube on the night table, rubbed some gel between his fingers and started massaging her intimately.

"Oh, Zeke!"

"Shh," he said soothingly. "Just feel."

How could she just feel? Quivering, she grasped his upper arm. She felt like a bow that was being pulled tight and then tighter.

Distantly, she heard Zeke crooning to her, and then he was there beside her, gathering her close, as his fingers continued to work and she went over the edge, shaking with her release.

When she finally came down to earth, she turned heavy eyes toward him.

"Now I want you," she whispered.

"Glad to hear that." His gaze intent, he moved

over her, positioning himself between her thighs. He gave her a quick, hard kiss. "I'll try not to hurt you. Just concentrate on kissing me."

His hands and lips soothed as he continued his inexorable move forward.

She felt stretched and full. Fear intruded for a moment, but before she could dwell on it, he thrust forward, burying himself within her.

She pulled away from their kiss and gasped. The pain had been sharp but fleeting. A feeling of fullness remained, and beneath that, pleasure.

"Did I hurt you?" he asked, his face etched with concern.

"It's better now. The pain was over quickly."

He smiled. "But this isn't."

He started to move then and taught her how to move with him, setting up a slow rhythm, while he whispered encouragement in her ear and described how she made him feel.

She felt wound tight, and the tension only seemed to build as he whispered intimate questions in her ear and coaxed answers from her.

In another life, she'd have been red with embarrassment. But tonight, she felt loose and carefree.

He was incredible, and he was absolutely devastating her. He crooned some sexy lyrics in her ear, and she nearly came undone.

His pace quickened then, and his breathing

became labored and harsh. Just when she thought the coil within her was going to spring free, he thrust once, twice….

Her release came seconds before his powerful climax. He tensed, thrust, jerked, and then went slack against her.

When their breathing had slowed and their hearts had stopped racing, she said huskily, "You've got great timing."

He guffawed and kissed her on the nose. "I'll take that as a compliment." He moved to her side, slung an arm over her and snuggled her close.

Zeke woke up happy, but the emotion was fleeting.

Sunlight streamed into the room. He could tell because, though his eyes were closed, a bright orange haze played before his eyes.

His lips turned up.

He'd dreamed long and well. He'd imagined himself composing a song—the song that had been torturing him for months.

He hummed a few bars. It was the first time that he'd woken up and been able to hang on to any piece of the song.

He figured there was a reason that he'd finally had a breakthrough, and that reason was lying next to him. *She* was the primary reason that last night had been superb.

He moved his arm, reaching for her…and came up empty. Just to be sure, he moved his arm again experimentally, patting the mattress. Nothing.

He blinked and sat up. Looking around, his happy mood fled as he realized her clothes were gone. He didn't hear movement in the suite, either.

Still, on the off chance that he was wrong, he swung his legs off the bed and padded out of the room naked.

After checking the bathroom and then the living room area, he had to face facts: she'd left without so much as saying Goodbye, thanks for a great time. And, to make matters worse, he didn't even have her full name.

His stomach plunged. Damn it. He battled the urge to punch a wall until common sense kicked in. He could picture the headline in tomorrow's paper if he gave in to frustration: Bad-boy Rocker Trashes Hotel Suite.

Stalking back to the bedroom, he raked his hand through his hair. He needed time to think. He had to find her—she was the key to his creativity. But he couldn't go around broadcasting the fact that he'd just spent the night with a woman that he knew only as Caitlin.

His eyes landed on a telltale blood stain darkening the bed sheet, and he cursed. She'd seemed innocent, and she had been.

He had to find her. He felt as though he'd finally found what he'd been looking for, and now that he had, he wasn't about to let her slip through his fingers.

He glanced at the alarm clock on the night table. It was still early.

While he mulled over what to do, he ordered breakfast from room service, then padded into the bathroom to shower and then dress. He knew from experience that before long, Marty and umpteen other people would be calling him about the day ahead. The only reason he'd gotten a bit of a reprieve this morning was because last night had been his last benefit concert for Musicians for a Cure for the time being.

By the time room service arrived, he'd hit on only one possible plan—other than hiring a private investigator. He figured Caitlin had probably bought herself a concert ticket in advance—probably with a credit card—so someone at the box office should have a full name on file. If he could just get access to that information…

Sitting down, he dug into a breakfast of pancakes, scrambled eggs and bacon. Absently, he flicked through the local newspapers that he'd requested be delivered to him along with breakfast.

Taking a sip of his coffee, he turned to Page Six of the *New York Post* to see if there was any mention of last night's concert in the gossip columns…and nearly spewed his coffee.

As coffee sloshed over the rim of his cup, he shot out of his chair to avoid getting burned.

There, staring up at him, was a paparazzi shot of him and Caitlin ducking into an elevator at the Waldorf last night. The first line of the article read: "Heiress Scarlet Elliott and rocker Zeke Woodlow's midnight encounter!"

Heiress?

What the hell?

Anger rose like bile in his throat. Had he been taken for a ride last night?

But no, she'd apparently been a virgin. Still, his brows snapping together, he wondered whether she'd just been fulfilling some odd fantasy about a rock star, a hotel room and losing her virginity.

His eyes flicked over the rest of the article. Apparently Caitlin was, in actuality, Scarlet Elliott, member of the powerful Elliott clan and heiress to the Elliott publishing fortune. Even he'd heard of the family and Elliott Publication Holdings.

If he remembered correctly, the Elliotts owned everything from the highly regarded news periodical *Pulse* to the celebrity-watching magazine *Snap*.

Well, at least now he knew how to track down "Caitlin." Page Six had done his work for him. Unfortunately, he now had another problem on his hands: Caitlin wasn't just another rock groupie. She was an heiress—one whom he'd just deflowered—

and the two of them were splashed all over the morning paper!

He hoped to God that the fact that her family was in the publishing business was a mere coincidence and not the reason Caitlin—or Scarlet, or whatever the hell her name was—had tracked him down. Otherwise, there was going to be hell to pay, and if he was going to pay through the nose, he was going to make damn sure that his Daphne look-alike did, too.

Picking up the phone, he punched in the number for directory assistance and asked for the address for Elliott Publication Holdings.

Summer stared at the wall of her cubicle at EPH's headquarters.

She couldn't believe how her life had changed in twenty-four hours.

Since when had she become so impulsive? So stupid? She winced. And, what was she going to tell John?

Thankfully, John was still away on his business trip. After all, what could she say to him?

Oh, hi. I'm so glad you're back. Yes, yes…no, nothing much happened. I just lost my virginity to a rock star. I guess you've heard of him? Zeke Woodlow.

She groaned, leaned forward and rubbed her face with her hands again.

She felt ill, as if her stomach muscles would

remain clenched for the rest of her life. Hysteria was barely being held at bay.

What had possessed her?

In a word: Zeke.

The answer popped into her head unbidden, and she felt herself grow hot.

In fact, she couldn't remember anything about last night without feeling herself heat up. It had been one of the most wonderful experiences of her life. Despite Zeke's reputation in the press as a player who changed women as quickly and easily as he changed clothes, he'd been sweet and gentle and considerate. She couldn't imagine a better way to have lost her virginity.

Still, she'd lain in her bedroom last night and agonized till the sun had come up over what had made her act so recklessly. She hadn't had much to drink. Sure, there'd been a couple fortifying glasses of wine back at *Charisma*'s offices while Scarlet had helped her dress. But those drinks had been hours before she'd stepped foot inside the Waldorf, and she'd only had a beer with Zeke in his dressing room.

No, she couldn't blame the alcohol, as much as that would provide an easy out.

Of course, she'd also recently been witnessing her family come apart as a result of her grandfather's ridiculous challenge. Certainly, there'd been more tension around *The Buzz*.

But whom was she kidding? She was a lowly copy editor. If there was pressure to be felt, it rested squarely on the shoulders of her uncle Shane, who was editor in chief of *The Buzz*.

Thinking of work, she winced as she remembered dragging herself to the office this morning. She'd been an hour late. Shane had seen her come in and quirked an eyebrow.

If she'd been productive in the hour since she'd arrived, she'd have felt better. Unfortunately, she'd managed the sum total of turning on her computer, making three trips to the pantry for coffee, water and more coffee, and staring at her cubicle wall.

There was no avoiding the last possible explanation for her uncharacteristic behavior last night: John. In the few weeks since he'd proposed, she'd felt jittery and unable to shake the feeling that she was making a mistake. Instead of planning her wedding, she'd found herself avoiding the subject of her upcoming nuptials whenever Scarlet or her grandmother had brought it up.

But had she slept with Zeke *because of* or *despite* her engagement to John? Had she unconsciously been trying to sabotage her engagement, or had she just been unable to resist Zeke?

She still couldn't believe she'd lost her virginity so casually after hanging on to it for so long. The formerly, sensible Summer Elliott had convinced a reluctant John to wait until their wedding night. She'd envisioned her wedding as the culmination of the careful screening process that she'd begun after college, winnowing down a small field of men to find The One. What more appropriate time to lose her virginity than on her wedding night?

It hadn't seemed like much of a hardship to wait. She'd known that if she kept to her five-year plan, she would be married by twenty-six. And, she'd reasoned, if pop star Jessica Simpson could resist the delectable Nick Lachey until their wedding night, she could certainly resist John.

Then, last night, she'd fallen into bed with Zeke after knowing him mere hours. Even more damning, she hadn't thought about John. Not once. Not until this morning.

She was whatever they called the female version of a cad. A fiend. Slime. She was only surprised that she hadn't grown scales and recoiled with horror when she'd faced the mirror this morning.

She sighed.

Whenever something had bothered her in the past, she'd always turned to Scarlet. This morning, she'd snuck back into the townhouse when it was still dark and had slept in, mumbling, when Scarlet had checked on her before leaving for work, that she wasn't feeling well.

She'd intended to keep last night to herself, to

bring it to her grave, if possible, or at least to avoid disclosing the facts as long as possible. But since her brain waves were on automatic pilot straight to Zeke, she figured she couldn't hold out against a teary confession to Scarlet much longer.

She got up. In fact, another two minutes was about as long as she could hold out.

When she got to the *Charisma* offices on the floor below, she walked toward Scarlet's cubicle until she heard her sister's voice coming from a nearby meeting room.

Bad timing, she thought. Scarlet was obviously in the middle of a conversation with someone else.

When she reached the open doorway to the meeting room, she saw her sister standing behind a conference table laden with photos and magazine clippings.

Scarlet's eyes widened as they connected with hers. Her sister made a quick, seemingly surreptitious, shooing motion with one hand.

Before she could digest the meaning, however, she took a step forward, and the man standing in front of the conference table turned around.

Her eyes collided with the impossibly blue, impossibly angry gaze of Zeke Woodlow.

Four

Zeke stared at the woman in the doorway. His eyes told him what his gut had already figured out: The woman behind the conference table was not the woman with whom he'd had a torrid night of mind-blowing sex. The woman in front of him was.

It all made sense now. Identical twins. Of course.

When he'd stepped into the conference room minutes before, he hadn't been able to shake the feeling that he'd tracked down the wrong person, despite her resemblance to the woman of last night. He just hadn't experienced that same kick-in-the-gut feeling of awareness…of being attuned to her.

But just what kind of game had these two been playing with him? The small part of his mind not given over to simmering anger took note of the fact that the woman he'd spent the night with was dressed much more like he'd imagined her. He hadn't been wrong last night when he'd thought that her clothes didn't suit her. She really was all cashmere and pearls.

His gaze raked her from head to foot before his eyes narrowed on the diamond ring on her finger.

Hell. She was engaged? What other surprises did she have in store for him?

Because she continued to stare at him, frozen in place, he glanced back at the woman behind the table, who'd done a good job of holding him off and attempting to cover for her sister. "Scarlet Elliott, right?" he sneered, before swinging back to the woman whom he'd last seen sprawled naked across his sheets. "And you're her identical twin…?"

"Summer," she supplied in a barely audible tone.

"Well, Summer," he said with false pleasantness, "there's no need to look horrified. I have to ask, though, how often have you and Scarlet played this identity-switching game? I'm finding it hard to believe I'm your first victim."

"How did you find me?" she blurted.

"Now, that's a good question, isn't it?" he asked in the same pleasant tone. He held out a copy of the

New York Post, folded and turned to Page Six. "Let's just say I got some unexpected help."

She took the newspaper from him and scanned it, her eyes widening.

"Yeah. Exactly." He glanced at Scarlet, then back at Summer. "Your sister tried to cover for you, but she's not that good an actress."

Scarlet bristled. "Look, Zeke, insult me all you want, but I resent having you take cheap shots at my sister. You may think, just because you're the current it-boy of the music world, that you can come in here and start flinging accusations, but I can have you thrown out so fast it'll make that rock-star hair of yours look more than artfully disheveled."

He raised his eyebrows. "Well, well, a debutante who doesn't bother with the kid-glove treatment. I guess that was your spandex-and-cleavage outfit that Summer was wearing last night?"

Summer took a step forward. "Stop it, both of you." She turned to him. "We need to talk."

"Yeah, we're in agreement on that at least. You owe me some answers."

"Not here, though," she said quickly. "There's another conference room upstairs, near my desk, that's rarely used. We can talk there privately."

As he turned to follow Summer out of the office, Scarlet threw him a warning look that blared: *Watch it. I can still have you thrown out of here on your ear.*

He gave her a parting grin that was full of insouciance.

As he followed Summer down the brightly patterned hall to the elevator bank, he noted that, if anything, she looked even sexier this morning than she had last night.

She was dressed in kitten heels, pearls and a twin sweater set. The retro look was demure, yet alluring. While last night's outfit had been like a green flag at a professional car race, this was more stop than go, and sexier as a result.

Realizing the direction that his mind was heading in, he put the brakes on his thoughts. Annoyed, he reflected that, while he had every reason to be mad as hell at her, he was still attracted to her.

When they got to the floor above, he noticed the decorating scheme changed from turquoise blue and edgy to red with lots of glass and chrome. He figured they were in the offices of another magazine in the EPH publishing empire.

As if reading his mind, she turned and said over her shoulder, "This floor houses *The Buzz*."

"Let me guess," he said dryly. "You work for *The Buzz*." He reined in his temper once again at the thought that he'd been taken in by some reporter's scheme to get access. Marty would have a fit.

"Yes," she acknowledged, then added, "Did anyone recognize you when you came in?"

"I'm surprised you didn't hear the squeals and screams up on the eighteenth floor."

She stared at him in astonishment.

"Worried?" he asked, unable to resist toying with her. Only after a deliberate pause did he explain, "This is New York City. Of course, anyone who recognized me was too blasé to care. That's why celebrities love New York."

When they got to the conference room, she shut the door behind them, and he sat on the edge of the conference table and folded his arms.

"Now, where were we?" he asked with outward pleasantness. He raised a hand as if to stop her reply. "Oh, yeah, you were about to explain how you forgot to mention you're a reporter, why you snuck out of my hotel room in the middle of the night and why you happened to be dressed like Scarlet." He added, focusing at the diamond ring on her finger, "Not to mention the fact that you've got a fiancé hidden away somewhere."

"He isn't hidden away. He's on a business trip."

"Even better." He felt a stab of jealousy. "I wonder how the future Mr. Summer Elliott will feel knowing his fiancée lost her virginity in a hotel room to a man she'd known only a few hours."

She flushed.

He cocked his head. "A little extreme, don't you think? Losing your virginity for the sake of a reporting assignment? Or was this just some prank that you and your sister concocted—sort of the last hurrah before the wedding?"

"Stop it! It's not the way you're making it seem."

"'Stop it,'" he mimicked. "Is that the best that you can do? Come on, Summer, let go of the uptown girl. Let's hear you really swear."

He was furious with her and even more furious with himself. He, who had a reputation for bad-boy ways and a sullen sulk, had been used and abused by Ms. Prim and Proper. The newspapers would have a field day.

"I don't need to swear," she snapped back. "And you're one to talk. Do you jump into bed with a different groupie every night?"

"Jealous?"

"That's ridiculous."

He decided not to enlighten her about his promiscuity or lack thereof. He wasn't a monk by any stretch of the imagination, but the news reports about him were usually overblown.

Besides, what could he say to explain jumping into bed with her last night? Whenever I see you, I hear a symphony? How corny was that? Not to mention that The Supremes had made it a hit song long ago. Yet, it was close to the truth. If only he could get that damn song down on paper...

Aloud, he countered, "You lied to me. Twice. First

not telling me you're an heiress, now this." He gestured at her hand. "You're engaged."

"I didn't lie."

He chuckled cynically. "Really, *Caitlin?*"

"That's my middle name. Summer Caitlin Elliott."

"And do you usually go by your middle name?"

Her shoulders lowered. "No, but I was only trying to buy a little time—"

"A little time till when?" he interrupted. "Until we were in bed together? Until the newspapers picked up the story?"

She threw up her hands. "Okay! You're right, I'm wrong! Is that what you want to hear?" She blew out a breath. "If you'd just let me explain."

"So explain."

She squared her shoulders. "I'm just a copy editor here, but my goal has been to become a reporter. Everyone knows you're the hottest thing in the music world right now. You're always getting mentioned in *The Buzz* and in other entertainment magazines. I thought that if I could convince you to do an interview…except I knew that you rarely granted interviews—"

"That's because I prefer to let my music speak for me."

So, he'd been right. She had been after an interview. *Screwed for an interview.* He shook his head. *Great.* There was a song in that, he could feel it.

She twisted her hands together. "I know it all sounds bad."

He quirked a brow. "Honey, it doesn't only sound bad. It *is* bad."

He'd begun to calm down, but being alone in the same room with her had his body humming. There were also things that still didn't make sense to him. For starters, she'd been a virgin. Now that he'd started to think logically about all that had happened and all that he'd found out so far, that piece of the puzzle just didn't fit. Unless, of course, she'd been swept away by lust, too.

Keeping his voice even, he said, "You still haven't explained how dressing like Scarlet figures into the picture."

She sighed. "I tried to approach you after the benefit concert on Wednesday night, but I couldn't get by security. Scarlet suggested I'd have better luck if I pretended to be a groupie." She paused. "Of course, I left my engagement ring at home."

He had one other question. "And sleeping with me?"

She flushed. "That wasn't part of the plan. It— I— It just happened."

Not the satisfaction that he was looking for, he thought, but it was something. He had every reason to be furious at her for misleading him and not revealing she was engaged. Yet, there was something about her that soothed his soul even as it inflamed his lust.

Besides, he figured her engagement couldn't be much of an obstacle if she'd been a virgin until last night. And, then there was the matter of *the* song. With that thought, an idea started to take hold.

She blinked rapidly. "I owe you a big apology. I never meant to mislead you. I was waiting for the right moment last night to tell you why I was there, but that moment never came." She drew a quivering breath. "I'm sorry."

He looked down for a moment, then back up at her. "What if I said I'll agree to do the interview?"

Her eyes widened. "You will? B-but why?"

His lips teased upward. "Maybe I've never had someone go to so much trouble just to get within speaking distance of me." *Or, for the matter,* he added silently, *into my bed.*

She looked uncertain for a moment.

"Well?" he said. "How about it?"

"We slept together!"

He shrugged and made sure to keep his voice neutral. "So? That's in the past—" albeit, the very recent past "—and it's not as if we have an ongoing relationship. Besides, this is the entertainment business, not global geopolitics. No one hesitates to use every connection, no matter how it comes about. And anyway, the press thinks I was out with Scarlet last night, not you."

She looked down, contemplating what he'd said, and he found himself holding his breath.

In the morning light shafting through the room's windows, she looked delectable, and he felt like the Big Bad Wolf. Last night hadn't sated his hunger for her. Not by a long shot.

Finally, she looked up at him with those amazing pale-green eyes. "Okay," she said, then added, "Thank you."

He let go of the breath he was holding. The seduction of Summer Elliott had begun, only she didn't know it yet.

"You slept with him?" Scarlet's mouth gaped open.

"A little louder," Summer said dryly. "The next table over hasn't heard you."

They were sitting in a booth in the employees' cafeteria on the fourth floor of EPH, where she and Scarlet regularly had lunch together. The cafeteria was a quicker and easier choice than beating the throngs that clogged the Manhattan streets downstairs at lunchtime.

"Didn't you tell him that you were there as a reporter?" Scarlet persisted.

"Er, we didn't quite get to that part."

"You didn't get to that part?"

Under other circumstances, Summer would have thought this scene was funny. For the second time today, she had managed to flabbergast someone: at the moment Scarlet, whom she knew to be usually unflappable, and earlier Zeke, who certainly appeared that way. Since she was a play-by-the-rules girl, this was a day of firsts for her. Aloud, she said, "Haven't you ever slept with a guy on a first date?"

"Never."

"Never?"

Scarlet shook her head.

Apparently, for once, she'd outdone her twin in outrageousness. She didn't know whether to laugh or cry, which was another sign, she supposed, that she was verging on hysteria.

"Anyway," Scarlet persisted, the salad in front of her forgotten, "this isn't about me and this isn't just about sleeping with a guy. This is about losing your virginity to some bad-boy rock star that you barely know when you said for years that you'd wait for your wedding night."

Summer knew that Scarlet had neither completely understood nor shared her vow of celibacy, but her sister had respected it. Now maybe even respect had flown out the window.

Summer winced at the thought, before joking weakly, "Thanks. Could you maybe make it sound more sordid and trashy?"

"And what about John?" Scarlet demanded, then shook her head. "I don't get it. Why lose your virginity now, when the wedding night is around the corner?"

Summer had been dwelling on the same question since leaving Zeke's hotel room.

After the confrontation with Zeke at the office that morning, she'd resigned herself to getting no work done and had popped outside and sat in a café, sipping tea, until lunchtime.

She'd had plenty of time to think, and to dwell on the fact that she'd never before experienced the same restless, I've-got-to-have-you-now attraction that she had last night with Zeke. The attraction defied explanation and logic—he was unlike her in many ways, and definitely didn't fit her normal taste in men—but there it was.

She'd also started to think that maybe her relationship with John was sexless because it was passionless. There was just no spark. Oh, she loved him, and he'd said he loved her, but maybe they'd both mistaken convenience and warm affection for sexual love.

She felt comfortable and safe with John and she understood him…but maybe that wasn't enough.

"What are you thinking?" Scarlet asked.

"I've been asking myself about John all morning."

"Yes?"

Summer shrugged resignedly, pushing her salad aside. She wasn't going to eat another bite. "I don't know. Maybe I wanted so badly to stick to my five-year plan and settle down that I ignored doubts I was having about my relationship with John."

And maybe she *was* crazy. After all, she was basing conclusions on one night of passion. Passion seemed like such an unreliable emotion compared to the solid and stable relationship that she had with John. Or rather, she amended, the solid and stable relationship that she'd *thought* she had with John.

"What are you going to tell him?" Scarlet asked.

"I don't know," she admitted. "He's still out of town, but I'll eventually have to tell him what happened." She smiled wryly. "However, the fact that the newspapers think it was you last night has bought me some time. Otherwise, I'd be afraid that John would have heard the gossip somehow even though he's out of town. This way, I get to break the news to him gently when he gets back."

She gave Scarlet an apologetic look. "Sorry for getting you mixed up in this."

"Don't worry about it. My reputation can use the spark right now," Scarlet said with dry humor.

A cell phone rang, and Summer realized it was hers. She dug it out of her purse and shrank as she noticed it was John calling.

"It's John," she said to Scarlet before pressing the Talk button and saying brightly, "Hi."

"Hey, yourself," John's deep voice sounded from the phone. "I've missed you."

What could she say to that? "How's your trip?"

"Great," he said, his voice reflecting his good

mood. "We got the deal wrapped up early, so guess what? I'll be flying back from Chicago this afternoon. In fact, I'm at the airport now."

Summer's stomach plummeted.

"How about catching dinner with me tonight?" John asked. "What about One If by Land, Two If by Sea?"

"Sure," she said weakly. One If by Land, Two If by Sea was reputed to be one of New York City's most romantic restaurants. It occupied a landmark eighteenth-century carriage house once owned by Aaron Burr.

"We're about to board," John said, breaking into her thoughts. "Can't wait to see you. Bye."

"Bye," she said before ending the call.

"Well?" Scarlet asked.

Summer looked at her, the weight of doom settling on her shoulders. "He's flying back early, and we're having dinner tonight."

Scarlet raised her water glass in a mock salute. "Showtime."

Five

John was waiting for her at the bar at One If by Land, Two If by Sea when Summer got there at six. She'd suggested an early dinner because she knew he'd be tired from his trip and, more importantly, she could meet him directly after work and thus circumvent having him pick her up at the townhouse. She wanted to avoid being alone with him tonight, given the news that she had to impart.

He slid off a bar stool. "Hey, sweetie."

She tried not to wince at the endearment. It reminded her that she was lower than a worm, that John had always treated her like a princess and that he didn't deserve what she was about to tell him.

When he leaned in for a quick peck on the lips, she looked away at the last moment so that his lips met her cheek.

She could see the slight puzzlement on his face as he pulled away.

"Is our table ready?" she asked cheerfully.

"I think so," he said.

He nodded to the bartender and settled his tab, then, with his hand at the small of her back, he guided her forward. A hostess showed them to their table, and John waited until Summer herself was seated before taking his own seat.

Settled in, he reached over and took her hand, rubbing the back of it in a circular motion with his thumb. "I missed you."

Summer smiled feebly.

What was wrong with her? Looking into John's caring dark brown eyes and catching sight of his disarming dimples, she questioned her decision and wondered whether she was about to compound one error with another. John was a man that any woman would be proud to be seen with. He was good-looking, hard-working, ambitious and reliable. In short, a catch in any sense of the word.

"I'm glad you're back," she responded, sliding her hand away. "Are you going to order some wine?"

He frowned. "Yes. I just hadn't gotten around to it yet." Nevertheless, he picked up the wine list and started reading it.

Summer took the opportunity to study him. The light from the overhead chandeliers caused his light brown hair to glint and gleam. He should have been perfect for her, but something had been missing.

Doubts. She'd been having them all along where John was concerned. Niggling doubts that hadn't gone away. But why, *why,* did she have to sleep with another man before she was willing to face them?

After the wine arrived, they ordered, then discussed John's trip. Because John traveled often for his high-octane career in advertising, he was often full of interesting stories about shooting TV commercials and developing promotional campaigns for new products.

"So, we sewed up the deal," he said, cutting into his beef Wellington. "Three print ads for watches by one of Hollywood's hottest actresses."

"I'm surprised she agreed to do it," Summer commented.

"So am I. A lot of film stars are reluctant to do ads in the United States because they're afraid it'll detract from their image. They'll do ads abroad, but only with the stipulation that those ads won't run in the U.S."

"So why do you think she agreed to do it?"

"Money," John replied. "This advertising campaign is going to cost our client a bundle, but the CEO thinks it's worth it because their target audience is the eighteen-to-twenty-four age group."

Summer had grown used to John throwing out advertising jargon as if it was second nature. He talked in terms of *target audiences, market share* and *campaigns.* She knew that being immersed in his career was part of what made John so successful at what he did.

As a waiter moved away with their plates, John said, "By the way, I saw that Scarlet was linked to Zeke Woodlow in today's gossip columns. Maybe she can convince him to do some ads."

Wine sloshed from the glass that Summer was raising to her lips. She watched as the spilled liquid caused a couple of angry red spots to spread on the formerly pristine tablecloth.

"Careful," John said.

She set down her glass with a thump and cleared her throat. She'd been waiting for the right moment to broach the subject of Zeke and now she was out of excuses. Dinner was over, and there was no time like the present.

"John, we have to talk," she blurted, waving off a waiter who had approached with dessert menus.

John looked at her inquiringly for an instant, then asked the waiter for the check. As the waiter moved off, he said, "So talk. You've seemed jumpy and distracted all night. I was wondering what was bothering you."

"This is hard," she began. Explain first and confess later, or confess first and explain later? She waffled.

"Yes?" he prompted.

"Something unexpected happened while you were away, and I—I came to some realizations."

He said nothing, just looked at her expectantly.

Tears threatened. She felt as if she were about to kick a puppy. Looking down, she said in a rush, "John, I can't marry you."

"What?" he said on a forced and skeptical laugh.

"It's not a joke."

"Why? I thought—"

She didn't let him finish. "I had sex with someone last night. Zeke Woodlow."

There it was. The harsh, glaring truth.

John looked as if she'd slapped him or thrown a bucket of ice water over his head.

"What did you say?"

"I slept with Zeke Woodlow last night. The gossip columns got it wrong. It wasn't Scarlet with Zeke. It was me." She took a deep breath, her eyes pleading with him for some understanding even though she neither deserved nor expected any. "I didn't plan it. I went to a Musicians for a Cure concert to try to land an interview with Zeke for *The Buzz*." She trailed off helplessly, "I don't know what happened…."

John snorted derisively. "Come on, Summer, you know what happened." His brows snapped together. "So you're now on a first-name basis with Zeke, are you?"

Realizing her mistake, Summer shook her head. "I don't blame you for being angry and hurt."

"Really?" he said sarcastically, then raked his fingers through his hair. "I go away for a few days and you sleep with someone else. Do you know how that makes me feel? You told me you wanted to wait for marriage."

"I know," she said guiltily, "and I've spent the past twenty-four hours wondering how and why last night happened. I wasn't drunk or too stressed out, but I realized I'd been pushing aside doubts about us."

"What doubts? We're perfect for each other. We want the same things out of life."

"Yes," she agreed, knowing she had to tread carefully, "but we lack spark. Maybe…maybe that's why it was so easy for us to put off sex for so long."

He said nothing.

"Maybe we love one another without being passionate about each other." She added softly, "You deserve to have some passion in your life, John. We both do."

John downed the rest of his wine in one swallow. "I could've been as passionate as any rock star, Summer, if you'd just given me the opportunity. Instead, I agreed to *your* terms about waiting until the wedding night."

She looked down, unable to hold his gaze. Catching sight of the engagement ring still sparkling on her finger, she tugged it off. Taking hold of his hand, she placed her ring in his palm and gently wrapped his fingers around it.

He stared down at their hands.

When the waiter came back to their table with the check, she reached for it, but John was faster.

Pulling his hand from hers, he said bitterly, "Allow me to pay for the last hurrah."

"You broke up with John," Scarlet repeated in disbelief.

Summer nodded. They were sitting in a bar near EPH, Summer having phoned Scarlet to meet her after her dinner with John.

"Why? Are you crazy?" Scarlet asked. "Why throw away a perfectly good relationship? So you slept with Zeke! So you made a mistake! That doesn't mean you should just throw away the man you love—the man you're going to marry. Everyone makes mistakes."

Summer shook her head. "You don't understand."

"Isn't John worth fighting for? If he can forgive you because he loves you, you two can put this behind you and move on with the life that you always intended to have together."

"It's not that simple. I'm not calling off the engagement because I slept with Zeke. I'm calling it off because sleeping with Zeke made me confront the doubts I'd been having about marrying John."

"Such as?"

"Maybe John and I love each other, but not in the sexual way that two people getting married should. Maybe it was easy for our relationship to remain sexless because it was passionless."

"Aren't you getting it backward?" her sister argued. "Maybe it was passionless because it was sexless."

"That's what I thought, but after last night I started to realize it was the other way." She paused. "John is a wonderful guy, but we just don't share that much passion."

Scarlet looked surprised, started to say something, and then stopped. Covering Summer's hand with her own, she said, "Are you sure you're not letting yourself be swayed by a night of great sex? Having sex for the first time can be heady stuff. It can screw up your thinking. You know, *Charisma* just ran a survey, and you wouldn't believe how many women, even today, feel they have to stick with the first man they sleep with."

"No," she said stubbornly, "it's not that, and I'm not confused. I have no intention of getting involved with Zeke just because I slept with him." *Just because I lost my virginity to him,* she added silently. She had no intention of compounding last night's mistake. "But if I'm sure of anything right now, it's that continuing to stay engaged to John would be wrong. I need time to sort things out."

"Are you sure this isn't just a case of cold feet?" Scarlet persisted.

"What?" she countered. "Cold feet from the day I got engaged? Months before the actual wedding?"

Scarlet sighed. "I guess you won't be the first woman to call off an engagement because she's realized it's a mistake."

Ironically, she found herself wanting to comfort Scarlet. She gave her sister a reassuring hug. "Cheer up! I finally let myself admit that John was so much like what I thought I wanted in a husband that I'd been ignoring the fact that I wasn't in love with him. At least the realization didn't strike at the altar."

"I guess I should be glad it didn't take that long," Scarlet murmured.

"What?" Summer asked.

"I said, I guess *he* should be glad it didn't take that long."

Summer nodded uncertainly. For a second, she'd thought Scarlet had responded with something completely different. Aloud, she said, "It's for the best, Scar. I'm sure of it. You'll see."

Zeke prowled around his hotel suite, half listening to his manager. It was almost nine o'clock on Friday night and within half an hour he'd be heading out to one of New York's hottest clubs, the celebrity hangout Lotus.

Like many celebrities, he was welcome with open arms at Manhattan's hot spots. Club owners were only too eager to toss free drinks and food at a star in exchange for free publicity, namely, having their club's name linked in the press with that of an A-list celeb.

Unfortunately, Marty had decided to stop by minutes ago from his own hotel room elsewhere in the building—ostensibly to discuss last night's benefit concert, but Zeke wasn't fooled.

Marty was a forty-something, balding music-industry veteran who'd been lucky enough and savvy enough to manage more than one great act during his career. But while his experience often made him invaluable, it also meant he could sniff potential trouble a mile away.

"So, you and Scarlet Elliott," Marty said, shaking his head. "I didn't even know you'd met."

"We didn't until this morning."

Marty frowned. "Come again? There was a photo—"

"I know about the damn photo," Zeke said irritably. "The reporter got it wrong. That was Summer Elliott last night." He added by way of explanation, "Scarlet's identical twin."

Zeke was still digesting everything that had occurred in the last twenty-four hours. *Damn it, she was engaged!*

"Elliott? As in Elliott Publication Holdings?" Marty asked.

"The one and same." Another piece of information, Zeke reflected, that she'd conveniently left out about herself. Hell, she'd known he'd assume she was some groupie.

Marty threw him a penetrating look. "Heiresses aren't your usual type. The publicist that we just hired for you has already been busy fielding questions from the media."

Zeke stopped in front of Marty. "What's he saying?"

Marty shrugged. "The usual. Fudging and leading the reporters on. You know, a half-hearted denial that you're involved with her, or rather, with the sister."

Zeke nodded. His public image was carefully cultivated. There was always a delicate dance with the media for maximum positive exposure and spin. Usually that meant leaving the public guessing about his love life, and appearing single and available and never too serious about any one woman for too long. Successive relationships helped keep his place as front-page news, and that suited him just fine. He knew he wasn't husband material, especially with a lifestyle that kept him on the road.

"So what's the truth?" Marty asked with his typical bluntness.

Zeke raked his fingers through his hair. "The truth is that she was a reporter after an interview with me."

He was not going to provide the intimate details about what had happened last night.

"I take it that you didn't give her the interview."

"That's right—"

Marty looked relieved.

"—but I've agreed to do an interview with her this week."

"What?" Mart stood up straighter. "I thought we'd been over this. All interview requests get vetted by me and the publicist. We want to make sure you're appearing in the right markets—"

"She works for *The Buzz.*"

"—and that the reporter knows the ground rules beforehand about what topics are off-limits—"

"Give me a break, Marty. This is going to be a short interview, not an in-depth profile for *Rolling Stone.*"

"It's not like you to cave in so easily to a request for an interview," Marty said, frowning.

Zeke shrugged. "This is going to sound nuts, but whenever I'm near her, I start hearing the song that's been playing in my head for the last few months and that I haven't been able to write. The only other thing that's been able to call it forth is a photograph that I have hanging back in the mansion in Los Angeles."

"She's your muse?" Marty asked, looking floored.

"Yeah, I guess you could say that."

Zeke watched his manager's face settle into unhappy lines. "Look, Zeke, I know you're into this songwriting stuff, but you're the hottest thing on the music scene right now. There are plenty of people who would love to be in your shoes, but they don't have your voice and they sure as hell don't have your sex appeal. Why mess with a good thing?"

They'd had this discussion half a dozen times. "Fame's fleeting, Mart."

"So? You can concentrate on the songwriting career later. For now, do yourself a favor and focus on putting out CDs and on touring to keep your name out there."

"I'm still mulling over that offer to write for a Broadway show."

Marty rolled his eyes. "Next thing you'll be telling me that you're getting serious about this Elliott chick. Remember, you've got an image as a heartthrob to maintain."

Zeke laughed and clapped him on the shoulder. "Marty, man, you're a damn pain in the rear."

<u>Six</u>

Emerging from the car, Summer looked up at The Tides and squared her shoulders. She felt as if she were twelve years old again and going in for a lecture from Gram and Granddad that was sure to end with her getting grounded.

Still, The Tides was home, and whenever she was stressed, she particularly welcomed its warm embrace. Probably not many people would think of the nearly 8,000-square-foot century-old mansion made of rusty sandstone as warm and inviting, but it was to her.

She breathed in the brisk sea air. Located in the Hamptons—an exclusive vacation community several hours east of New York City—the five-acre Elliott estate sat on a bluff overlooking the Atlantic Ocean.

Ever since her parents had died in a plane crash when she and Scarlet were only ten, she and her sister had been raised by Gram and Granddad at The Tides. Even now, she and Scarlet spent most weekends there.

Except, this morning Scarlet had begged off going out to The Tides, mumbling that she had things to do in the city. And when she'd tried to ask her sister where she'd gone last night—because Scarlet hadn't been home when Summer herself had finally gotten back to the townhouse after staying on at the bar with some coworkers after her sister's departure—Scarlet had clammed up.

She hoped Scarlet wasn't mad at her for breaking up with John in the way that she had. Her sister had seemed understanding enough yesterday, but this morning she'd been cool, abrupt and aloof, refusing to say where she'd been or with whom. They'd never kept secrets from each other in the past, so Scarlet's behavior had hurt.

Summer waved to Benjamin Trent, her grandparents' long-time groundskeeper, then climbed the steps to the front door.

Home. She put down her bag and tossed her jacket onto a nearby chair, looking around the house as she did so and taking in for the thousandth time the understated and elegant decor that was a testament to Gram's fine taste.

Footsteps sounded on the marble floor and a few seconds later, Gram emerged from the living room at the back of the house.

"Summer! What a lovely surprise!" Gram said, her voice colored by an Irish accent. "I wasn't sure if you were coming this weekend, with the wedding planning and all."

Wedding. She was reminded again of the conversation that lay ahead. Nevertheless, she smiled, then kissed her grandmother on the cheek. "Hello, Gram."

Her grandmother had been a nineteen-year-old seamstress in Ireland when Patrick Elliott had swept her off her feet. Now, though she was seventy-five, one could still detect some freckles on her pale skin and some auburn in the white hair that she always wore in an updo. Despite her somewhat frail health, she radiated warmth and cheer.

When Summer pulled back, she noticed Gram's eyes went to the door, then back to her.

"You're just in time for lunch. Scarlet hasn't joined you?"

"No, she said she had things to do in the city this weekend." She linked her arm with Gram's, and they started toward the breakfast room at the back of the house. "We'll have a lovely lunch anyway, won't we?"

"With you here, of course!"

She'd always felt protective toward Gram. Not only had Gram lost her son Stephen and his wife—Summer's parents—in a plane crash, but she'd also lost her seven-year-old daughter Anna to cancer. Adding to the strain, Granddad hadn't always been on the best of terms with his and Gram's surviving adult children.

When they got to the breakfast room, Olive—Benjamin's wife and the housekeeper at The Tides—greeted them warmly, and Gram asked her to set another place at the table.

Noticing that only three places were to be set, Summer asked, "Aren't Aunt Karen and Uncle Michael here?"

"Michael had to get back to the office yesterday to deal with pressing business and won't be back till this evening," Gram responded as they took their seats. "And Karen is resting." Gram's face clouded. "She's too tired to come down and will take her meal in her room later on."

"How is she doing?" Summer asked quietly. Her aunt, her uncle Michael's wife, had recently been diagnosed with breast cancer and had undergone a double mastectomy.

"Karen is never one to complain. I'm thankful the cancer hasn't spread, but the chemotherapy that she's taking as a precaution is going to take its toll."

Summer knew her cousins were concerned about

their mother, whose diagnosis remained guarded. The only bright light, Summer reflected, was that her cousin Gannon had just gotten married, and his younger brother, Tag, had recently gotten engaged to a wonderful woman. The celebrations had given her aunt something to look forward to.

Of course, Summer's own wedding, or nonwedding, was a different story.

She nearly jumped when her grandfather entered the room.

"Well," Patrick Elliott said in his usual booming voice, "if it isn't the return of the vagabond grandchild."

Unlike his wife, her grandfather showed gruff affection at best, but Summer was well used to it. She rose from her seat and kissed him on the cheek. "Granddad, you know I was here just last weekend." Settling back into her chair, she added, "It's just me this time, though. Scarlet decided to stay in the city."

Patrick Elliott took his seat as Olive, humming, came in with their bowls of chicken soup. "So how's your vagabond sister?"

Summer let out a half laugh.

"Patrick, you're incorrigible," Maeve said. "Stop teasing the poor girl."

Patrick's only response was a slight movement of his bushy eyebrows as he raised a spoonful of soup to his lips. Summer knew that if there was one person who could bring her grandfather to heel, it was Gram. He adored her.

Over lunch, they talked about current events and Maeve's charity work, as well as happenings in and around the Hamptons.

Just when Summer was starting to relax, however, and they were finishing up lunch over fresh berries and cream, Patrick nodded at her hand and said, "What happened to your sparkler?"

Darn. Leave it to her grandfather to zero in on her ringless hand. He'd probably noticed as soon as he'd come in and sat down, but, in typical Patrick Elliott fashion, he'd let his victim relax before going in for the kill.

Gulp. "I've called off the engagement."

"Have you now?" her grandfather asked pleasantly, as if they were discussing the weather.

"Oh, Summer," Maeve said. "Why?"

The million-dollar question, she thought. She wished she had a good answer. She knew that saying she'd lost her virginity to a globe-trotting musician whom she barely knew wouldn't play well with her Irish-Catholic grandparents.

"Um—" She cleared her throat. "I realized John and I just weren't suited for each other."

Maeve's brow furrowed. "But he seemed like such a nice man, and you two were like two peas in a pod."

"I think that was part of the problem," she said.

"We had no spark. We were too alike." Good grief, this was an awkward conversation to be having with her grandparents.

Patrick removed his napkin from his lap and set it down next to his plate, shaking his head. "Too alike? In my day, you met a fella with a steady job, you got married. You didn't worry that being responsible adults made you too alike."

Summer groaned inwardly.

"Patrick, do be quiet." Maeve patted her hand. "It's all right, dear."

Patrick stood. "I need to get back to work—like a responsible adult."

Watching her grandfather's retreating back, Summer said, "I guess I was speaking a foreign language to him."

Maeve sighed. "He'll get over it."

"I know he liked John." She looked at her grandmother. "They're similar in many ways. Smart, ambitious, hard-working." She hoped her grandfather didn't think her rejection of John amounted to a rejection of his values as well.

"He just wants to see you happy," Maeve said, "and he understands John." She added, her eyes twinkling, "After all, your grandfather's been a devoted husband for fifty-seven years. Naturally he's an expert on the formula for marital bliss."

"Naturally," Summer concurred.

Then they shared a laugh.

Thank God for her grandmother, Summer thought. She could defuse almost any situation, which was one of the many reasons that she also made an excellent hostess.

Not that breaking the news to her grandfather had been all that bad. Within the range of Granddad's reactions to news that he didn't want to hear, his response had been mild. It was almost as if, notwithstanding his subsequent bluster, her news hadn't come as a complete surprise to him. She wondered, too, whether she'd only imagined the flicker of respect in his eyes for a moment.

"I'll never understand Granddad."

Summer didn't realize she'd spoken aloud until Maeve said, "He has his reasons."

She looked at her grandmother. "You know the atmosphere at EPH has become downright chilly since he made it a competition among the magazines to name his successor. It's true that I haven't felt it much because Uncle Shane remains fairly easygoing, but I know Scarlet's felt the pressure at work because Aunt Finny is working harder than ever to make sure *Charisma* is at the head of the pack."

She didn't have to mention the strained relationship between her aunt Finny and her grandfather. She knew Granddad had mellowed with age, but he'd always run a tight ship. While building his empire, he'd sometimes cared more for appearances than for his family, and he'd paid for his mistakes by alienating some of his children and grandchildren.

Maeve looked sad. "I'd hoped Patrick's challenge wouldn't put additional strain on his relationship with Finny."

"But why?" Summer asked. "I just don't understand why he had to set up this rivalry within the family. It's started to pull people apart."

Maeve looked thoughtful for an instant, then said quietly, "As I said, your grandfather has his reasons for doing what he does, and he'll never back down on this one. I have faith that the family will pull through without falling apart."

Summer wasn't so sure.

She was alone again with Zeke in his hotel room and keenly aware of him. Summer tried to forget the last time she had been here.

Today he was dressed in blue jeans, a white T-shirt and an open button-down shirt. Of course, now she knew what lay beneath those clothes: hard, sculpted muscles, smooth sun-kissed skin, powerful thighs....

She yanked her mind away from her wayward thoughts. She was here to do the interview that he'd promised her and nothing else.

She knew from reading the newspapers that Zeke's publicist had issued a denial that the two of them—or, rather, he and Scarlet—were more than friends. With any luck, the whole story would soon fade away. It would, she promised herself, as long as she managed to get her interview and get out of here.

When she'd returned to work yesterday morning, after having spent the weekend torturing herself about her recent behavior, Zeke had called to schedule an interview for Tuesday afternoon.

Of course, she'd agonized over what to wear. She wanted to look professional but not prudish. She'd tossed aside her twin sets and an angora sweater, and had finally settled on a fitted silk Chinese-style jacket over black pants and half boots.

She really needed to go shopping. If not for the Chinese-style jacket that Scarlet had tossed at her at a designer sample sale, she didn't know if she'd ever have found something appropriate to wear.

"Have a seat," he said, breaking into her thoughts and making her jump. "Can I get you something to drink?"

"J-just some water. Thank you."

He smiled as he headed to the kitchenette.

Was it her imagination or was his grin tinged with wickedness? Was he remembering that the first time they'd met she'd drunk more than just water? Maybe he thought she was trying to avoid past mistakes.

When he returned, he handed her a glass of water

and took a seat in a chair perpendicular to the couch that she was sitting on.

She took a sip. It was almost a relief to be away from EPH and, instead, here interviewing Zeke. She hadn't heard from John since Friday, and she supposed he was traveling again. Scarlet was still distant, and her family's reaction to her broken engagement had ranged from shock to dismay.

"Don't you have a photographer with you?" Zeke asked, breaking into her thoughts.

"I'm taking the photos." With her free hand, she raised the case holding her camera.

He gave her a quizzical look. "You're the photographer?"

She shrugged self-consciously. "I've taken classes. It's a hobby." She put her glass down on an end table.

He gazed at her intently, and she shifted. What was he thinking?

"You look different," he said, his voice—that incredible voice—as smooth as honey and as deep and rich as chocolate.

Concentrate, Summer, she scolded herself. "Mmm, really?"

"Yeah, at the concert you were rocker girl, and at work on Friday you had a white-gloves-and-pearls retro look. Today, though, you look exotic." He cocked his head. "I'm still trying to figure out which of you is the real Summer Elliott."

Maybe she was, too. "Maybe all of them are."

He shook his head. "I don't think so. I think you're still trying to figure out who you are."

"I thought I was the one doing the interviewing," she said lightly.

His lips twitched. "Isn't an interview just a two-way conversation? Besides, the more I get to know you, the more I find you intriguing."

"Thank you—I guess."

"For instance," he went on as if he hadn't heard her, "do you *ever* wear your engagement ring?"

She thought about lying, but decided it was best to come clean. He'd probably find out the truth soon enough from the newspapers anyway. "I broke off the engagement."

She saw a flare of heat in those amazing blue eyes of his before he banked it. "You told him."

"I told him," she confirmed, then added defensively, "You're not the reason that we broke up, if that's what you're thinking. You just made me realize John and I would be making a mistake by getting married. I broke up with him before I told him what had happened between us on Thursday night."

"What did happen on Thursday night, Summer?" Zeke asked, his voice deep and smoky.

"I—I still don't know."

"It was incredible. *We* were incredible."

"Stop it. You promised—"

"What did I promise?"

She remained silent.

"I don't remember promising anything. I remember saying I wanted to see you again."

"For an interview," she clarified. He was twisting around the conversation that they'd had. "Your manager and publicist called yesterday after you did, and they peppered me with questions about the timing and substance of this interview."

"Sorry to hear that."

She looked around. "Where are they, by the way? I had the impression they wanted to be here."

His eyelids dropped, concealing his expression. "They both had things to do."

She thought that was odd, but decided not to remark on it. Instead, she brought out the tape recorder that she'd carried along with her. He was making her nervous, and the only way to avoid any more dangerous conversation was to get down to business. "Well, let's get on with the interview, don't you think?" she asked briskly. "I don't want to waste your time."

The look that he gave her was an invitation to sin. "You're not wasting my time."

A shiver chased down her spine. She cleared her throat and switched on the tape recorder. "What's your biggest challenge as a musical artist?"

He laughed. "Diving right in, aren't you?"

She raised an eyebrow.

He sighed. "Okay. The biggest challenge is to avoid repeating myself. I think that's what every artist worries about. I want my music to stay fresh and vital and to still be commercially successful."

To Summer's surprise, the interview unfolded easily after that, the conversation flowing smoothly. He talked about the success of his latest CD and his involment with Musicians for a Cure.

Eventually, she decided to move the interview to a different topic. "There haven't been any stories about you and drugs, or getting arrested, or brawling—"

"Sorry to disappoint," he quipped.

"But," she went on, "you've been described in the press as 'surly' and 'a bad boy.' How do you think you've come by your reputation?"

"Simple. I usually refuse to give interviews."

A laugh escaped her before she could stop it. "You've got different legs of an international tour for the rest of the year. What's up next?"

"Houston is next, at the end of the month, then L.A., and I'll be going abroad soon." He paused. "But I'll be staying in New York until the end of the month."

"Oh?" she said, tamping down an annoying little thrill.

"Yeah, I'll be catching up with family."

She knew from her background research that he'd grown up in New York. "I'm sure they'll be happy to see you." She turned off her tape recorder because she'd gotten what she needed for her article.

He gave her a sly grin. "Unlike you, you mean?"

She refused to take the bait. "The bio on your Web site says only that you grew up in New York."

"That's purposeful. I like my privacy." He tossed her another quick grin. "But if *you're* curious, I grew up on the Upper West Side."

She wondered whether he'd lived within a stone's throw from where she lived now.

"My father's a professor at Columbia University," he elaborated, "and my mother's a psychologist in private practice."

She tried to picture him as the son of an academic and a shrink, and failed.

He gave her a wry smile. "Yeah, I know. Hard to believe." He paused. "But not as bad as it sounds. My father's an archaeologist, so we spent most summers on digs in South America and the Middle East." He shrugged. "That probably explains why I picked a career that requires lots of travel."

"Did you always know you wanted to be a musician?" she asked.

"You mean, a rock star?" he asked mockingly, then shook his head. "No. For a while I followed the path that my parents expected of me, but a month before graduating from Columbia, I landed my first recording deal."

"What did you major in?" she asked, surprised he'd graduated from a prestigious Ivy League university. He certainly didn't have the pedigree of a typical rocker.

"Music. On and off campus. What about you?"

"English, with a minor in journalism." She added, "At NYU."

"High school?"

"Private school in the Hamptons. What about you?"

"Horace Mann," he said.

They smiled at each other until she cleared her throat. The conversation had gotten way too personal. How had that happened? "Okay, I'll just need some photos of you to accompany the article," she said.

He stood up. "Right. Where do you want me?"

She gave him a quick look. Was he coming on to her?

He just looked back at her blandly.

She stood, her digital camera in hand. "Er, somewhere bright but not in direct sunlight. Also, we'll want a backdrop that's not too busy."

"How about if I sit on the arm of that chair over there?"

She nodded. "Sounds good. Then we can take some of you standing in front of the living room wall. That'll provide a solid, off-white background."

As soon as he was ready and she'd adjusted her camera, she started snapping shots.

"Big smile," she said, and he obliged, giving her a disarming smile.

He was a natural in front of the camera, changing the angle of his head but still looking great in every shot.

She warmed as he looked at her through the camera's viewfinder. What she read in his blue eyes was enough to quicken her pulse. It was a good thing that the camera was between them, she thought, mitigating the power of his potent appeal.

All the while, she somehow continued to coax reactions from him. "Don't smile. Give me serious," she said, snapping away. "Now tilt your head down and look up at the camera." *Snap, snap.* "Now turn your head to the side and slant me a look." *Snap, snap.*

By the time he'd posed straddling the chair, and then moved to pose in front of the wall, the air in the room had become sexually charged.

"Now give me smoldering," she said unthinkingly.

He did, and she thought, *Oh, my.*

It was like experiencing vertigo. She was felt dizzy and breathless.

She lowered the camera and pretended to fiddle with it. "Okay, that's it."

He walked toward her and when he reached her, he slid his hand under her hair and around the back of her neck, exerting subtle pressure to force her head up to his.

She barely had time to close her eyes before his

lips feathered across hers. Once, twice, three times, and then he was there, claiming her mouth in a kiss that was so sweet, so deep, so satisfying that her knees nearly buckled. The hand holding her camera went limp by her side.

When he finally pulled back, she whispered, "Why did you do that?"

"Because I wanted to," he said.

She looked at him mutely.

"Because you were turning me on. Because I wanted to confirm that what I experienced on Thursday night wasn't just a fluke."

"We can't."

"Can't or shouldn't?"

"Both."

"Why? You're not engaged anymore, remember?" He rubbed his thumb across her lips. "What are you doing Friday night?"

"I've got plans. There's a party for *The Buzz* at my cousin's restaurant, Une Nuit."

"Invite me."

The letters M-I-S-T-A-K-E flashed across her mind.

"Come on," he coaxed. "Don't I deserve a thank-you for submitting to an interview? Besides, you'll be helping *The Buzz*. I'm sure the staff there would love a personal connection to another celebrity."

He was persuasive, she'd give him that.

He bent for another kiss, and she ducked. "Okay,"

she relented as she scooted past him to gather her stuff and, more importantly, to put some space between them.

For *The Buzz,* she promised herself. Only for *The Buzz.*

Seven

Une Nuit, located on Ninth Avenue on the Upper West Side, wasn't what Zeke had been expecting. He'd looked up the restaurant before coming over, so he knew it was known for its French-Asian fusion cuisine, but he was still surprised by the ambience. The decor was seductive with low red lighting, black suede seating and copper-top tables.

At Summer's insistence, they'd planned to meet at Une Nuit rather than at her place. He figured she didn't want to draw any unnecessary attention to them as a couple.

After getting a drink at the bar, he scanned the

crowd that was standing and milling about and spotted Summer laughing with some guy who looked like a male model.

Frowning, he made his way toward her, aware of the glances thrown his way. He was used to looks and whispers when he was recognized.

When Summer spied him, laughter still lurked in her eyes and she exclaimed, "Zeke, you're here!"

Apparently not a moment too soon, he thought dryly. He bent and kissed her on the cheek, grazing the corner of her lips—and staking his claim. She was dressed in black, as was he, and she looked fantastic.

As he straightened, he gave her an intimate smile. "Hi."

"Zeke, have you met Stash?" she asked, gesturing with the hand holding her wineglass.

Zeke looked Pretty Boy in the eye and noted the amusement on the other man's face. Stash? What the heck kind of name was that? And why didn't Stash go stash himself somewhere else right now?

Aloud, he said, "I haven't." He stuck out his hand. "Zeke Woodlow."

The other man grasped it. "Zee pleasure iz all mine."

Zeke almost rolled his eyes. A Frenchman? He had to compete with the lure of Stash's foreign mystique?

"Stash is the manager of Une Nuit," Summer said. "Zeke is—"

"I know who iz Zeke Woodlow, *chérie,*" Stash

said. A smile curved his lips. "I am afraid that work calls, however, so I weel leave you to your friend."

Zeke watched as Stash kissed Summer on the cheek and then sauntered off, tossing him another amused look as he went.

Stash, Zeke thought sourly, seemed like the type who could charm honey away from bees. Turning his gaze back to Summer, he asked, "You two know each other well?"

"Stash has been the manager here a long time."

Hardly reassuring, Zeke thought.

Summer beckoned to him, and with narrowed eyes, he followed her as she moved deeper into the gathered crowd.

She greeted people as she went until she was stopped by a man who looked to Zeke to be a quintessential smooth operator. The guy was around his own height of six foot one but looked to be about a decade older—perhaps in his late thirties.

Great. Was he destined to spend the whole evening batting away potential rivals?

Standing next to the dark-haired playboy type was a curvy green-eyed blonde. She gazed up at the playboy admiringly, but he hardly seemed to notice—*his* attention was directed at Summer.

Damn. He took another step forward and moved closer to Summer.

Summer looked up, seeming to realize all of a

sudden that he was still there. "Zeke," she said, "this is my uncle Shane Elliott, the editor in chief of *The Buzz*, and his executive assistant, Rachel Adler." To Shane and Rachel, she added, "This is Zeke Woodlow."

Zeke's shoulders relaxed. He needed to get a grip. His attraction to Summer was starting to drive him crazy—even if right after their interview, he'd been able to get down a major chunk of the melody and lyrics for the elusive song in his head.

Zeke shook Shane's hand and noted that Shane's grip was just as firm as his own.

"It's good to meet you," Shane said. "Summer tells me that the interview went well."

"The interviewer did her homework."

Shane laughed. "In any case, I appreciate your taking the time. We're in a heated race and every little bit helps."

The talk then shifted to a discussion of the music industry and who was topping the music charts, or would be soon, with new CDs.

When the conversation eventually ended and he and Summer had moved on, Zeke asked, "What did he mean 'we're in a heated race'?"

"I'll tell you later."

"Tell me now."

She sighed. "My grandfather, who founded Elliott Publication Holdings, recently announced that the head of whichever EPH magazine is the most profitable by the end of the year would succeed him as CEO."

Zeke whistled. "So basically he's letting his kids duke it out over who will succeed him?"

"Yes."

"So that's what made you desperate enough to try to beard the lion in his den. You were hoping an interview with me would help the home team."

He watched her shrug. "I did it for myself *and* for *The Buzz*. I'm just hoping Granddad's challenge doesn't tear this family apart."

Zeke grimaced. "It's at times like this that I appreciate growing up an only child." He gave her a wry smile. "No matter what, the parents still have only me."

"And you still have them."

The look in her eyes made him stop. He'd done some digging into her background on the Internet, and surprisingly, while there'd been plenty of mentions of her grandparents and assorted other Elliott relatives, there'd been none connecting her to her parents.

Before he could ask, however, she said, "My parents died together in a plane crash when I was ten."

"God, I'm sorry," he said.

"I've had fifteen years to learn to cope, but, you know, the hurt never completely goes away."

Before he could respond to that, their conversation was interrupted by a man Summer introduced as her cousin Bryan, the owner of Une Nuit.

"Stash sent me over," Bryan said before Summer could say any more. "He told me that he'd run into the two of you together by the door."

From the way Bryan pronounced the word *together* and from the look in his eyes, Zeke could tell he'd come over to check things out himself.

Doing some sizing up of his own, Zeke estimated that Bryan was about his own age—twenty-eight. In contrast to Shane, however, there seemed nothing laid-back about this Elliott cousin. If anything, Bryan seemed to be constantly watchful, taking in everything and giving nothing away. He was like a panther ready to pounce.

Zeke looked Bryan in the eye as they shook hands, and a certain recognition and mutual respect passed between them.

"Bryan has the perfect life," Summer joked.

"Really?" Zeke asked, looking from Summer to Bryan and back.

"Yes," Summer said, throwing her cousin a teasing look. "He has this fantastic bachelor pad above the restaurant that lets him just fall out of bed and go to work. Not only that, but he's got a job that keeps him well away from EPH and us other Elliotts. Or, I should say, one Elliott in particular, namely my grandfather. And on top of it all, Bryan gets to travel to fantastic places for the restaurant."

Interesting, Zeke thought. Not only was the statement revealing about Bryan, but it was intriguing that Summer thought the perfect job was *away* from EPH.

"Summer's exaggerating," Bryan said.

"No, I'm not."

"Where do you travel for the restaurant?" Zeke asked.

Bryan shrugged. "Europe mainly. Paris."

"I was in Paris just a month ago. What did you think of—?"

"Excuse me, will you?" Bryan said suddenly. "I just spotted someone I've been trying to catch up with all evening."

Strange, Zeke thought, watching Bryan's departing back. He got the distinct impression that Bryan wanted to avoid talking about his travels.

Zeke watched as another guy who'd also been observing Bryan's departure turned back now and said, "I see you've met the clan's International Man of Mystery."

Turning to Summer, the guy gave her a peck on the cheek and said, "Hey, honey. Long time no see."

"Zeke, this is—"

"Let me guess," he said dryly. "Your cousin." The guy bore a striking resemblance to Bryan. They shared the same coloring of jet-black hair and blue eyes. In personality, however, this cousin seemed as smooth and laid-back as Shane.

"Cullen Elliott," the man before him said, his eyes glinting. "I'm Bryan's younger brother." Holding up his thumb and index finger a half an inch apart, he added, "But only by that much."

"Cullen is the director of sales for *Snap*," Summer supplied.

Zeke feigned shock. "You're from the rival camp? What are you doing here?"

Cullen grinned. "I'm invited everywhere." He added, "So Summer's filled you in on the family rivalry, has she?"

"Yeah," he said. Turning to Summer and jerking a finger at Cullen, he asked, "If he's here, where's Scarlet? Doesn't she work for an EPH magazine, too?"

Zeke watched Summer frown. "Scarlet decided not to come. She went skiing with friends this weekend."

Cullen turned to him and raised an eyebrow. "I saw the piece about you and Scarlet in the *Post*," he teased. "Are you wondering if you're out with the right sister?"

If only Cullen knew, Zeke thought. Beside him, he noticed that Summer froze for a second, then pasted a lighthearted smile on her face.

"Don't listen to Cullen," Summer said, swatting her cousin playfully. "He's broken more hearts than I can count."

"Yup, that's me," Cullen said, obviously playing along, though Zeke noticed a shadow flit across his face. "I'm giving Shane a run for his money for the title of Playboy Elliott."

They talked to Cullen a little more, then Zeke suggested to Summer that they head to the bar and refresh their drinks.

When he'd asked the bartender for a bourbon on the rocks for himself and another glass of white wine for Summer, he turned to her and said with dry amusement, "I've run the gauntlet for you tonight with your relatives."

"They're just curious," Summer responded. "They know I broke off the engagement to John, and now, tonight, I show up with you."

"Did you tell them that it was you and not Scarlet at the Waldorf?"

"No, but they're curious nevertheless."

"Do they have anything to be curious about?" he couldn't resist countering.

She cast him a sidelong look. "Not anymore."

He noted, however, that, when their shoulders accidentally brushed, she moved away self-consciously. She was clearly not as cool and collected as she wanted to appear.

He handed her drink to her and took a sip of his own. "I like your cousins. They're interesting characters."

"Interesting?"

"More than they seem," he elaborated.

She tilted her head inquiringly.

"Bryan and Cullen seem like they have a few secrets. Bryan in particular."

Summer looked doubtful. "You know, Cullen was joking when he said Bryan was the International Man of Mystery. It's just that, more than most of the rest of us Elliotts, Bryan has a separate life away from the family."

He arched a brow. "Something tells me there's more to it than that."

Summer looked skeptical, but then smiled. "I've known them my whole life and, believe me, there's never been anything mysterious about them. Bryan is a restaurateur at heart, and Cullen...Cullen is exactly what he said he is. He's a magnet for women."

Zeke decided not to push the point further, though he remained unconvinced Bryan and Cullen were as uncomplicated as baby cousin Summer thought they were.

He followed Summer to a buffet that had been set up at the back of the restaurant and they helped themselves to items such as fried Kumamoto oysters, crab and avocado millefeuilles, and a lobster and melon salad with Asian pear and Thai mango dressing.

Later, Cullen joined them again, and Zeke met a few more of Summer's coworkers, who all seemed curious about him.

Eventually, however, they were left alone at a

corner table, and an awkward silence reigned—a novel situation for him where women were concerned.

Slowly, though, he succeeded in drawing her out. They talked about the places that he'd traveled to, and he regaled her with stories about strange and unusual fans and even weirder tabloid headlines.

They discovered that they both knew how to speak Spanish well and French badly, that they loved Malta in the summertime, and that they preferred their Mexican food really spicy. They debated whether they'd had better skiing in Vale or the Alps, and which were the best places to go on St. Bart's.

"So," he finally joked, "what're your musical tastes? Who do you like?"

"They're all dead."

He laughed. He supposed he shouldn't have been surprised. "Classical?"

She took a sip of her wine. "Yes, and oldies. Sinatra. Nat King Cole."

"Are you just being diplomatic and trying not to admit you prefer my competition?" he teased.

She looked at him from beneath her lashes. "If I did, would you mind?"

Realizing that she was flirting with him, he banked his satisfaction. "I'd be heartbroken, but I'd console myself with the thought that we're both Beethoven fans."

A smile tugged at her mouth. "I enjoyed your concerts. You're very good."

"Only very good?" he teased again.

She looked into his eyes. "Compelling," she said softly.

As he continued to look into her eyes, he felt himself go up in smoke. Man, she had an effect on him.

He decided to let her—and himself—off the hook. "Actually, chances are I'll be leaving the performing behind sooner rather than later."

He could tell he'd surprised her. "Really?"

"Yeah, I see myself concentrating on songwriting instead." He looked around. The crowd had thinned a bit, though the party was still going strong.

"Are you ready to leave?" she asked.

"Yeah." He looked at her. "I'm ready, are you?"

It was a loaded question, and he knew it, but he wanted her badly. Being near her and holding back was torture.

"Yes," she said, "let's go." She gave no indication that she'd taken him at other than face value.

They wound their way to the front door, saying good-night to people on the way, and he retrieved her coat and his jacket from the attendant at the cloak room.

Fortunately, Shane and Cullen were nowhere to be found. Bryan, on the other hand, just tossed him a significant look that said Zeke had a modicum of his trust and shouldn't do anything to waste it. Zeke gave him the barest of nods that said the message had been delivered and noted.

He held the front door open for Summer, and when they got outside the restaurant, he pulled a baseball cap out of his jacket pocket and pulled it low over his eyes.

She looked at him questioningly.

"Keeps me from being recognized by paparazzi," he explained. "Can I get you a cab?"

"No, thank you," she said. "Home is just a few blocks away."

"I'll walk with you, then."

She hesitated for a second. "Okay."

Eight

She was burning up. It was crazy, of course. It was only thirty degrees outside. But beneath her cashmere coat and underneath her wraparound top, she was burning up.

And it was all due to the man beside her.

Zeke.

Her lover.

When they arrived at the Elliott townhouse, Summer watched as Zeke looked up at the huge gray structure, taking it in.

She was used to people being impressed by the place that she and Scarlet used as a weekday residence and that her grandparents used when they were in town.

She tried to see it through his eyes, as if for the first time. The three-story mansion boasted white trim and was set ten feet back from the street, shielded from curious passersby by a black wrought iron gate covered in ivy.

Zeke looked at her. "Your grandfather wasted no words in making a statement, I'll say that for him."

His insightfulness surprised her. Most visitors' observations ended with the physical structure before them. "Granddad started the EPH empire," she said. "On his way up, I think appearances were very important to him."

"Yeah."

"Jealous?"

A smile quivered at his lips and he glanced at her. "More like envious of his privacy." He added, "And feeling like an idiot now for thinking you'd be impressed by my suite at the Waldorf."

She flushed. She didn't like being reminded of how she'd misled him that night, but he didn't look angry now, only as if he was enjoying teasing her.

Still, now that they'd arrived at the townhouse, an awkwardness fell over her. Trying to cast off the feeling, she heard herself ask, "Would you like to see the inside?"

"Sure."

As they made their way up to the front door and

inside, she had time to rue her impulsive offer. She should've said goodbye outside.

Should've, could've, hadn't.

Instead, after they had deposited her coat and his jacket and cap in the front hall, she showed him around. The house was quiet because of the late hour, the few servants asleep or gone for the day.

She was very aware of him behind her as they made their way from the grand entry hall, with its impressive stained glass skylight, to the library and then on to the dining room and living room. She showed him the family room and kitchen, and they looked out at the back porch, which overlooked a private garden.

Eventually, he followed her up to the next level, where bedrooms for family and guests were located, and then to the top floor, where she and Scarlet had sleeping quarters.

Finally, he stood in the open doorway of her bedroom.

Trying to gauge his reaction, she babbled, "And this is my room. It's been redecorated over the years. Fortunately, Scarlet and I never had to share a bathroom. I'm not sure our relationship would have survived otherwise."

She looked around at the white-and-cream color scheme that contrasted dramatically with the antique cherrywood furniture, and at her brass bed with its matelassé cover.

What was he thinking? Too cozy?

He said nothing, just looked around, and she stopped fidgeting.

Finally, he murmured, "Very feminine."

He strolled in and stopped by the closed laptop and paperwork on her desk. Looking down, he asked, "You've started writing up our interview?"

"Yes." She walked over to him. She'd forgotten she'd left her draft sitting out.

He picked up some sheets of paper and cast her a curious look. "Do you mind?"

"No—I mean, no, I don't mind." She gave a nervous laugh. "As long as you don't expect the right to censor it."

He quirked a brow. "Don't worry," he murmured. "Given all the stuff that's already been written about me, I doubt I'll be shocked."

She waited nervously as he read.

She'd labored over every word of the article so far. And every word had brought back in stunning detail thoughts of him and of that night at the Waldorf.

She'd toiled over how to describe him without sounding trite or love struck. *Zeke Woodlow, soul of an artist, body of a sex symbol,* she'd written before deleting the words. She'd called herself ridiculous and more, then had stared at the blank computer screen for ages.

Finally, she'd decided to open with the heart of the matter: a quote from Zeke himself on striving to keep his music fresh and relevant.

Just then, he broke into her thoughts. "Very good," he said. "I like it."

"Really?" Realizing she'd sounded embarrassingly surprised, she tried again, "I mean, really?"

A smile played at his lips. "Yeah, really. I have just one criticism."

"Oh?"

He put the article down. "It needs more research."

"I'm not sure there's anything else I need to know."

He moved closer until he was standing within scant inches of her, and she felt her breath catch in her throat.

"Are you sure?" he murmured. "Because there are lots of things I need to know about you."

Their sexually tinged banter was causing her skin to prickle with awareness. "Such as?" she whispered.

His hand came up to cup the side of her face, the pad of his thumb tracing over her lips. "Such as whether your skin is always so soft." He drew her closer and bent his head. "Such as whether your mouth is always as kissable as it looks," he whispered against her lips.

His mouth fit over hers expertly, and soon she was lost in the same sensations that had swirled between them that first night at the Waldorf.

She clung to him until he lifted his head and looked down at her, his eyes lingering on the deep *V* created by her wraparound top. "I like what you're wearing tonight," he said in a low voice.

"I went shopping," she confessed. She'd finally nabbed some time and headed to the stores, determined to have something to wear for tonight that sent the right message. She hadn't spent too much time analyzing why it mattered so much what she wore.

"Very sophisticated."

"Maybe it's the emergence of the new Summer Elliott," she joked.

"If it is, I'd be only too happy to help with the process in any way I can," he said seductively.

She felt a strange fluttering in her stomach. This dance of desire that they were engaged in was still new territory for her. "We were talking about the interview."

"Yes…and research."

"Are you trying to seduce me?"

"If I am, is it working?" His gaze lingered on her chest, where her nipples pressed against the material of her top. "You seem kind of turned on."

"You're not really my type." Was she trying to convince him or herself? "Everyone that I've dated has had conservatively short hair." They'd also had desk jobs. A closet full of business suits. *They hadn't been rebels.*

He laughed. "Learn to live dangerously."

Did she dare?

"And you're definitely my type," he teased.

She looked at him disbelievingly.

"Authentic," he clarified. "Fresh and natural and lovely."

She looked into his gorgeous blue eyes and felt her self-control slip, but she said, "For once, I'd like to think of you outside a haze of desire."

He laughed. "Why? Some people say the luckiest ones are those that never emerge from the haze."

Maybe he was right, she thought. Ever since the night at the Waldorf, a question had lingered: Who was that passionate woman who'd tangled the sheets with Zeke Woodlow? An aberration? Or a part of herself that the sensible Summer Elliott had kept bottled up, fearing to let loose?

She wanted to find out, and Zeke seemed all too willing to oblige her.

He shifted closer at the same time that she took a tiny step toward him. She fit seamlessly into his embrace, and mouth met mouth.

Summer felt Zeke's hand fit over her breast and rub her nipple, bringing it to a peak and making her want him all the more. When his lips moved away from hers, he feathered kisses over her eyelids, along the side of her face, and down to the hollow of her throat.

She tugged at his crewneck shirt until it came free

from where it was tucked into his jeans. He finally obliged her by yanking it over his head.

Not waiting for an invitation, she trailed her fingertips over his chest, feeling his hard muscles flex under her touch.

When he stilled abruptly and cursed, she raised her eyes to his. "What's wrong?"

"I didn't bring any protection."

"I have some."

"Why, Ms. Elliott," he drawled, "were you planning to seduce me?"

She batted her eyelashes at him. "Not until tonight, but I happen to know Scarlet has some condoms in her bathroom. Scarlet's a better-safe-than-sorry kind of girl."

Sure enough, Summer located an unopened pack in her sister's bathroom cabinet. As she returned to her own bedroom, she thought she heard Zeke humming. Walking into the room again, she discovered he'd lit some of the candles. The faint scent of roses hung in the air.

"Now, where were we?" he asked coming toward her. He took a foil packet from her hand and tossed it on the night table.

He took her in his arms and kissed the corner of her mouth, pulling at the tie of her wraparound top until it came undone. Pushing the delicate material off her shoulders, he exposed her breasts, encased in a lacy bra.

He looked up at her, his lips quirking. "I'll say this for you. You've got fantastic taste in lingerie."

She smiled, embarrassed. The truth was, she'd taken to heart Scarlet's advice from the night of the concert: dress sexy and you'll feel sexy. So, she'd gone out and bought more sexy underwear. "It's a recent development."

"Well, hurray for small changes." He cupped her breasts and stroked them, arousing her.

"Zeke…"

"Yeah?"

Take me. I've got to have you inside me. She longed to give him the kind of sexy words that he'd whispered to her on the first night they'd made love, but she found she couldn't speak.

"What do you want, Summer?" he asked, his voice low and seductive. "Tell me."

"Kiss my breasts."

"Mmm," he said, his eyes hooded. "Kiss them? You mean like this?" He bent and placed open-mouthed kisses at the cleavage revealed by her bra. "Is that what you want?"

"No," she said, her voice tinged with frustration. He knew what she wanted.

He seemed to pretend to consider. "No?"

All at once, she knew what she had to do. Two could play at this game. He was teasing her, and suddenly there was every reason to shed her inhibitions.

Keeping her eyes steady on his, she took a step back.

"Where are you going?" he asked.

"Nowhere," she said seductively. "Why don't you have a seat, Zeke?"

His eyes widened a fraction, but he sat down on the bed.

"Comfortable?" she asked as she went to the bedside lamp and dimmed the lighting.

"Yeah."

"I hope you like jazz," she said as she turned on soft music. "Some people say it puts them in the mood. Do you agree?"

"Come here and find out."

A thrill coursed through her at his words. She moved toward him, and, while she did so, she unclasped her bra and let it fall to the floor. Reaching him, she pushed him back against the bed until he rested on his elbows, and then she straddled him.

His face registered surprise and then delight. "Now that you've got me, what are you going to do with me?"

She bent and kissed him, deeply and languorously. When she pulled back, she said, "Kiss me." She gazed into his eyes. "I want you to kiss my breasts. I want you to do all those wonderfully erotic things that you did that night in your hotel room."

He sat up. "With pleasure."

She guided him to her and when his mouth closed over her breast, she sighed, her fingers tangling in his hair and her eyes fluttering shut. He played first with one breast and then with the other, until she thought she couldn't stand any more.

Clasping her, he tumbled her down onto the bed and came down beside her, his leg wedged between the two of hers. She could feel his erection pressing into her hip.

He kissed her, making love to her with his mouth, his hands caressing her while hers stole up and down his arms, playing over hard muscles.

When the air between them had become charged to a fever pitch and they were both breathing deeply, he levered himself off the bed.

He stripped the remaining clothes from her and then shed his own jeans and shoes.

She surveyed him unabashedly. He was aroused and gorgeous.

"Feel free to touch," he said.

She wanted to.

She sat up and reached out, taking his erection in her hand and stroking him.

He closed his eyes, his breathing becoming deep and harsh.

When he groaned, she bent and took him in her mouth.

"Ah, Summer," he sighed, his voice throaty.

She'd never felt so powerful and sexy.

When she finally pulled away, Zeke came down

beside her on the bed, a helpless laugh escaping him. "Wow. That felt good."

She smiled at him, suddenly a bit shy.

He looked at her closely. "What's this? Embarrassment from my seductress?" He cocked his head. "Maybe I should really give you something to blush about."

Moving over her, he kissed and stroked his way down her body, leaving her hot and aroused and wanting. When he reached her inner thighs, she moaned and tried to clamp them shut.

"Shh," he soothed.

He took his time until his questing mouth went to the very core of her, which was warm and wet and wanting him.

Summer felt the world close around her like a warm cocoon. There was only Zeke and the wonderful things that he was doing to her…until the universe exploded behind her eyes and she shook with ripples of pleasure.

When she finally returned to earth, she heard the sound of ripping foil, and then Zeke was beside her again, taking her into his arms.

He held her and kissed her, and this time his entry was smooth and uninterrupted, though he seemed to go slowly to give her time to adjust to him.

Once he was inside her, he rolled over so that she lay on top of him.

She looked down at him in surprise, the curtain of her hair shielding them from their surroundings.

"Take me where you want to go, Summer," he said huskily. "You're in control."

She hesitated for a second, then moved experimentally. His responding groan was all the encouragement she needed.

She let him guide her in setting up a rhythm, following him as he quickened the pace. She watched as his eyes closed and his muscles became taut, his face tensing with pleasure.

She closed her eyes, too, concentrating on the pleasure building between them.

When her climax came, she gasped, spasmed and then stilled as Zeke grasped her hips and thrust into her.

Zeke groaned and, a split second later, joined her in going over the edge to sweet oblivion.

She fell against him then, and he held her.

"Ah, Summer, you do it for me every time," he said, stroking her hair. "You are so passionate."

"I've never thought of myself as passionate," she said, her voice muffled against his shoulder.

"You're kidding."

She shook her head, then raised it to look at him. "John and I never shared much passion."

He shook his head. "Well, take it from me. You're one of the most responsive women I've ever met. I just can't believe you remained a virgin this long."

"It was all part of the five-year plan."

"Huh?"

"The five-year plan," she repeated. "I drew up a life plan, and part of it called for getting married by twenty-six."

He laughed, then asked curiously, "And what else did it say?"

"Oh, you know, the usual stuff. Aim to get promoted to management by thirty. Have a baby." Somehow, giving voice to her goals seemed like confessing something embarrassing.

"You can't live life by a neat plan."

"It's important to have goals," she said defensively.

"Yeah, but not when they interfere with examining your evolving feelings. Sometimes plans can get in the way of getting what you really want."

"You sound like an expert."

He grinned. "You can take it from me. I'm the son of a psychologist, and I'm also someone who gets paid big bucks for singing about emotions."

"Yes, I noticed. I thought I heard you humming something under your breath a little while ago before we were, ah, otherwise occupied. I didn't recognize the tune. What was it?"

"Nothing," he said obliquely. "Just a song that I kind of know."

"Hmm," she said, running her foot along his leg.

His hand clamped down on her moving leg and

stilled her, his face taking on a seductive intensity. "On the other hand, I don't just *kind of* know you."

As he pressed her into the bed, she laughed breathlessly and gave herself up to tonight, for once not thinking about tomorrow.

Nine

The next morning, Summer woke up feeling happier and more content than she could recall being in a long time. She looked across at the man lying asleep next to her.

Zeke.

She'd never before woken up next to a man. She wondered why she never had, and yet she knew how she was feeling now was due to Zeke himself.

Looking at him, she itched for her camera so she could snap his picture. In repose, unguarded, his features relaxed, he looked even more heart-stoppingly handsome than on stage.

A part of her couldn't believe *the* Zeke Woodlow had taken an interest in her. She knew he couldn't be attracted to her for her money, since he was very wealthy in his own right.

She recalled the events of last night and flushed. They'd fallen asleep and woken up to make love twice more during the night. After the last time, Zeke had sung her to sleep. Just thinking of it now, she felt warm and cherished all over again.

She was pleased he'd liked the write-up that she'd done of their interview. She'd walk on hot coals before she'd admit it to anyone, but she'd played back the tape of their interview repeatedly, just to hear the sound of his voice.

She watched as Zeke opened his eyes and smiled, rolling on his side toward her and stroking her with his hand. "Hi."

She smiled back at him. "Hi."

He pulled her toward him and nuzzled her neck. She laughed and squirmed, and soon there was no more talking.

Much later, he asked, "Any plans for the weekend?" He waggled his eyebrows. "Spending it in bed, I'm hoping."

She laughed. "Actually, I usually go to The Tides."

At his confused look, she added, "My grandparents' estate in the Hamptons. It's where Scarlet and I were raised after my parents died."

His hand caressed her thigh. "Take me along."

"I couldn't!"

The words were out of her mouth before she had a chance to think. Yet, of course she couldn't bring him to The Tides! Last night Une Nuit, and now The Tides? She'd be flaunting him right after her breakup with John.

He cocked his head and gave her a look of mock offense. "What's the matter? I'm good enough to sleep with but not good enough to be seen with?"

"Isn't that my line?" she responded. At the moment she still had to figure out how to sneak him out of the townhouse without alerting any of the servants. Fortunately, there was a secondary entrance from the outside directly to the living quarters that she shared with Scarlet. She just had to get downstairs to retrieve his jacket and cap, which they'd left in the foyer last night, and sneak back up.

Zeke just continued to look at her in amusement, and she wondered for a second whether he'd read her mind.

"Anyway," she asked, "aren't you busy? Don't you have things that you need to be doing this weekend?"

He smiled. "Nope. I'm all yours."

"We'll have to take separate bedrooms," she warned, weakening despite herself. "My grandparents are traditional." She didn't add that, of course, she wouldn't give him the room that John used to stay in. *That* would be a little much all around.

He gave her an intimate smile. "I can be fun out of bed, too."

She heated. "You're incorrigible."

So it was that, later that day, they pulled into The Tides' parking garage. Because they'd gotten a late start and had had to swing by the Waldorf, it was already after lunchtime when they arrived.

As they walked along the breezeway that connected the garage with the rest of the mansion, she watched Zeke look around, then arch a brow. "Even more impressive than the townhouse."

She shrugged half-apologetically. "To me, The Tides has always been just home."

"Some home," he said as they walked into the house.

They dumped their overnight bags in their rooms, and Summer was relieved when she was told by Olive that her grandparents were out and would not be back until dinner. At least she didn't have to deal with those introductions just yet.

"How is Aunt Karen?" she asked Olive.

"Michael brought her into the city to see her doctors. The both of them are not expected back until Monday."

Uh-oh. She'd been hoping her aunt and uncle would be around to act as a buffer between Zeke and her grandparents.

Olive served them a quick late lunch, and afterward Summer said to Zeke, "Come on, I'll show you around the estate."

They went back to their rooms for jackets to guard against the blustery March weather. On the way out Summer grabbed her camera and slipped it into her pocket. She always left one of her digital cameras in her room at The Tides. She liked to amuse herself on weekends by taking pictures of the surrounding landscape, playing with light and shadows and capturing the changing seasons.

Outside, they toured the grounds together, taking in the pool house, the helicopter landing pad that her grandfather used when commuting to work in Manhattan, and the site of the English rose garden that Maeve lovingly tended and that bloomed in warmer weather.

Finally, they stopped at the top of hand-carved stone stairs that led down from a bluff to a private beach and boat dock.

Summer drew the camera from her pocket.

She saw Zeke grin as he spotted it.

"What's so funny?" she asked.

"You. I still think you're more suited to be in front of the camera than behind it."

"Oh." She flushed. "I thought that was just a line you were giving me when we were in your dressing room after the concert."

He arched a brow. "Distrustful sort, huh?" He shook his head. "No, I really meant it. With your coloring, you're model material."

"Will you pose for me?" she asked, skirting a subject she wanted to avoid.

"I thought you'd want to capture the landscape."

She shrugged. "I often do, but today I want to photograph you. You have an interesting face." A compelling face. She didn't want to admit just how fascinated she was by it. By him.

He gave her a wicked grin. "Okay, I'll pose for you. I like where this led last time."

She remembered, too. It had led to kissing and would probably have led to much more if she hadn't fled after their interview. *Careful, Summer.*

Soon, though, she was snapping photos of him from different angles, first as he looked out at the water, and then as he stood on the stone steps.

"Did you ever do photo sessions with John?" he asked when she was done.

"No," she answered, then realized how that sounded. She lowered her camera and busied herself with shutting it off and putting it away.

"Hey," Zeke said as he came back up the steps to join her, "I want to see how those pictures turned out."

"I'll e-mail them to you."

She was troubled by what she'd admitted to Zeke—and to herself. She'd never been fascinated by John's face, had never had a compulsive urge to snap his picture.

Good grief, what was wrong with her? She'd

nearly convinced herself to marry a man who'd really been not much more than a good friend. On the other hand, maybe it was her current fascination with Zeke that was abnormal.

When she looked up, she caught Zeke gazing at her thoughtfully.

"It's okay if you find me more fascinating than you do other men," he teased.

He saw too much, she thought with chagrin. "Let's get back."

Later that evening, as she sat across the dining table from Zeke, Summer realized dinner was going to be as much of a trial as she'd thought. Olive had informed her grandparents that Summer had brought a "male friend" along with her.

Summer had started to count the number of times that her grandfather's eyebrows had risen and fallen with suspicion, and now she wondered if civility would hold sway at least until the end of the meal.

Even her grandparents had heard of Zeke Wood-low and, of course, her grandfather was no fool. If her cousins had seemed to sense there was more to her relationship with Zeke than met the eye, then certainly Patrick Elliott wouldn't be fooled. Last weekend she'd announced her broken engagement, and this weekend she was showing up at The Tides with a different man in tow.

At that thought, she caught her grandfather's penetrating look and nearly winced as she got a good idea of his thoughts: *Well, Summer, my girl, these are the sorts of shenanigans that I'd have expected out of your sister and not from you.*

Zeke cleared his throat, breaking the uncomfortable silence that had descended. "So, Summer tells me you're in the process of choosing a successor. Do you already have big plans for your retirement?"

Summer groaned inwardly. The word *retirement* didn't exist in her grandfather's vocabulary. Not really, and certainly not as applied to him.

She wondered why Zeke would bring up a touchy subject. She'd already told him how the competition among magazines was exacerbating family tensions. She tossed him a quelling look that he either didn't see or refused to acknowledge.

Summer watched as her grandfather leisurely finished buttering a roll and took his time answering. She knew from experience that one of her grandfather's techniques for making his targets uncomfortable was to draw out the silence.

Zeke, however, appeared to remain completely at ease. It was she who felt like squirming.

When Patrick finally looked up, he said, "Some of us never really stop working. For others, though, the party never seems to end." He bit into his roll.

Argh, Summer thought.

She watched as Zeke took his time chewing his food and swallowing. "Yes, sir. That's all too true. I'm glad we fall into the same camp on that score."

Patrick huffed, as though he couldn't believe Zeke had the audacity to claim that he—the up-by-his-bootstraps, self-made founder of a publishing empire— had anything in common with a bad-boy rock star.

Summer noticed her grandmother hide a smile. Well, at least Gram seemed to be rooting for the underdog.

Patrick stopped eating and addressed Zeke. "You mentioned that your parents are a professor and a psychologist. Do they approve of your career choice?"

"They weren't too happy at first, but they realized I was entitled to pursue my own dreams. How about yours?"

Summer thought she heard her grandfather say something under his breath that sounded suspiciously like "insolent pup." She wanted to crawl under the table, or at least throw her napkin over her head.

Maeve appeared to catch the pleading look that Summer sent her and said, "When Patrick first came calling, my father disliked him intensely."

"Then I'm glad he's only continuing a family tradition," Zeke said.

Maeve looked greatly amused, while Patrick lowered his eyebrows.

To Patrick, Zeke added, "I'm like you. Ambitious, hard-working and willing to start at the bottom and work my way up in a field in which I had no connections."

Patrick studied Zeke thoughtfully. "But still with time to dally, it seems. First with one granddaughter, now with the other, eh?"

At Summer's gasp, her grandfather turned to her and added, "Don't look at me like that, my girl. I'm still able to read, and, yes, news of Scarlet's appearance with Zeke in the *Post* did make its way back to me. I may need reading glasses, but I'm not dead yet."

"That was me, not Scarlet, Granddad!"

The minute the words were out of her mouth, Summer regretted them.

Patrick sat back, a curiously satisfied look on his face.

Summer flushed. "I mean—"

Zeke looked Patrick in the eye. "There is no explanation."

Summer recovered enough to add, "I still meant what I said last weekend. I realized that John and I wouldn't suit, that we're too alike, so I called off the engagement."

"Your grandfather understands," Maeve interjected. "After all, there was a time when he was young and impetuous himself."

"Never," Patrick declared.

"Why," Maeve continued, as if she hadn't heard her husband, "my father swore that Patrick was heading for the shortest courtship on record."

Maeve then steered the conversation to a safer topic and asked Olive to bring in some fresh fruit.

Summer was relieved when dinner wrapped up soon after that. Afterward, she sat with Maeve in the small tearoom, which was done up with chintz-upholstered furniture, and sipped some herbal tea from a porcelain cup. Her grandfather and Zeke had disappeared into the library, and Summer worried about their conversation.

"I think Patrick likes him," Maeve said.

Summer jerked up her head to look at her grandmother. "You're kidding. How can you tell?"

Maeve gave her a fond little smile. "Zeke refused to be cowed. He put me in mind of Patrick nearly sixty years ago when he came to Ireland and courted me."

Summer mulled over her grandmother's comment, and later that night, when she finally caught Zeke alone, she said, "I did try to warn you about Granddad."

Zeke laughed. "His bark is worse than his bite."

"What did you talk about in the library?" she asked curiously.

"We smoked cigars and shot the breeze. He showed me his impressive collection of first editions." He added with a wink, "Don't worry, I like him."

Her eyebrows shot upward in surprise, but Zeke just laughed again.

* * *

On Wednesday night, Zeke picked up Summer at work in his rented sports car. They'd made plans to eat at Peter Luger Steak House in the Williamsburg section of Brooklyn, just over the bridge from Manhattan, and then take in a photography exhibit at an art gallery in nearby Fort Greene, which was known as an artists' haven from Manhattan's high rents.

He'd never met anyone quite like Summer, Zeke reflected. She was a bundle of contradictions. An heiress with few pretensions and not a few insecurities. A throwback to another era, but one who had career ambitions. A recent ex-virgin who could send him from relaxed to heavily aroused in less than a minute.

Maybe that was why he found her so fascinating.

He glanced over at her now as they strolled the streets of Fort Greene. She had on a short, fitted leather jacket and, under it, a black-and-white striped top that dipped low and was gathered enticingly between her pert breasts. He hadn't been able to stop his gaze from wandering back there again and again during their recently ended dinner.

In fact, he'd had to stop himself from whisking her back to his hotel room in order to spend the evening in bed, engaging in hot and satisfying sex.

"Here we are," she said, smiling and turning to him, interrupting his thoughts.

He looked at the storefront behind her. The store windows were draped with red velvet curtains that shielded the inside, and there were no signs indicating what lay within except for a discreetly placed plaque beside the front door with the words Tentra Gallery in black.

As he soon discovered, however, the space inside was light, airy and loft-like, with a second-floor accessible by elevator. Photographs hung on the walls, each marked by a nameplate and a brief description.

The gallery had attracted a sizable but not overwhelming crowd. And because he didn't want to be recognized, he kept his baseball cap on.

He and Summer started at one end of the gallery and, taking their time, gazed at each photograph individually.

"Remind me again of why we're here," he murmured.

She laughed softly. "Because Oren Levitt is a good friend and one of the photographers whose work is being shown."

"How good a friend?"

She cast him a sidelong look. "Jealous?"

"Do I have reason to be?"

She looked at him from beneath her lashes. "No." Then she added, "Oren's engaged to his longtime girlfriend."

"Good." Irrational relief washed over him. He couldn't recall ever being this possessive—or passionate—about a woman before.

Just then, a lanky guy whose look was all grunge approached, accompanied by a petite woman with dyed black hair and heavy eyeliner.

Summer made the introductions, and Zeke gave a nod of acknowledgment to Oren and his fiancée, Tabitha.

Both seemed impressed and enthusiastic to be meeting *the* Zeke Woodlow, and, as far as Zeke could tell, the only awkwardness came when Oren asked Summer about how John was doing and she had to divulge their recent breakup. If Oren and Tabitha wondered about Zeke's own relationship with Summer, however, they kept their thoughts to themselves.

After Oren and Tabitha had moved on to greet some new arrivals, Zeke glanced down at Summer and said, "Not exactly the type of friends that I'd have thought a debutante like you would have."

She arched a brow. "Are you saying you think I'm a snob?"

"I'm just surprised, that's all. Until recently, you were all pearls and cashmere, and you've still got the posture of a comportment-school grad and the manners for afternoon tea with royalty."

Summer sighed. "I met Oren in photography

class. I met a lot of different people in my photography classes. I *like* meeting different types of people."

"And yet," he mused, "you were about to marry a guy who's apparently just like you."

Turning, he sauntered over to the nearest photo on the wall, leaving her to mull over that observation.

He noticed that she said nothing, but eventually she walked over to join him.

It seemed to Zeke, from what was on display, that Oren liked to do funky portraits. His work was sort of a cross between the photos of Annie Leibovitz and the art of Andy Warhol.

When they made their way up to the second floor, Zeke discovered more of Oren's photographs.

"This is some of Oren's earlier work," Summer said, then added with a frown, "I didn't know he'd have some of these on display tonight."

Zeke spared her a glance as he walked toward the nearest photographs. One was of a clown, another of someone dressed as Marie Antoinette, the ill-fated queen of France.

Turning a corner, he saw other photos hung on the back of a flat pillar—and was brought up short.

Daphne.

It was the same woman who graced the photo that now hung in his mansion back in L.A. The same woman who glorified his dreams. He could swear it was.

Except the woman in this photograph was dressed in a Victorian ball gown, her hair in an elaborate twist on top of her head, her face made-up and partially obscured by a fan.

His eyes went to the nameplate accompanying the photo: "Daphne Victoria."

"What's wrong?" Summer asked as she joined him, glancing at his face and then at the photo on the wall.

He heard her sharp intake of breath before she looked back at him.

With Summer and Daphne now side by side, Zeke found he could finally really compare the two. The pale-green eyes were the same, but as with "Daphne at Play," the hair of the woman in the photo was a couple shades darker than Summer's own auburn.

"The resemblance is uncanny, isn't it?" he murmured. He tore his eyes away from the photo and looked at Summer. "Are the photos on display tonight for sale?"

"I suppose so."

"Good." He nodded at the photo in front of him. "I'll take that one." He glanced around. "In fact, if there are any others like it, I'll take those, too."

"Zeke."

He turned back to face Summer, who stood chewing on her lower lip.

"What's wrong?"

She hesitated. "Oren took that photo."

He gazed at her for a moment, then realization slowly dawned.

Of course. He should have guessed. He wanted to laugh.

"It's you, isn't it?" he asked. If it hadn't been for the heavy makeup and the difference in hair color, he'd have guessed right away.

The woman who haunted his dreams didn't just resemble Summer. She *was* Summer.

He watched now as Summer nodded. "Please don't tell anyone."

"What? Why?" He paused, then asked as suspicion dawned, "No one in your family knows?"

She nodded again. "I posed for Oren once as a favor in order to help him with his career, but only on the condition that he use a pseudonym for me and never publicly link me to the photos."

"So that's why the woman is identified as Daphne."

"Yes.

Another thought occurred, and he drew his brows together. "There aren't any nudes, are there?"

Her eyes widened. "What? No!"

"So what's the problem?"

Her face shuttered. "I just didn't want to cause my family any embarrassment."

"What's to be embarrassed about?" He frowned. "Are you sure your motivation was simply that you didn't want to embarrass your family? Or was this your little private act of rebellion against the strictures of being an Elliott?"

When she didn't answer, he said, "Let me guess. Striking provocative poses for an up-and-coming but unknown photographer didn't mesh well with the image of Summer Elliott as the oh-so-proper publishing heiress and Manhattan debutante."

"Oh, shut up."

He grinned. "Tsk, tsk. Not very polite."

"I'm glad you find this so amusing."

"In fact, I do," he concurred. "Amusing and fascinating. You see, I already own a photograph of Daphne, er, you."

She looked surprised. "You do?"

He nodded. "It's hanging in my home in Los Angeles. That's why I asked you that first night after the concert whether you'd done any modeling."

"I denied doing any because no one was supposed to know about it."

He grinned. "Caitlin, Daphne, Summer. Are there any other personas that I should know about?"

"Very funny."

He regarded her thoughtfully. "Daphne has darker hair, though."

"My hair was digitally enhanced in the photos to make it a couple of shades darker than its natural color."

"Ah." No wonder both Summer and Daphne called forth the song for him: they were one and the same person. In his mind's eye, he saw "Daphne at Play." The woman's face was heavily made-up, her body draped sensuously on a chaise longue.

"You know," he mused, "I love the photograph of you that I have back in L.A. It was the reason I was so dumbstruck when you walked into my dressing room after the concert."

"You do? You were?" She looked pleased, flattered, and—he hoped this wasn't just a figment of his fevered imagination—as if she wanted to jump his bones.

"Let's get out of here," he said huskily.

She nodded.

He wanted her badly. As he punched the button for the elevator, he just hoped he could hold out until they got back to the Waldorf. He didn't want to think of tomorrow's newspaper headlines if they got caught having sex in his car.

Before leaving the gallery, however, he stopped long enough to convince Oren to consider selling him the copyright to all the Daphne photos.

He'd pay whatever it took. If one photo of Daphne could stir his imagination, who knew what a roomful of photos would do for his creativity? And then, of course, there was the stimulating idea of possessing Summer's little secret.

Ten

Summer looked around Zeke's mansion again as she waited for him to return from running an errand. It was a bright Sunday morning, and she relished the mild southern California weather. She couldn't remember being happier.

After leaving the art gallery on Wednesday night, they'd wound up back at Zeke's hotel suite, where they'd made love until the early hours of the morning and then fallen asleep in each other's arms.

On Thursday, they'd dined with his parents, whom she'd found to be smart, witty and charming. Sort of, she thought with a smile, like their son.

And then, somehow, she'd let Zeke talk her into coming out to L.A. this weekend. She'd announced at work that she wouldn't be in on Friday, so the two of them had been able to fly out to the West Coast together.

Now, as she walked from room to room in Zeke's Beverly Hills mansion, she was struck anew by how impressive his estate was. When they'd arrived on Friday afternoon, he'd shown her around a bit, but she didn't have a chance to form more than a general impression. She'd seen that the landscaped grounds boasted an indoor pool, a tennis court and a guest cottage. The house itself, a two-story in the Spanish Mission style, had a red-tile roof, arched doorways and a wonderful veranda, where they'd dined their first night al fresco because of the unseasonably warm weather.

This morning she picked up details that she'd missed in her first walk-through. She loved the way his decor blended antiques of different periods for a look that was stately but still warm and welcoming.

Gram would have approved. She herself approved. Very much. His style reflected her own tastes.

As she walked to the back of the house, she couldn't help thinking that, so far, their time in L.A. had been idyllic. Yesterday she'd snapped photos of him shirtless, then he'd laughingly taken the camera from her and snapped pictures of her. They'd played tennis, then taken a dip in the pool, which had led to their making love in the pool house, despite her half-hearted protests that someone might stumble upon them. At night, they'd eaten dinner at the Hotel Bel-Air, which had one of the city's swankiest restaurants.

On top of it all, Zeke was having a subtle but sure influence on other aspects of her life. Her wardrobe had become sexier and more stylish—in no small part, she realized, because she wanted to entice him. And, of course, thanks to him, she was playing hooky from work—and liking it—for the first time in her life.

Summer stopped as she entered Zeke's music room, where, he'd told her, he liked to play and compose. She looked again at the photograph that hung over the mantel.

She remembered when Oren had taken that shot of her as Daphne, the Greek goddess. She'd been nervous because she'd felt as if she were rebelling, just as Zeke had guessed.

It gave her a thrill to think Zeke had seen "Daphne at Play," and known that he had to have it. It made her believe that it hadn't just been she who'd felt an instant connection, as if they'd known each other forever, when they'd met for the first time. It made her think that something significant had started that night—significant enough to necessitate breaking off her engagement to John.

"I see you've spotted the photo," said a voice behind her.

She turned from the photograph to face the man who was sauntering into the room.

"Hello, Marty," she said. She'd been introduced to Zeke's manager yesterday. He'd struck her as an experienced music-industry operator who always kept his eye on his client's interests and who'd perhaps seen too many rising music stars combust on their way to the top.

Marty stopped beside her. "You know, when Zeke told me that you'd walked into his dressing room back in New York, I thought, what an amazing coincidence."

She smiled. "Wasn't it?"

"And lucky, too. But then luck's always seemed to be on Zeke's side. His first album was released just when the public seemed to have a hankering for romantic and sexy ballads."

"I didn't know it was considered lucky that Zeke met me," she said, unable to keep from feeling flattered.

"He was going through a real dry spell as far as getting down songs for his next album. Sort of a writer's block." Marty nodded at the space over the mantel. "The photo was the one thing that could unblock him and get the creative juices flowing again." He looked back at her. "Of course, having you in the flesh has been even better."

Summer wondered uncomfortably if there was a double meaning in Marty's last words, but he just looked at her placidly. Surely he couldn't have meant "having her in the flesh" literally. Aloud, she said, "I didn't realize I was helping Zeke's creativity."

"Didn't you?" Marty returned, then nodded. "Yes, you're more or less his muse for the time being."

Something in Marty's tone gave her pause.

Marty looked from the photograph to her again. "You know, at first I was worried. A deep entanglement wouldn't be good for Zeke's career. Millions of women see him as a sex symbol."

She managed a nod of agreement. She wasn't sure where this conversation was heading.

"But then," Marty went on, "once Zeke explained his involvement with you was for, uh, artistic purposes, I realized there was nothing to worry about."

"I see." Summer felt a tightness growing and taking hold in the pit of her stomach.

Marty sighed. "Unfortunately, a celebrity of Zeke's caliber has an image to maintain and a publicity machine that needs to be fed—with the right kind of publicity, of course."

"Of course." She was beginning to dislike Marty, but then again, was she just blaming the messenger? Working at an entertainment magazine, she, more than most people, knew the truth in Marty's words about the nature of a celebrity's existence.

Zeke was at the top of his game. He was young, talented and blessed with movie-star good looks. As a sex symbol, it wouldn't be good for him to get deeply involved with someone or, heaven forbid, engaged or married at this point.

"You work for *The Buzz*, don't you?" Marty said. "Of course, you understand how these things work. Just in the last couple of days, I had to plant a story linking Zeke to a supermodel and then issue a non-denial to a competing newspaper. Zeke's got to stay in the public eye, and my job is to keep tongues wagging, but about the right type of stuff."

Summer nodded. She really needed for this conversation to end. She felt sick. She should have known someone like Zeke wouldn't have been attracted to someone like her unless there was an ulterior motive. They were…different.

How naive could she be? Very, she answered herself.

Aloud, she said, "Would you excuse me, Marty?" The comportment-school grad in her kicked in. Politeness under the most distressing situations. Especially in the most distressing situations. "I have a phone call to make." A little white lie, sparingly used, could rescue anyone from the worst circumstances.

"Of course," Marty said. "Enjoy the rest of your stay in L.A."

"Thank you," she managed, then turned and walked toward the door, her head held high and her back ramrod straight. A part of her couldn't shake the feeling, however, that she was fleeing…and Marty knew it.

* * *

"You're leaving?" Zeke asked in disbelief. "Why?"

He'd thought they'd agreed to fly back to New York City together on the redeye tomorrow night. He had a meeting to attend tomorrow morning with his talent agency in L.A., but then he'd be free to accompany her back to New York.

Instead, here she was packing and announcing she was leaving on an overnight flight tonight.

Summer tossed her bathing suit into her suitcase. "I decided I needed to get back. I have a job, remember? A job that I want to advance in."

He was distracted by the bathing suit. He remembered taking it off her yesterday and what had happened afterward.

"I know you have a job," Zeke said, forcing his gaze back to Summer, "but I thought we'd agreed to leave tomorrow night."

"I changed my mind," she said, continuing to pack.

"Damn it, Summer," he said, his patience finally snapping as he grabbed the skirt that she was about to toss into her luggage. "Would you look at me? What is this really about?"

Probably because she didn't have a choice, she stopped. After a moment, she said, "This weekend has been wonderful, but it's also made me realize we're two completely different people with two completely different lifestyles."

He just looked at her. What had happened? He thought they'd been heading toward…something.

She grabbed the skirt back from him and tossed it into the suitcase. "I need to get some perspective, and for *that,* I think there needs to be some space between us."

"Perspective? Perspective on what?" he asked, dumbfounded. A part of his mind understood what she was saying, but he just didn't want to believe it.

Usually, *he* was the one having to let the woman down easy. He'd never liked doing it, and had never boasted about the number of times that he'd had to do so, but it was just a fact of life, given who he was. There would always be women who were ready to appear on the arm of a rock star, however briefly.

He watched as Summer took a deep breath. "Our lives are totally different, Zeke. You tour a lot, and I'm committed to climbing the ladder at EPH."

"Are you?" he asked. "I've started to wonder, you know. You're a great photographer, and you have a real passion for it."

"Becoming a reporter at *The Buzz* is my goal," she said emphatically. "It's the reason I met you, remember?"

"I remember," Zeke said, "but I've also realized that EPH was your grandfather's dream. It doesn't have to be for all his kids and grandkids."

"I know, but it's been my dream for forever."

He wanted to say more, wanted to argue with her, but he decided it would be more productive to change tactics. "Look, even if EPH is what you want, that doesn't mean we can't be together."

"For how long?" she countered.

He had no answer to that. Marty's admonition sounded in his head: *Don't get serious with anyone.* It wouldn't be good for his career.

"I don't want the globe-trotting lifestyle," Summer continued, "and you're not ready to settle down."

What could he say to that? He hadn't really thought about where their relationship was heading. He'd just been happy to take each day as it came. That was how it had been in every past relationship.

Yet, Summer seemed ready to cut her losses now.

"You need to feed a voracious publicity machine," she went on. "You need to stay in the public eye with the right type of publicity, and that's not me. That's not what I want."

Again, he couldn't argue with her. In fact, she was sounding a lot like Marty with her harping on the requirements of his career.

He tried the only tactic that he had left. "Come on, Summer. You've come a long way from where you were just three weeks ago. You're finally breaking out of your shell. Don't back away now. Seize the opportunity."

"Maybe the shell is who I am," she said quietly,

"and you should stop kidding yourself or thinking I'm transforming into someone else."

She turned her back to go to the dresser and get more of her clothes, and Zeke knew that, from her perspective, the conversation was over. They were over.

"Summer."

"Hmm."

"Summer."

Summer swiveled around in her chair at work and noticed her uncle Shane lurking at the opening of her cubicle. She started guiltily. Ever since she'd left L.A. three days ago, she'd had trouble focusing on work. It was now Wednesday, and she was still trying to concentrate.

Shane rested his arm on top of the cubicle's partition. "Good news."

She could use some. "Oh?"

Shane grinned. "You're getting promoted. Next month, you'll be a reporter here at *The Buzz*."

She forced a smile, the news arousing mixed emotions. "Thanks."

"You came through for *The Buzz*, kid, with that interview with Zeke Woodlow. You've helped us keep up with the competition in this game that Granddad started, and you deserve to be rewarded."

In Summer's opinion, Shane had coped with Granddad's challenge better than most of the rest of the family. But then, Shane seemed to view the competition among EPH magazines as a game—a game that perhaps would be interesting and amusing to win.

Shane cocked his head to the side. "What's wrong? I thought you'd be elated about the promotion." He looked at her quizzically. "Isn't this what you've been gunning for?"

She had been. She'd come out and said so last year in her annual employee review. So, what was wrong with her?

For Shane's benefit, she tried a game smile. "Of course, I'm happy." *No, you're not.* "It's what I've always wanted." *Until now.* "I'm just trying to absorb it all. After all, I've been aiming for this promotion for a long time."

Shane nodded, then winked. "Great. We'll have a celebratory drink on Friday."

The staff of *The Buzz* sometimes converged at a nearby bar for TGIF—Thank God It's Friday—drinks, but this time Summer found it hard to work up any enthusiasm. "Thanks, Shane."

When her uncle had left, Summer found herself staring at her computer screen. She wished she could confide in Scarlet, but her sister had been distant and remote lately, not to mention rarely home. Summer couldn't help thinking Scarlet's behavior was due to her breaking up with John and hooking up with Zeke, though Scarlet had never come out and said as much.

She was still morose when she got home that night. As usual, Scarlet wasn't home when she got there, though Summer heard her come in after she'd gone to bed.

It had been three days without a word from Zeke. Summer knew she had no reason to expect him to call, but, perversely, she wanted him to.

After tossing and turning in bed without being able to sleep, she gave up in the early hours of the morning and went to sit on the couch in the living room, staring ahead as the city lights outside created a dim glow in the room.

She was so confused. Today, she'd hit another milestone in her five-year plan by getting her coveted promotion.

She should have been happy, ecstatic even, but she wasn't. She should have been celebrating with John, but she wasn't.

She remembered Zeke's words: *You can't live life by a neat plan.*

She mulled over what he'd said, and wondered if that's what she'd been doing. Had she been trying to make life nice and tidy when, by nature, it was messy and full of the unexpected?

She'd realized she was marrying John just because he fit in with her long-standing plans, but maybe he wasn't the only aspect of her life that she should have been questioning. Maybe trying to move up at *The Buzz* had become something she did unthinkingly, without examining why she was striving for it anymore.

What was it that Zeke had said? *Sometimes plans can get in the way of getting what you really want.*

What did Summer Elliott really want? She almost feared opening that door and finding out what lurked inside, but she forced herself to.

What did she want?

Just as Zeke had said, she was a far cry from the Summer of even a month ago. Gone were the twin sets and pearls and kitten heels. Today she'd gone to work dressed in a bottle-green V-neck top, a snug blazer that outlined her breasts, pants that rode low on her hips and black pumps. The look was sophisticated but soft. Thanks to several after-work shopping trips, her style wasn't Scarlet's, but neither was she the conservative retro chick that she'd been when dating John.

Will the real Summer Elliott please stand up? she thought wryly.

She closed her eyes and thought about the transformations of the past month. She let her mind loose, freed it to think about her most secret desires.

Release your inner goddess.... Release your inner goddess....

Scarlet's words came back to her.

She thought about what she really wanted and realized it wasn't being a reporter, or *The Buzz*, or even EPH. She'd enjoyed interviewing Zeke, but what made her happy was photography. She loved capturing the world around her with a camera.

She hadn't let herself seriously pursue photography because…well, because of fear. Fear that she'd never be good enough to be more than an amateur, and fear of family expectation. She'd assumed—more than been told—that she was expected to work at EPH, just like everyone else in the family did.

She wondered now whether she'd sold herself short. Where would Granddad have gotten if he'd been afraid to succeed in publishing? If he'd let himself be bound by the customary fields of work for the son of Irish immigrants?

What was it that Zeke had said? *EPH was your grandfather's dream. It doesn't have to be for all his kids and grandkids.*

Maybe she'd gone about it all wrong. Maybe remaining true to Granddad's example meant pursuing her own dream rather than her grandfather's.

She opened her eyes and exhaled. *Yes.*

She didn't know what she'd do yet, but she did know her future wasn't tethered to EPH or *The Buzz*. She wanted to find out how much talent she had as a photographer. She'd love to have the sort of gallery exhibit that Oren had had recently.

Zeke's words echoed in her head. *You've come a long way…. Don't back away now.*

Finally, she knew what he'd meant. It wasn't just about John or her love life. It was about her life. Period.

She felt a smile touch her lips. How many times tonight had she thought about what Zeke had said? She didn't care whether it was due to having a mother who was a psychologist, or because he was in tune with emotions because of his music, Zeke Woodlow had taught her a lot about herself.

Her smile widened. She'd learned something— something profound—from a bad-boy rock sensation.

And, with that thought came another.

Release your inner goddess.... Release your inner goddess....

Her inner goddess, she realized, wanted Zeke Woodlow.

Her heartbeat kicked up a notch. She not only wanted Zeke's, she loved Zeke.

He was smart and funny, and he made her a better person by challenging her. And they had amazing chemistry. Sure, she'd learned a lot from him in bed, but she'd learned even more out of it.

She didn't have to wonder whether she was being swayed by Zeke having been her first lover. Intuitively, she knew she'd never have had the same chemistry with John or any other man even if she'd gone ahead and slept with any of them.

It all made sense now. She loved Zeke.

Yes, his career would often put him on the road,

but it would make life with him an adventure. And if she was going to be a serious photographer, a career on the road might be ideal. She'd never lack for interesting subjects and scenery.

It no longer mattered to her that she wouldn't be getting married at twenty-six…or even in the foreseeable future. She realized that life couldn't be lived according to a neat plan.

What mattered to her was that she and Zeke were committed to seeing where things led between them. She knew he'd remain a heartthrob to his fans, but she also knew she could accept that—as long as he felt as strongly about her as she did about him.

That thought should have buoyed her. Instead, she slumped back against the sofa cushions. The problem was that three days ago, she'd kicked Zeke out of her life.

She looked at the glass clock on the end table. It was one in the morning in New York, but only ten in the evening in Los Angeles.

She could call him, but she'd much rather talk to him in person. Then she remembered Zeke had said he had a concert in Houston at the end of the month.

Picking up the phone again, she got in touch with the airline that she usually used.

She was going to Houston, and this time, thanks to *The Buzz*, she hoped to have a press pass to get backstage.

Eleven

Zeke strummed his guitar, played a few bars and paused to jot down some notes.

Then, becoming distracted again, he tossed aside his pencil.

Damn. It was no use.

Since Summer had left four days ago, he'd found it hard to concentrate.

It was now Thursday, and he was still in L.A. He looked around his music room. If time apart was what she wanted, then that was what he'd give her. Anyway, the truth was, he'd been hanging around Manhattan for the past month mostly to be near her, rather than for any pressing business reason.

He had the song down now, and it was about her. It had always been about her, he realized. In a fit of inspiration last weekend, before she'd left, he'd finally gotten the song down—lyrics, melody and all—during the small hours of the morning while she'd slept.

Too bad that now she was gone, his writer's block had returned with a vengeance. He was unable to make any progress on another song, his thoughts straying again and again to Summer.

At a sound from the doorway, he looked up. "Hey, Marty." He looked back down and experimentally played a few notes.

Marty walked into the room. "How's it going?" his manager said, adding, "The housekeeper let me in."

Zeke put the guitar aside and stood up from the couch. "I wasn't expecting you."

"It's sort of an impromptu visit."

"Can I get you anything?" he said. It was almost lunchtime.

"Just some iced tea, if you have it. I want to talk to you."

Zeke nodded. Marty only ever stopped by to talk business.

When they were seated at a table on the veranda, he with a beer and Marty with his iced tea, Zeke said, "So shoot."

"How's work on the next CD going?"

"It's going," he said. "Slowly, but it's going."

Marty nodded, looked off into the distance, and then back at him. "Look, Zeke, I want you to consider something and keep an open mind about it."

Zeke thought he could guess what Marty was going to say.

"For this next album, I was thinking we could have you do remakes of some classic songs, and even get you a little help with the songwriting on new material."

"Marty, no." He raked his hand through his hair. "You know writing songs is what I want to do, and I need to establish my credentials. Get a few more hits under my belt."

"Zeke, under your contract, you need to have another CD out next year."

"I'll make the deadline," he responded, "but then I'm committing myself to doing the songwriting for the Broadway musical that I've been approached about."

"What? Look, I thought we'd discussed this."

He gave Marty a steely look. "You work for me, Marty."

He rarely had to pull rank, but he did it now.

More and more, he and Marty were seeing his career in different terms, and Zeke wondered how much longer they'd be able to work together. In the past, Marty had steered him right in many ways, but this was a decision that he felt strongly about. It was a question of vision—vision about what to do with *his* life.

"Zeke, be reasonable. At the moment, you can't even seem to get started on the songs for your next release."

"I was doing fine until Summer left," he grumbled.

Marty sighed heavily. "For a while there, you really had me worried about this Elliott woman."

Zeke cocked his head, sensing they were getting into dangerous territory. "How so?"

"You seemed to be getting hung up on her," Marty said, adding, "We both know that getting serious about any woman would be bad for your image. Women love you, Zeke, because you're the sexy bad-boy rocker that their mothers always warned them about."

"What made you realize I wasn't hung up on her?" Zeke asked, keeping his voice even.

Marty shrugged. "You said it yourself. She was your muse. Or rather, her photo was, initially. She wasn't your usual type, but once I realized why you were hanging around her, it all made sense."

Zeke remembered Marty had stopped by on Sunday when he'd been out, and he started to form a hunch. He nodded and said, "Summer was really taken with the coincidence of my owning 'Daphne at Play.'"

"I'll bet," Marty responded. "It's not every day that a woman realizes she's the inspiration for a major rock sensation. Very flattering."

Zeke forced himself to nod placidly. "You know, I never did get around to telling her that part."

"Yeah," Marty said, "it seemed to come as a bit of a surprise when I mentioned it to her."

"And did you also mention she should be flattered?" he asked, his voice too quiet.

Marty held up his hands. "Hey, Zeke, look—" He stopped and looked around. "Where is she, by the way? I was surprised when you left a message with my secretary saying you wouldn't be returning to New York on Monday like you'd planned."

"Summer's gone back to New York." Zeke stood. "And you're leaving."

Marty looked up at him uncomprehendingly for a second, until an astounded expression crossed his face. "What? Why? Do you have an appointment to keep somewhere?"

Zeke realized Marty figured he must be joking, but this was no joke. "You need to leave, Marty, before I give in to the urge to deck you." He added, "Believe it or not, I'd hate the bad publicity as much as you would."

Marty wiped his lips with his napkin before standing up. "When you've calmed down, you know where to reach me."

"I'm as calm as I'll ever be," Zeke replied. "What exactly did you say to Summer?"

Marty eyed him. "Is it my fault you didn't mention to her it was her photo that got you hot and bothered?"

Zeke waited, holding his temper in check.

Marty finally shook his head. "I pointed out the

obvious, including the requirements of your career right now." He perked up. "I planted a story about you and that hot Czech model in the press this week. Did you catch it? Nice touch, eh?"

Zeke shook his head. "You're just not getting it, Marty."

"Getting what?"

"For a while, I've thought that the two of us weren't on the same wavelength as far as my career was concerned. I chose to ignore the feeling—until now." He looked the other man in the eye. "You're fired, Marty."

"What?" Marty blustered. "You can't fire me. You need me. I'll sue your pants off."

"Take it to my lawyer," Zeke said coldly. "I think our contract allows me to pay you off to dump you. It's a price I'm willing to pay."

"This over a nice piece of ass?" Marty sneered.

Zeke didn't need to think about it. He threw Marty out on his ear.

Much later, Zeke sat in his living room gazing sightlessly at the television.

Marty had echoed some of the same things that Summer had said on Sunday: she wasn't his usual type, and they were different in a lot of ways. And, yeah, he couldn't deny that he did have his career to consider.

He wondered, though, how much of what Summer

had said was due to her reaction to Marty's words and how much was due to her own feelings coming to light.

Zeke's jaw tightened. He couldn't lose Summer. He'd never felt this way about a woman before. Unfortunately, that also meant he was in uncharted territory about how to make things right.

When the phone rang and he heard a familiar voice, he was only too happy for the distraction. Minutes later, when he hung up, he knew what he had to do.

Zeke's concert was the same as the first two she'd attended. At least this time, Summer thought ruefully, she knew what to expect.

She was surrounded by thousands of Zeke Woodlow fans, all gyrating and bumping and singing and hollering their way through Zeke's repertoire of songs.

This time she was dressed more appropriately, too. She wore hip-hugging jeans and a deep scoop-neck top.

She looked up at Zeke on stage, and her heart swelled.

He strode around the stage as if he owned it—the mark of any great performer. He picked up his guitar, he sang along with one of his backup musicians, and he egged on his fans with teasers. And always he was in sync with his audience.

She hungrily took in every inch of him. He looked gorgeous. It had been almost a week since they'd parted, and she couldn't believe how much she'd missed him.

She rubbed damp palms against her jeans as she mouthed the words to one of Zeke's most popular songs.

She was a little nervous about the reception that she'd receive from Zeke, but she was going for broke. He was the man she loved, and she wasn't going to let him walk out of her life without telling him so.

Once or twice, she thought she caught Zeke staring straight at her in the audience, his gaze intense and magnetic. But she dismissed the thought as fanciful. There were thousands of people in the audience, and though she had one of the better seats, the lighting was dim and she was several rows back and off to one side.

Besides, if there was one thing she'd come to know about Zeke, it was that he was able to make every audience member feel connected to him.

She couldn't wait to get backstage at the end of the concert. This time, thanks to some last-minute wrangling and imploring Shane to pull strings, she had a good seat *and* a press pass.

Of course, she'd had to explain to Shane why she couldn't just approach Zeke for access, and the truth—well, some of it—had come tumbling out of her. She'd admitted she and Zeke had recently become romantically involved.

Shane hadn't been too happy at the news, given

that it made it awkward that *The Buzz* was publishing an interview with Zeke under her name, but he'd eventually waved her off, especially when she'd told him what she was considering in terms of her career.

He'd just looked at her and sighed. "Ah, Summer," he said. "You're the last Elliott that I'd have expected to even think about doing something like this."

"I know," she'd said somewhat guiltily. She knew that, no matter how lightheartedly Shane had taken Granddad's challenge up to now, he probably wouldn't mind winning, and she'd just announced a potential setback for *The Buzz* in the race among EPH magazines.

Shane had finally waved her out of his office. "Okay, kid, go get your man, and good luck to you. Never say that I stood in the way of true love."

"Thanks, Uncle Shane!" she'd said gratefully, then kissed him on the cheek before beating a hasty retreat.

And now, here she was at Zeke's concert, the moment of truth soon to be upon her.

On stage, Zeke flashed a grin at the audience as he took a break between songs. "I've got a surprise for you."

The crowd hooted and hollered.

"Are you ready?"

The audience responded even more loudly.

Zeke slung the strap of his guitar over his neck.

"For the grand finale, I'm going to unveil a new song just for you."

The crowd went wild as the music struck up.

Zeke played some notes experimentally. "It's called 'Days of Sunshine and Summer.'"

Summer froze in mid-clap. He didn't... He hadn't... The title was just a coincidence, she told herself. Surely, he meant the season, and not the woman. Not her. Surely, he hadn't written a song about their breakup—a song that he was about to play for the thousands of people around her.

Zeke nodded to the band behind him, then launched into a ballad of heated intensity about unexpected love. The song was a play on the word *summer,* so that it seemed as if the woman that he sang about was the same as the season: hot, bright and uplifting. "Summer she called to me/Sunny and inviting as a beautiful day," he sang.

Summer held her breath. The song didn't contain a word about heartbreak or betrayal or breakup. Its mood was upbeat and inspiring. And, if the words of the song were true, then Zeke loved summer—loved *her.*

The song brought tears to her eyes. There was no way that Zeke could know she was in the audience. Had he just used their romance—however brief it had been—to fuel his songwriting? Or, as she wanted to believe, were the words of his song true and heartfelt?

When the final notes of the song drifted away, Zeke seemed to look straight at her, and this time Summer could swear she wasn't wrong.

Moving to the microphone, he said, "Everyone, I'd like you to meet Summer."

Before she could blink, a spotlight shone on her. Under other circumstances, Summer was sure she would have reacted like a deer caught in headlights. But right now, her gaze was captured and held by the look on Zeke's face.

Zeke held out his hand to her. "Summer, come on up here."

Crazy as it was, it seemed that only she and Zeke existed, and her feet impelled her toward him.

She walked up onto the stage, the security guards making way for her. Her gaze was fixed on Zeke, the periphery of her vision a blur.

When she finally reached him, he took hold of her hand. The look on his face stole her breath. It was heated and adoring, and it contained just a touch of mischief.

He cast a sidelong look at the audience. "Sorry to embarrass you like this, sweetheart," he said, sounding not the least bit apologetic.

The crowd laughed.

"What are you doing?" she whispered.

He gazed into her eyes and whispered back, "Do you love me?"

"Yes," she answered. She didn't have to think about it.

To the audience, he said, "She loves me."

In response, there was whooping and laughter and clapping.

"You crazy man," she said, trying to keep her voice low enough not to be picked up by the mike in front of him. "What are you doing? Your career—"

He silenced her with a passionate kiss that had the crowd clapping and laughing some more.

Summer clung to him. The kiss quickly brought forth the electricity that always crackled between them.

When he lifted his head and let her go, she watched in disbelief as he sank down on one knee and pulled a ring from his pocket, his eyes never leaving hers.

"Summer, I love you. Will you marry me?"

Her hands flew over her mouth, and tears welled in her eyes.

There were several calls from the audience of "Say yes!" And this time Summer knew there wasn't a doubt in her heart.

Lowering her hands, she cried, "Yes!"

Zeke beamed at her, his face breaking into a grin.

He took her trembling hand and slipped onto her finger an antique band with a diamond flanked by two emeralds. Then he stood up, gathered her into his arms and bent her backward for a deep kiss.

When they broke apart, he flashed her a grin. "I hope you don't mind the PDAs."

"The new Summer Elliott likes public displays of affection a lot," she responded breathlessly.

Minutes later, in the privacy of Zeke's dressing room, Summer found herself in Zeke's arms.

"How did you even know I was in the audience?" she asked, resting her hands on his chest.

Zeke nibbled at her lips. "Mmm…Shane told me."

Her eyes widened. "He did?" Because her voice sounded squeaky, she tried again. "I mean, he did?" She didn't know whether to thank her uncle or not.

Laughter lurked in Zeke's eyes. "How else do you think he got his hands on a press pass and a last-minute ticket for one of the better seats in the house? The concert's been sold out for a while."

Summer's eyes narrowed with suspicion. "What did he say, exactly?"

"Exactly? I don't remember."

She swatted him playfully. "Try."

A smile hovered at the corners of his lips. "He didn't say too much. He just said you were desperately looking for a ticket and a press pass in order to get backstage to see me." He added, "Given how things had ended between us, Shane's call was enough to make me hope you weren't showing up just to put the final nail in the coffin of our relationship."

"He used the word *desperate?*"

Zeke laughed. "You look like you're not sure whether to give Shane an earful."

"Mmm-hmm."

"I'm sure he was just trying to help, and, you know, everything turned out well in the end." He gave her a quick kiss. "Just out of curiosity, though, if I hadn't called you on stage and proposed—"

"Yes, that was a surprise. In front of all those people, Zeke!"

He grinned unapologetically. "But if I hadn't done it, what were you planning to do?"

"Get backstage, lock you in your dressing room and refuse to let you out until you realized our relationship deserved a real chance."

"I've known that all along."

"But Marty said—"

"I know what Marty said. Forget it." For a second, Zeke looked fierce.

"You do? How do you know what he said?"

Zeke relaxed his hold on her. "He stopped by the house on Thursday, and his conversation with you came up." Zeke shrugged. "Let's just say Marty and I had a parting of the ways."

Summer's eyes widened. "What? Zeke, no. Not because of me."

"It wasn't just because of you, Summer, though that brought it to a head. Marty and I have been drifting in different directions. He thought I should concentrate on being a sex-symbol rock star, but songwriting is my real passion."

Zeke stepped back, letting her go. "After this international tour is over at the end of the year, I'm settling down in one place for a while." His lips turned up at one side. "I guess New York City is as good a place as any."

She moved toward him. "Zeke, you don't have to do that on my account. I know I said I didn't want to be on the road all the time, but—" she bit her lip "—that's because I was so hurt when I thought you were just using me to get through your songwriting block."

His smile widened. "Too late. I've signed up to do the songwriting for a musical that's being put together by one of the biggest producers on Broadway. That'll be my next big commitment after I fulfill my contract by recording another CD."

She clapped her hands. "Oh, Zeke! I'm so happy for you!"

He shrugged. "Writing for the Broadway show is an offer that I've been toying with for a while. I was approached about it a couple of months ago, but Marty hated the idea, and at the time, I wasn't prepared to part ways with him."

His gaze softened as he looked down at her. "Besides, doing Broadway will give me some time closer to my parents. And," he teased, "I'm assuming you'll want me in New York for the wedding."

"Of course!" She gazed down at the ring that he'd given her and said, "The ring is perfect."

"I'm glad you like it. I thought you'd like something old and unique. The emeralds remind me of your Irish eyes."

She looked up at him. "I didn't think you were ready to settle down."

"I realized I was waiting for the right woman to come along," he said thoughtfully. "The rest was just a public image carefully cultivated by Marty supposedly for the sake of my career."

She nodded, her heart catching on the words *the right woman*.

"It's true that the photo of Daphne was my songwriting inspiration after a dry spell," he said. "In fact, the photo inspired 'Beautiful in My Arms.'"

"I love that song!" she said. She loved it even more now that she knew the song was about Daphne—or, rather, her.

"Yeah, well," he said, looking amused, "I composed it after a particularly hot dream about Daphne—er, you."

She laughed.

"Of course, after that," he went on, "I couldn't get another song written—until I met you. I'd been dreaming about another song but I couldn't seem to hold on to it when I woke up. But when I was around you, the song started coming to me, and last weekend I finally wrote 'Days of Sunshine and Summer.'"

His eyes held hers. "You may have started out as my muse, but you became so much more than that."

"Oh," she said, caught by the look on his face.

His hands clasped her loosely around the waist. "Given the way the fans reacted to the marriage proposal tonight, I've got to wonder whether Marty was a little narrow-minded about what was good for my career."

She laughed. "How ironic."

He looked confused. "What is?"

"That just when you're ready to settle down, I'm planning to give notice to Shane that I'm taking a leave of absence from *The Buzz* and EPH—probably in anticipation of my eventual resignation. In fact, I've already hinted as much to him."

A look of surprise crossed his face. "What?"

"How else am I supposed to follow you as you travel the world?"

"Aw, Summer." He kissed her, and when the kiss threatened to become deeper, he pulled back and looked at her soberly. "I hope you're not taking the leave just because of me."

She shook her head. "No. It's for me, too. I finally decided to give myself permission to pursue what I really want. You…and photography."

"Good for you."

"Thanks. I'm going to freelance, which should give me maximum flexibility for planning a wedding and spending time with you." She shrugged. "Maybe some of my work will end up in EPH's magazines. I think Shane would be open to acquiring some of my photos."

"Sure. I know I would."

"You're not exactly unbiased," she joked, then added more somberly, "I wonder how Granddad will take the news."

"Something tells me, better than you think."

Summer looked at him in surprise. "What makes you say that?"

"It would be hypocritical of him to do otherwise, don't you think? After all, he went off and pursued his dream."

"Mmm." It was only recently that she'd come to look at matters the same way herself.

"You know," Zeke continued, "I wondered whether working your way up at EPH was another way of pleasing your family, just like getting engaged to John was."

"It may have been," she said. "My grandparents sort of stepped into the shoes of my parents after the plane crash. Instead of trying to please parents, I was trying to please grandparents."

Zeke nodded. "Maybe your preoccupation with planning stems from the plane crash. You know, it's an attempt to impose order and predictability on life, which you learned at an early age can be surprising and scary."

His insightfulness surprised her, though she supposed it shouldn't anymore.

"Anyway," he said teasingly, "I guess you wound up sticking to your five-year plan after all."

"What do you mean?"

"You'll be getting married by twenty-six."

When she realized he was right, she wanted to laugh.

He pulled her closer. "Tell me again that you love me," he murmured.

"Every day," she said just before his lips met hers.

Then there was no more talking. Instead, she gave herself up to the happiness that she'd discovered in his arms.

* * * * *

THE FORBIDDEN TWIN

by
Susan Crosby

SUSAN CROSBY

believes in the value of setting goals, but also in the magic of making wishes. A longtime reader of romantic novels, Susan earned a BA in English while raising her sons. She lives in the central valley of California, the land of wine grapes, asparagus and almonds. Her chequered past includes jobs as a synchronised swimming instructor, personnel interviewer at a toy factory and trucking company manager, but her current occupation as a writer is her all-time favourite.

Susan enjoys writing about people who take a chance on love, sometimes against all odds. She loves warm, strong heroes; good-hearted, self-reliant heroines...and happy endings.

Susan loves to hear from readers. You can visit her at her website, www.susancrosby.com.

For Mabel, a woman of grace and humour.
Mum knew best.

One

Early March

John Harlan clutched a two-carat, brilliant-cut diamond engagement ring in one hand and a Glenfiddich on the rocks in the other, his third in the past hour. Cold had settled in his bones, his heart, his soul. It probably didn't help that he hadn't turned on the heat or even a lamp since night fell hours ago. Only the lights of New York City through his huge picture window illuminated his living room, making a hazy silhouette of the bottle of scotch on the coffee table. What more did he need to see than that, anyway?

A few hours ago his fiancée—former fiancée—had gently placed the diamond ring in his palm. He hadn't let go since.

John had thought he knew and understood Summer Elliott. She was goal-oriented and orderly, like him, and together they were dynamic, a power couple with great lineage and an amazing future. At twenty-nine, he was at a perfect age for marriage, and at a perfect point in his career at his advertising agency. Everything according to schedule.

She'd ended all possibility of a future together that afternoon.

He hadn't seen it coming.

They'd dated for months, long enough to know the relationship worked. They'd gotten engaged less than three weeks ago, on Valentine's Day, appropriately, romantically. And now, while he'd been in Chicago working with a new client this past week, she'd found herself another man—a rock star, of all people. Calm, sedate Summer Elliott, the woman whose personality matched his, had found herself a rock star.

John downed his scotch, relished the burn and was contemplating another when the doorbell rang. He didn't move. The bell rang again. He picked up the bottle and poured, the ice from the previous drink almost melted. Knuckles rapped on the door, and a female voice called his name.

Summer? No. She wouldn't come here.

Curious, however, he set the glass on the table and stood, taking a moment to shove his fingers through his hair and to find his balance. Although it was uncharacteristic of him to have more than a glass or two of wine in an evening, he wasn't drunk. At least he didn't think so, maybe just slightly off-kilter.

He opened his door and did a double take at the sight

of Summer standing at the elevator ten feet away, her back to him.

"What are you doing?" he asked, squinting against the light and stepping into the hall just as the elevator pinged, indicating its arrival on the fifteenth floor, his floor.

She spun to face him but said nothing. He registered that she looked different in her short red dress, but couldn't put his finger on exactly why. Her scintillating light auburn air caught the light, the soft, natural curl caressing her shoulders and drifting down her back. Her light green eyes were focused directly on him, her expression open and caring. Caring? Why should she care? She'd dumped him. Unceremoniously. Emotionlessly.

Which pretty much defined their relationship. Emotionless. Sexless. A partnership with a future based on a solid friendship and healthy respect for each other, if without passion. But he'd loved her and believed she'd loved him. He'd always figured the passion part would fall into place at some point, and had respected her wishes to save herself for the marriage bed.

Had she realized her mistake in breaking it off with him? Was that why she was here?

Why wasn't she talking? She'd come to see him, after all.

"Are you here to apologize?" he asked. Did he *want* her to apologize?

"Made a mistake," she said so low he could barely hear her. She walked toward him, her hand outstretched. "A big mistake." Her fingertips grazed his chest, then she pulled back as if burned, curling her fingers into a fist that she pressed against her heart.

His gut tightened. Her touch had been light, but lethal

to his equilibrium. Hope tried to shove hours of hurt out of the way. The hurt resisted giving way…until she reached out again and was suddenly kissing him—kissing the hell out of him. Caught off guard by her new, surreal level of passion, he kissed her back until she moaned, even as a cautionary voice in his head shouted at him not to forgive the woman who'd never slept with *him,* her fiancé, yet who'd given herself to a man she'd just met.

When she pressed her hips to his and moved against him, he was grateful he hadn't had that fourth drink and could still think clearly enough to know what to do next. Resisting wasn't an option, even though he'd spent months doing exactly that. Not this time, however. Not this time.

He scooped her into his arms, carried her to his bed and laid her on the comforter, deciding that the reason she looked different was that she'd come dressed to seduce him—something she'd never done before.

An unexpected warmth spread through him at the thought that she'd made that kind of effort for him.

"This is out of the blue," he said, turning the words into a question, wanting to trust her motives, but afraid to. What did it say about him if he so easily forgave her?

"I never expected to make love with you."

He frowned. "What do you mean?"

"Just that."

It wasn't an answer, but apparently it was all he was going to get. Had the bad-boy rock star already dumped her? Did it matter? Yes. But…*but* John wanted to show her what she'd been missing as he'd reined himself in all those months, honoring her self-imposed pledge of chastity. His ego even demanded it.

He turned on a bedside lamp, pulled off his tie and un-buttoned his shirt, his movements jerky. She wasn't tell-ing him to stop. She was really going through with it?

He shrugged off his shirt and tossed it aside, reached for his belt buckle and pulled his belt out of the loops, letting it drop to the floor, noticing her spiky red high heels there, as well, a vivid reminder of the strangeness of the evening. He'd never seen her wear heels that high, which put her equal in height to him.

Equal. Was that the point? To make them equals? She'd suddenly become aggressive, not merely assertive?

His jaw tightened painfully as he searched her face, seeking answers to questions he didn't ask because he wasn't sure he wanted the answers. Not only did she not tell him to stop, she didn't even flinch and instead studied his every move, not a hint of virginal shyness in her eyes. He toed off his shoes, slipped his trousers down and off, along with his socks.

His briefs were black and tight, had gone tighter in the past few minutes. She made a leisurely inspection of him that was more exciting than any kiss or touch he could remember. She swallowed and lifted her eyes to meet his again. Her nipples pressed against her dress. His heart thundered; his fists clenched.

If he took off the briefs, would she run? She'd kept him at arm's length for months and months, yet after she'd slept with another man, she wanted *him* now? What kind of sense did that make? Comparison? It was totally out of character for her.

And if he slept with her now, would it be in forgive-ness…or out of revenge? He wasn't sure if he even wanted to find out, but an irrational force made him continue, even knowing he might be shot down or stopped. Or humiliated.

Except she'd said she'd made a mistake....

He pushed off the briefs. She rose to her knees and reached out to touch him, her fingertips gliding down him like warm, silky water. He sucked in a breath, knelt on the bed and peeled her formfitting dress over her head, discovering a red lacy bra and matching thong underneath. He pushed the satin straps down her arms, the weight of her breasts taking the fabric temptingly lower, the lace hanging up on her nipples. Her lemony scent drifted up to him.

His mouth went dry. He'd imagined Summer as a white-bra-and-panties woman....

He lifted his gaze to hers as he laid his palms on her breasts, feeling the smooth, warm firmness of her flesh, the heels of his hands grazing her hard nipples. She was so different from what he'd expected. So sexy. So willing. So...

So not Summer.

"Scarlet?" he managed to ask, taking his hands away, sure of her identity even as he asked the question. No wonder she was different. Not Summer, but her identical twin sister. Scarlet had a wild reputation, but he never would've guessed she would pretend to be her sister. What purpose did it serve? She'd always been standoffish with him, as if she didn't like him.

She sat back, confusion in her eyes. "Have you ever seen Summer wear a dress like that?"

He could tell her he was three-quarters drunk, but it would seem like an insult. "I thought she'd come to seduce me."

Scarlet's lack of answer could mean anything. He wouldn't try to second-guess her.

Mistaken identities aside, he was acutely aware that his arousal hadn't suffered at the recognition of Summer's twin. If anything, the shock of the revelation excited him even more, though he didn't stop to determine why—didn't want to determine why, except he'd endured a long abstinence.

"What are you doing here?" he asked, tired of waiting, frustrated by her actions and his own wayward thoughts.

She rose to her knees again and set her hands on his chest. For several endless seconds their gazes locked. "Does it matter?"

Not at the moment, but soon it would probably matter a lot. Her words about never expecting to make love with him echoed in his head. "You hadn't intended to make love? Then what—"

"Maybe you shouldn't be thinking so hard," she said, drawing him closer.

Her touch erased all thoughts, banished all doubts, and he let go of his curiosity and kissed her instead. He forgot about Summer and opened himself up to Scarlet….

Scarlet, who made incredibly sexy, needy sounds that vibrated from her throat, whose hands wandered over his body as he sought her in the same way. He flicked open her bra, tossed it aside, captured a nipple between his lips, then tongued the hard contours before drawing it into his mouth and savoring as she arched her back, her fingernails digging into him to keep her balance. He took as much care with her other breast, but need pounded him relentlessly, especially when she wrapped her hand around him as he throbbed and ached.

He jerked back, trying to slow down. This was probably the stupidest thing he'd done in his life, but he couldn't stop— Yes, he could. He just didn't want to.

He set his hands on her waist to help her stand, then he eased her thong down her legs. Grasping his head, she leaned over to kiss him, kissed him as he'd never been kissed before, with lips and teeth and tongue, until he couldn't wait another second. He shoved her onto her back and moved her thighs apart. He watched as he entered her, clenched his teeth at the hot tightness that enveloped him, felt her contract, heard her long, low moan that quickly escalated in volume and tempo. He squeezed his eyes shut, holding back, waiting for her, then he exploded inside her. Sensation bombarded him, starting deep and low then racing through his body, even into his mind, blocking everything but feeling, hot, overwhelming feeling. It was good. She was good. Incredible....

He resisted the return of logic and sanity, which came regardless of his wishes. He rolled onto his back and stared at the ceiling. She lay silent beside him. Silent and still. He couldn't even hear her breathe. Her perfume mingled with the earthy smell of sex. He wouldn't soon forget it.

He would *never* forget it.

He turned toward her—

The mattress jiggled as she rolled away from him and off the bed. She gathered up her clothes and hurried to his bathroom, shutting the door.

Shutting him out.

Scarlet tried to let her mind go blank as she dressed inside John's elegant bathroom. She focused on the black fixtures and brushed-nickel faucets. She avoided the mirror as long as she could, then she had to look.

Mascara smudges under her eyes made her skin look paler and her eyes darker than usual. She dampened a tissue and cleaned off the smudges, then finger-combed her hair, stalling, not wanting to face him again.

What had she done?

She'd only come to tell him she thought Summer had made a huge mistake in ending their engagement. Then somehow they were kissing. Scarlet had told him the truth. She'd never expected to kiss him—ever—much less make love with him. She may have cultivated a reputation for outrageousness in the past, but this was over the top, even for her.

The problem was, Scarlet had been in love with John forever, feelings she'd had to keep to herself when she realized he and Summer had discovered an affinity for each other—then they'd realized they were in love just about the time when Scarlet was going to tell Summer how she felt about John herself.

Scarlet had envied the way John had treated Summer, the way he looked into her eyes when she talked, the way he touched her whenever he was near, a sweep of a hand down her back or the surprisingly sexy brush of her curls with his fingers. But it was his consideration of Summer that had made Scarlet the most envious—how much time he spent with her. How they never seemed to run out of things to say, their discussions deep and long. How he always called to say good-night and good-morning.

Scarlet had never had a man treat her like that.

Well, consider the source.

She closed her eyes for a moment, not wanting to dwell on her own shortcomings.

She'd ignored those tender feelings she'd had for John for a long time, had avoided ever having a private discussion with him, fearing he might see how she felt. She'd thought she had those feelings well under control, had made herself stop thinking about him in a romantic light when her sister had gotten serious with him, but seeing him tonight, seeing his pain, had made her realize she hadn't stopped caring, that she'd only shoved everything aside because of Summer.

And now Scarlet needed to kill those feelings once and for all. She and John couldn't have a relationship. Propriety would be reason enough, never mind that he wouldn't want to have anything to do with her beyond this night, since it would keep him in proximity with Summer, as well. This was a once-in-a-lifetime opportunity. Over and done. Relegated to the memory book.

She brushed her hands down her dress then opened the bathroom door. He was still lying in bed, his hands tucked under his head, the sheet pulled up to his waist.

She hunted down her shoes, put them on, wobbling some because she was shaking.

He threw back the covers, climbed out of bed and set his hands on her shoulders. "Take it easy, okay? Nothing—"

"You could at least cover up," she said, wincing at her snippy tone.

After a moment he grinned, revealing heart-tugging dimples. She stopped a sigh from escaping. He was one fine-looking man, with those intense dark brown eyes and sandy brown hair. Who would've guessed that hidden under his boring business suits was such a remarkable body, strong, muscular and toned. Tempting.

"You're leaving, I guess," he said.

"Of course I'm leaving. Do you think I'm an idiot?" She closed her eyes. "Scratch that question." Her behavior already gave her idiocy away.

He looked at her curiously, then grabbed his briefs and donned them. "Why did this happen, Scarlet?"

She searched for a reason he would believe. The only thing that came to mind was what Summer had confided earlier that day when she'd told Scarlet that she was ending her engagement with John—that even though she'd loved him, there had been a complete lack of chemistry between them. For months she'd thought she was just sublimating her passion, so that she could avoid sleeping with him until their wedding night. One hour with rock star Zeke Woodlow had changed all that.

But Scarlet couldn't believe that Summer had been talking about the same man who'd just made love to *her*. Lack of chemistry? Not a chance. The man Scarlet had just made love to took passion to a whole new level.

"Cat got your tongue?" John asked.

All she could do was give him a weak smile.

"Why did this happen?" he repeated.

"Because we got carried away?"

"I know why I would, but why would you?"

She couldn't tell him she loved him, so what could she say? After a few seconds, she felt him touch her cheek. The tenderness of the gesture almost made her throw herself into his arms.

"I figure you know I never slept with your sister."

She nodded. "She was wrong, though. You are a passionate man."

His mouth quirked. "Maybe it's just you. Maybe you brought that out in me." He brushed her hair behind an ear, then rubbed her earlobe. "How about helping me hone my skills? I never want to disappoint another woman."

"This is no time to joke. You don't need lessons, and we have no future together. What happened shouldn't have happened, and I'm sorry."

He narrowed his gaze. "Sorry? For what?"

"I know you must be hurt and angry, and you probably even want revenge, but please, please, don't tell anyone what happened," she said, then walked away before he could say or do anything to stop her. She was confused, not sure why she had done what she'd done, or what she could do about it now. She needed to get away and think. She grabbed her purse off the living-room floor and raced out the door, then hurried down a flight of stairs just to get away fast. She picked up the elevator on the next floor.

The doorman called good-night as she left the building. She stepped into the cold, damp evening and realized she'd forgotten her coat. She couldn't go back for it.

She couldn't go home, either, to her grandparents' town house where she and Summer shared the top floor. Summer probably wasn't even home, might even be with Zeke, but Scarlet didn't want to take the chance. She would get a hotel room for the night, order a bottle of wine, take a hot bath and figure out where she'd gone wrong.

Except that it hadn't felt wrong—not when she was in John's arms. It had felt so...right. He wasn't her sister's fiancé anymore. She hadn't violated any codes of ethics, sibling or otherwise. She and Summer had made a pact when they were eight years old that they would never pretend to be the other, and while she'd gone to John's apartment as herself, she knew fairly soon that he'd thought she was her sister and she hadn't corrected his mistake until it was almost past the point of no return. If he hadn't realized it on his own, she would've told him, though—wouldn't she?

Yes, of course. Probably.

So…a bath, some wine and some reflection. She would put John Harlan out of her mind once and for all.

And by morning she would be fine.

Just fine.

Two

Early April

Scarlet glared at her watch. A quarter past noon. She checked her cell phone, making sure it was turned on. It was. No missed calls. No voice-mail messages. Irritation whipped through her. It was unlike Summer to keep her waiting, especially for fifteen minutes. But then, Summer had lost her predictability. She'd even gotten herself engaged to Zeke Woodlow less than a month after ending her engagement to—

Scarlet went no further with the thought. At least there was a sparkle in Summer's eyes and a lightness in her step that hadn't been there before. A totally different kind of aura surrounded her, and for that Scarlet thanked Zeke.

He'd just better not ever hurt her....

Pasting on a smile, Scarlet returned a wave to a fellow employee then stabbed a piece of avocado in her Cobb salad. Seated in the company cafeteria, she was grateful she'd been able to grab a booth. She hated eating alone in public—Summer knew that. And it was especially bad here where noise bounced off the walls and the steel tabletops, the modern decor not helping to absorb sound, not letting a person think clearly. Plus, the entire twenty-five-story Park Avenue building was owned by EPH—Elliott Publication Holdings, her family's business. Or rather, businesses, their many magazines, so that a lot of people could pick her out of a crowd. Plus she was an Elliott, one who'd already caused enough talk.

She should've told Summer to meet her at the deli down the block.

"Who are you waiting for?"

Scarlet looked up to find Finola Elliott, editor in chief of *Charisma* magazine and Scarlet's boss for the past two years—and for twenty-five years, her aunt Finny.

"Summer. She's late."

"That's unlike her."

"I know."

Fin lowered her voice. "Are you okay?"

Surprised, Scarlet focused on her aunt instead of the cafeteria entrance. "Sure. Why?"

"You've seemed tense lately."

"I'm fine," she said, resisting the temptation to make a similar comment to Fin, who was under a great deal of stress since her father, Scarlet's grandfather, had issued a challenge regarding who was to fill his shoes when he retired at the end of the year—a challenge which had only added to the long-standing tension existing between Fin and her parents. The fact that Fin was eating in the company cafeteria instead of the executive dining room indicated her discomfort, as well.

"I'd ask you to join us, Fin, but Summer called this meeting. Here she is now."

"No problem," Fin said as Summer hugged her then slipped into the booth. "I'm meeting Bridget. See you later."

"Sorry I'm late," Summer said, her eyes shimmering. "Cute outfit. Can I borrow it?"

Scarlet smiled. Even though Summer had made sweeping changes recently, her wardrobe still wouldn't include anything like the purple-and-red minidress that Scarlet had designed and made this past week. "My closet is your closet," Scarlet said.

Summer laughed.

Scarlet could usually anticipate what her sister would say, but not this time. Not for the past few weeks, actually. She only knew that Summer was revved about something. "What's up?"

She linked her fingers together and set her hands on the table. "I'm taking a leave of absence from *The Buzz*."

Shock heated Scarlet from the inside out. "Why?"

"I want to go with Zeke on his international tour."

"For how long?"

"A month."

Scarlet could barely find words. "We've never been apart for more than a week."

"Life is changing, Scar. *We're* changing."

"Separating." *I used to be able to read your mind. We used to finish each other's sentences.*

"It was bound to happen someday." Understanding *and* determination rang in Summer's voice.

"I can't believe you're giving up your dream job, and an imminent promotion, for a...man."

"Not just any man, but Zeke. The man I love." Her calm voice was offset by a stubborn glint in her eye. "The man I'm going to marry."

"When do you leave?"

"Tomorrow."

"So soon?" Scarlet felt more vulnerable than ever. Her link to life as she knew it was breaking. It had been hard enough this past month not to confide in Summer about her night with John Harlan, especially when Summer had asked her where she'd been all night.

"Don't be jealous," Summer said, laying her hand on Scarlet's.

"Jealous? I—" She stopped. Maybe she was, a little. She'd been wanting to try her hand at fashion design but hadn't had the nerve to quit her job as assistant fashion editor for *Charisma*. "Granddad will accuse you of being ungrateful," she said to her sister instead, reminding herself of that fact, as well—the main reason why she hadn't quit her job herself.

"That's what I'm afraid of. But Zeke has tried to convince me otherwise. Loyalty matters more than anything to Granddad, but I need to do this. I want to do this. I'm *going* to do this."

And everyone thought Summer was the meek twin. "Have you told him?"

"I'm telling you first. I'll tell Shane after lunch. Then Gram and Granddad."

Shane—Uncle Shane—was Fin's twin and the editor

in chief of *The Buzz,* EPH's showbiz magazine, where Summer worked as a copy editor, and was about to be promoted to reporter. Scarlet didn't envy Summer telling Shane or, worse, Granddad.

"I'm going to miss you like crazy," Scarlet said, nearly crushing Summer's hand.

"Me, too," she whispered, her eyes instantly bright. "I'll call lots. I promise. Maybe you could meet us somewhere on the tour for a weekend."

"Three's a crowd." Scarlet made an effort to keep things as normal as possible. She dug into her salad again. "Want some?"

"Butterflies," Summer said, patting her stomach.

Scarlet nodded. "What I said about my closet being your closet is true, you know. If you'd like to take some of my stuff on the tour, you can."

"Zeke likes me as I am."

So had John, Scarlet thought. Summer was so much easier to be with—not anywhere near as demanding of equality or independence as Scarlet. At least, not openly.

"There you go again," Summer said, tapping the table next to Scarlet's salad bowl.

"What?"

"You've been zoning out for, I don't know, about a month now."

"Have I?"

"Yes. Right after you spent the night away from home and wouldn't tell me where you'd been. Seems to me you've been keeping a secret, and that's a first for us, too."

Scarlet wanted so much to talk to Summer about John, about that night, but that was impossible. There was no one she could talk to, except the man himself, maybe, but he hadn't contacted her at all, and she both resented and appreciated his self-control. Except for having her coat delivered to her office the next day, without a note, they hadn't existed for each other.

Except that her body hungered in a way it never had.

"Can we spend the evening together?" Scarlet asked, changing the subject altogether, then noting the hurt in her sister's eyes. But Scarlet couldn't confide. Nothing would ever change that. Some secrets would be taken to the grave.

"You'll help me pack?"

"Sure."

"I don't know what time I'll be home. I'm taking the helicopter to The Tides to tell the Grands."

"I'll wait up. We'll have margaritas. You'll need one." Scarlet added teasingly, "Better you than me this time."

Summer grinned. "I know. The shoe's finally on the other foot. For years you've made it your goal to irritate Granddad with your men of choice, and I've always tried to get you to stop doing that. The Grands have taken their role as guardians seriously since Mom and Dad died. I guess after fifteen years in that role it's hard to change. And of course, Granddad still cares about image."

"He cares too much about image." And Scarlet thought, they hadn't really been her "men of choice," but men she'd chosen specifically to irritate her overbearing grandfather. Men came and went. Very few had been lovers. Most were just friends.

Then there was John. She missed him. How had that happened? But she couldn't reach out to him—she, who'd never been known for her patience, had controlled her impulse to contact him, made easier by the fact that he'd left town, or so the rumor went. In mourning for losing Summer?

"I need to get going," Summer said. "I'll call you when I'm headed home, as long as Granddad lets me take the copter back. If not, it's a long ride from the Hamptons."

"I'll go up the elevator with you," Scarlet said, not wanting to stay in the booth alone.

They waited at the doors. Scarlet would get off at the seventeenth floor, Summer one higher.

Scarlet swept her into a big hug as the elevator rose with silent speed. "Promise you won't change."

"Can't."

Scarlet pulled back and brushed her sister's hair from her face. "Is it wonderful, being in love?"

"Zeke is an amazing man."

The simple statement, layered with tenderness, almost made Scarlet cry. She wanted that for herself—a partner, an amazing partner. One who cared for her more than anyone, who thought *she* was amazing. Someone who was hers, and hers alone, as she would be his alone.

"I love you," Scarlet said as the elevator door opened.

"Me, too, you."

Scarlet stepped out of the elevator and headed for her cubicle, past the dazzling sign with the company slogan—*Charisma, Fashion for the Body.* The bright turquoise color scheme and edgy, bold patterns seemed to shout at her. Everything was topsy-turvy. She needed a little peace.

She would find none in her cubicle, which was filled with photos and swatches and drawings—colorful and eye-catching, not soothing. She grabbed her sketch pad and flipped to a blank page. She drew almost without thought—a wedding gown for Summer, with a long veil and train, something fairy-tale princesslike, a fantasy dress, layered with organza, scattered with a few pearls and crystals, but nothing flashy, just enough to catch the light. Elegant, like Summer.

Scarlet turned the page and sketched another wedding dress—strapless, formfitting, no train, no veil, just a few flowers threaded in the bride's long, light auburn hair—hers.

She stared at it, her pencil poised over the pad, then tore off the page, crumpled it into a ball and tossed it in the trash can. Turning to her computer, she opened a work file. She wasn't the Cinderella type. She would skip the grand ceremony, the stress of the spectacle and have something simple instead, if she ever married. Married was married. It didn't matter how it happened.

Her phone rang. Her one o'clock appointment had arrived. She stood, hesitated, then pulled the wadded-up design from her trash can. Her hands shaking slightly, she smoothed out the wrinkles and tucked it back into the pad behind Summer's design.

It was a good design, she thought, something she should redo and put in her portfolio—that was the reason she'd retrieved it. She didn't throw away good work.

Liar. The word bounced in her head, as much in accusation as relief, but above all, honest, a trait that seemed in short supply these days.

Three

At 9:00 p.m., two days later, John stood in front of the Elliott town house near 90th and Amsterdam. The gray stone building sported stately white trim and a playful red front door. He put his hand on the ivy-covered, black wrought-iron gate meant to keep out passersby. He knew of another entrance, however, a private entrance that would take him to the third, and top, floor—Summer and Scarlet's living quarters, comprised of a bedroom suite for each and a communal living room.

The home's owners, Patrick and Maeve Elliott, patriarch and matriarch of the Elliott clan, spent most of their time these days at The Tides, their estate in the Hamptons. Summer and Scarlet were raised there by their grandparents after their parents' deaths in a plane crash. Now the girls lived mostly in the city, occasionally going home to The Tides on weekends.

John's family owned an estate neighboring the Elliotts' in the Hamptons, yet they'd had little contact through the years. John was four years older than the twins. He'd headed to college when they were just entering high school. A couple of years after Summer and Scarlet graduated from college, he'd met them as adults and became an occasional companion to Summer, their relationship escalating from there. No big romance, just an increasing presence and steadily growing relationship.

This last month away from New York had given him perspective. He and Summer had never been suited for each other. They were too much alike, both with their five-year plans, career focuses and even-keeled personalities.

She'd changed, apparently. He'd read in some Hollywood gossip column that she'd accompanied Zeke Woodlow on tour to Europe. Amazing. Who would've guessed that such an adventurous spirit lived inside her?

Over and done, he reminded himself. Now he needed to see Scarlet. The month's separation had allowed him to acknowledge the absurdity of anything happening beyond their one stolen night, but he knew they would run into each other now and then, so they needed to settle things between them.

He hadn't called her, although many times he'd picked up to the phone to do so. Nor had she called him. And as bold and direct as she was, the fact that she hadn't made contact spoke volumes. It had been a one-night stand for both of them.

He reached for his cell phone to alert her he was there, then didn't make the call. He knew he should—

it was unlike him not to be courteous. He had no idea if she was even at home, or alone, but he wanted to catch her off guard and see her real reaction to him, not something manufactured while waiting for him to climb the stairs, so he punched in the security code to enter the half-underground four-car garage, slipped inside the door and strode past the indoor pool and up the staircase to Scarlet's floor.

Nerves played havoc with his equilibrium. The thought caught him by surprise, keeping him from ringing her bell immediately. Maybe he should've worn a suit, shown her—and himself—that he meant business. Instead he'd pulled on a sweater, khakis and loafers, as casual as he owned. At the last minute he'd slapped on some aftershave, something with a citrus base that reminded him of Scarlet's perfume, which had lingered on his skin for days, it seemed, showers not ridding his memory of the fragrance. He'd gotten hard every night in bed just thinking about it, about her, about the way she'd admired and touched him, about the way she kissed, and moved, and—

Hell, things were stirring *now*.

He rang the bell, needing to get the conversation over with so that he could move on with his life. After a few seconds, a shadow darkened the peephole, then came a few long, dragged-out seconds of anticipation. Maybe she wouldn't even open the door, or acknowledge she was home….

The doorknob turned; the door opened slowly.

The living room lights were off. Behind her the open door to her bedroom spilled enough light to cast her in silhouette. He saw only her outline, her hair around her shoulders, a floor-length robe. Her perfume reached his nose, drifted through him, arousing him the rest of the way.

"John?"

How he'd ever confused her voice with her sister's the other time was beyond him. Scarlet's was silky, sultry…sexy.

"Are you alone, Scarlet?"

"Yes." She gestured toward the living room. "Come in."

He looked around, as if seeing it for the first time. He'd been there often with Summer, yet everything seemed different. He saw Scarlet's modern influence now instead of Summer's more homey leanings, the eclectic mix of antiques and minimalist furnishings effective and dramatic.

"Have a seat," she said, indicating the couch in front of the picture window overlooking the street. She pulled her robe around her a little more, tightened the sash, switched on a lamp, then sat at the opposite end of the couch.

Her breasts were unrestrained; her nipples jutted against the fabric. He could hardly keep his eyes off her. He knew she was waiting for him to start the conversation, to let her know why he'd come. He wasn't sure of his reasons anymore.

"How have you been?" he asked finally, starting slowly, gauging her reaction to him being there without an invitation.

"Fine. And you?"

"Okay." *Inane. Say something important, something honest.*

She smoothed the fabric along her thighs. He wanted to do that, too, then lay his head in her lap.

"Where did you go?" she asked.

"L.A. My partners and I are expanding the markets for some new clients, growing the firm. It seemed like a good time to go."

"So your decision was because of business, not because of—"

She didn't finish the sentence. Would she have said "Summer" or herself?

She angled toward him a little, which created a gap in the robe, allowing him a glimpse of the upper swell of her lush breast. He really needed to stop fixating on her body.

"Business," he said. Which was not entirely true. He'd manufactured some business that needed one of the partners' attention, then had volunteered to go. His ad agency was already hugely successful, but there was always room to expand.

"I see."

A long silence followed.

"Why are you here, John?"

He finally remembered the reason. "I just wanted to make sure you were okay with…what happened. I don't want things to be awkward between us, since we're bound to run into each other now and then."

"I think picturing you naked will remove any sense of awkwardness for me."

Her eyes took on some sparkle. He was glad to see it.

"It's vivid for me, too," he said.

"It was good, John, but emotionally charged. We need to remember that. Make it real, instead of…"

"Surreal."

"Exactly. A fantasy, nothing more."

"And a one-time thing." He added the tiniest inflection at the end, turning the phrase into a question if she chose to hear it that way.

"Absolutely." Definite. Certain. No question.

He looked away. He had his answer. "Okay. I'm glad we cleared that up."

"Me, too."

He shifted a little. "I didn't use protection."

"We both got carried away. But there's no problem."

"Good. Great." He stood. "I'll go, then."

He heard her follow him. The air seemed thick. Breathing took effort. He turned when he reached the door, wishing he could read her mind.

"Is there something else you want?" she asked, reaching toward him then pulling back.

"You," he answered, catching her hand, tugging her toward him. "I want you."

"John…." There was hunger in her voice, need in her eyes.

Then they were in each other's arms, kissing, moaning, hands wandering, bodies pressing. She tipped her head back as he dragged his mouth down her neck, her robe separating, revealing her naked body, warm and dewy, as if she'd just stepped out of the bath.

"You're all I've thought about," he said just before drawing a nipple into his mouth, cupping the most feminine part of her with his hand. "You. This."

"Me, too." Her voice was deep, breathy. "Come with me."

He went willingly into her bedroom. Lights were on full. Sketches were everywhere—tacked on corkboard on the wall, scattered over the floor, even on the bed, an unmade jumble of linens. She swept the papers away.

They drifted to the floor, as did her pale blue robe, pooling around her feet, making her look like a goddess rising from the sea.

He jerked his sweater over his head, got rid of his shoes and socks. He touched his belt. She brushed his hands away and undid it, all the while looking at his face. Her color was high, her cheekbones sharp, her eyes a deeper green. Her lips were swollen from kissing, and parted slightly. He felt his slacks drop to the floor and kicked them away. Then she hooked his briefs and tugged. As she knelt to remove them, her hair brushed his abdomen, then his thighs, his shins.

He dug his fingers into her scalp, pulled her hair into his fists, squeezed his eyes shut. A month of fantasies became reality. Hell, not just a month, a lifetime, but a month of specific fantasies about one particular woman.

When her exploration became more daring, he pulled her up, moved her back and made her stretch out on the bed. He wanted to drag it out, make it last, but he lost all sense of control and finesse. He plunged into her. She arched into him. His body blasted apart in a long series of hot, explosive, rhythmic sensations. She clenched him from inside and climaxed with him, her face contorted, her mouth open. Then their movements slowed…stopped. He rolled over, taking her along. She stretched out on top of him and he wrapped her close.

For a long time, neither spoke.

Scarlet had spent the better part of the past month—months, really—convincing herself that she didn't love John, that she'd merely been infatuated because he was so different, attentive to Summer in ways that no man had been attentive to her. She'd been envious, that was all, and had created a fantasy about him. Now she was back at square one. Because she did love him.

Now, how could she keep him in her life long enough for those feelings to run their course? Obviously absence hadn't helped. And obviously they couldn't go public. People would assume that John and Summer had slept together, so the idea of Scarlet sleeping with her sister's ex-fiancé was— She couldn't even come up with the right words.

Appearances were important, especially for John, personally and professionally. And while Scarlet had a reputation, such a liaison with John would be beyond her usual outrageousness. How could they get past that? Not to mention him coming in contact with Summer.

And also not to mention she was probably a kind of substitute for her sister, a way to end his curiosity about her. Why else would he have come on this strong? He would certainly want closure; *she* would, in his shoes. Since he'd missed out on a physical relationship with Summer, having one with Scarlet *could* give him closure. Of sorts.

The thought that she and Summer might be interchangeable in his mind made her a little sick to her stomach. But maybe he wasn't thinking that way at all. Maybe she was just imagining it.

So, now what? It seemed to Scarlet they needed to let the attraction burn in a controlled environment or it might be a bank of embers forever, taking on too much importance as time passed, always waiting to flare.

She had an idea....

"Do you still want lessons?" she asked, burrowing against him, not wanting to see his face.

His arms tightened around her, and he drew a long breath, as if she'd awakened him. "Lessons?"

"Last time you asked for help honing your skills."

"You said I didn't need lessons."

"Not in bed. But you could learn something about being more romantic if you want to woo a woman into bed...in the regular way."

After a long, drawn-out moment of silence, he rolled to his side with her, then propped himself on an elbow to look her in the eyes. His were filled with humor. His dimples deepened. "Woo?"

She shoved his shoulder as he laughed, apparently at her use of such an old-fashioned term. "You have to admit you could use lessons."

His smile faded some. "I admit it. Instinct doesn't seem to be serving me well. Except—" he slid a hand down her back and pulled her closer "—where you're concerned."

"Only in regards to sex, then." She knew he didn't return her feelings.

"No stronger instinct, is there?"

She shrugged.

He stroked her hair, tucked it behind her ear. "So, you'd be willing to advise me on how to properly *woo* a woman? What would that entail?"

Lots of time together. Lots of touching. Lots of— "Lessons," she said instead.

"Homework?"

She hadn't thought about that. He would have to experiment on other women, to see if the lessons worked.

That would never do. "You'll practice on me. If you can make *me* fall under your spell, then you know it can work on any woman."

"She says humbly."

"I'm not being egotistical. I'm just immune to the games of most men."

"What happens if you do fall under my spell?"

She had no answer for that. She'd dug a ditch she couldn't climb out of, however.

"Seems to me this is a game with potentially disastrous outcomes," he said.

"Or fun ones." She laid a hand along his face. "It's very selfish, I suppose, to want this."

"But if we're both in agreement, what's the harm?"

"We're adults, after all."

He said nothing for a few seconds, then seemed to relax. "When would we start?"

"Sometime when we're dressed."

He grinned. "In the meantime…" He hooked a leg over hers, bringing her closer then kissing her until she forgot everything but the feel of his mouth. "Will this be part of the wooing?" he asked, dragging his lips along her jaw.

Huh? Oh. He was talking to her.

She didn't answer immediately. She understood that he was trying to figure out what the parameters of their relationship were going to be. She wanted more than sex, but she knew that was all she could have. Too much stood in their way, especially how quickly they got together after the breakup. Should she settle for only sex? Would the desire fizzle in time?

"I'm enjoying this as much as you are," she said

truthfully, testing his own expectations. "Although we both know—"

He put a hand over her mouth. "We do. And we don't need to talk about it."

She moved his hand away. "I wouldn't have guessed that you were an avoider of truth."

"It's my superhero role. That's why you never see me in tights and a cape, and only in suits."

"Oh, *that's* why. I did wonder."

"When do we start Woo University? Tomorrow?"

So, they weren't going to define their relationship yet. Maybe that was a good thing for now. "Why wait?" she asked.

"I'm not done registering for class yet." He rolled on top of her, bent to kiss her. "Haven't finished uploading from my hard drive."

She laughed. Who would've thought the man could be so playful? "You're not what I expected."

"In what way?"

"In every way. You always seem so serious."

"You'd never seen me naked."

She smiled. "I guess it does make a difference."

He nuzzled her neck. "You're not what you seemed, either."

Her body tingled from the feel of his warm breath against her skin. "How?"

"Less bold."

"I thought I'd been plenty bold."

"Sexually, you have been."

"What other way is there?"

He didn't answer. The hand that had been roaming over her body stilled. "Do you really want to spend our time analyzing this?" he asked, pulling away, locking gazes.

No. It was a time to enjoy him, to make memories. He would change her life—she knew that without a doubt—but her obsession could finally end and she could move on, once and for all. Her relationship with her sister would never have to be tested, nor would Scarlet give the publicity hounds something to sniff out. If Summer could change, so could she.

"No," she said, looping her arms around his shoulders and pulling him down to kiss him. "No analysis necessary. Although I do plan to study your moves."

"As a mentor?"

She smiled slowly. "As a woman."

"Nothing like putting on the pressure."

His words may have indicated a lack of self-confidence but his actions didn't. He knew exactly what to touch, and how, and when. She couldn't remember being aroused so skillfully. But was that all there was—skill? Was his heart engaged even the slightest?

He cupped her face. She opened her eyes, sensing a question coming.

"You don't seem to be in the moment," he said.

"I am completely in the moment," she replied honestly, although his interpretation was probably different from her own. All her desires, all her fears raced through her mind. She wanted to ignore them. They refused to go away.

His silence lasted several long seconds. He started to pull away. She wrapped him close, drew him down… and gave him no more reason to wonder.

Four

John picked up his office telephone the next day, started to punch in a number, then stopped. His first homework assignment was to ask Scarlet for a date in the way he usually asked a woman out. He had to think about it. When he was seeing Summer they'd talked every day and decided together what they would do. He'd never *wooed* her, since they'd just sort of fallen into the relationship gradually. It had been a long time since he'd asked out a woman.

He ran a hand down his face, then dialed Scarlet's work number, feeling like a novice at this dating game instead of a twenty-nine-year-old veteran.

"Scarlet Elliott," she answered, all businesslike.

Which turned him on. He pictured her as she was last night, leaning against her headboard, her hair tangled, face flushed, the sheet tucked over her chest but drifting bit by bit while they talked, until he'd tugged it away and gathered her close.

"Hel-lo?" she singsonged.

He ignored his body's stirrings. "Good morning."

A pause, then, "Who's calling?"

"The man who heated up your sheets last night."

"Stop that," she said in almost a whisper. "You're supposed to have just met me and are asking for a date."

Role-playing? He considered that for a moment. It might be fun—for a day or so. "Not my fault. My mentor didn't give me a syllabus for my first Woo U class."

He heard her laugh briefly.

"Start over." She hung up before he had a chance to say a word.

John sat back in surprise then began to laugh. He redialed.

"Scarlet Elliott."

"Good morning, Ms. Elliott. This is John Harlan of Suskind, Engle and Harlan. We met at the *Charisma* open house over the holidays."

She sighed. "If you have to add the name of your firm, you didn't make much of an impression in the first place. Start over." She hung up.

He was tempted not to call her back, but after a minute, he did.

"Scarlet Elliott."

"Good morning, Ms. Elliott. This is John Harlan. We met at the *Charisma* open house over the holidays."

"I remember. You defended the existence of Santa Claus quite well."

He smiled. "Someone told me your name was Virginia."

"Friend or foe?" she asked.

"Someone who wanted me to embarrass myself, apparently, by calling you by the wrong name."

"You didn't. Embarrass yourself."

Was there double meaning in her remark? "That's good to hear." He was aware she wasn't calling him by name, probably so that no one could overhear her. "I'd like to get to know you better. I was wondering if you would have dinner with me."

"When?"

"Saturday night." This was too easy. How long could he draw out the lessons? He'd have to play dumb just to drag it out.

A long pause ensued. "This is Friday," she said coolly.

"Would you rather go out tonight?"

Dead silence.

He brushed a speck of dust from his slacks. Something told him he'd just messed up his first assignment, big-time. "Scarlet?"

"You don't think it's a little insulting to ask me out the day before? You don't think I would have other plans already?"

"We only started this class today," he countered. "If we'd started on Monday, I would've asked you then." Although he'd would've asked her for Tuesday, but he wasn't about to tell her that. "Do you have plans for Saturday night?"

"Yes, I do."

He wasn't sure what to say. Should he ask her for the following Saturday?

"Start over," she said, then hung up.

He decided to make her wait. When he finally redialed fifteen minutes later, he got her voice mail.

"Ms. Elliott," he said, starting from the beginning. "This is John Harlan. We met at the *Charisma* open house over the holidays. I was wondering if you'd like to have dinner with me a week from Saturday. Here's my private line." He recited his phone number. "I look forward to hearing from you."

He'd barely hung up when his private line rang.

"It's a good thing I came into your life," Scarlet said. "Has that method worked in the past?" She said *method* as if it were something that stank.

"What method?"

"Leave a message for a woman asking her on a first date?"

She sounded either shocked or disgusted.

"I asked for more than a week from now."

"You asked her answering machine."

He massaged the bridge of his nose and closed his eyes. "Which is apparently the wrong thing to do. I'll start over," he said, hanging up before she could. Normally he would've been frustrated by that kind of game by now, but he found it stimulating. She challenged him. The trick would be to challenge her in return.

He lifted the receiver, then hesitated. She would be expecting him to call back.

"Not this time, Ms. Elliott," he said as he flipped through his Rolodex. He wanted an A on his first homework assignment.

She'd gotten him thinking outside his normal box. He wanted her to see what he'd already learned.

* * *

"Somebody likes you," a woman said as she rounded Scarlet's cubicle.

She smelled the flowers before she even looked up from her computer and spotted the bouquet, not something neat and tidy like a dozen roses, but an exotic bundle of baby orchids in a variety of deep colors. Her heart did a little dance at the sight. She hadn't been sent flowers in a long, long time. Even so, she resisted the temptation to bury her face in the blossoms as the vase was set down in front of her by Jessie Clayton, the vivacious twenty-three-year-old intern assigned to work with her.

"Shall I read the card?" Jessie asked, green eyes sparkling behind trendy glasses as she snagged the tiny envelope and held it over Scarlet's head.

"I write your performance reviews."

Jessie laughed and handed Scarlet the card. "I don't suppose you're going to read it out loud."

"Good guess."

Alone, Scarlet held the envelope to her lips for several seconds before opening it. Inside was a phone number. No flowery sentiment. No invitation to dinner. Just a phone number.

She smiled, slowly. Score one for John.

She picked up the phone and dialed.

"John Harlan."

She heard expectation in his voice, maybe because he was trying to cover it. "Nice move."

"Who's calling?"

She grinned. "Let me start over." She hung up and redialed. After he answered, she said, "The flowers are exquisite. Thank you."

"So you remember me?"

She slipped into the role. "Of course. We met at the *Charisma* open house over the holidays."

"You were wearing a green dress the color of your eyes," he said.

Her breath caught, even though they were talking about an imaginary occasion. He made it sound real, as if he'd seen and admired her in that dress. "You were wearing a suit and tie," she countered.

"Lucky guess. I hope you're wondering why I sent the flowers."

"I'm curious, yes."

"I'd like to get to know you. Would you have dinner with me? Maybe a week from Saturday?"

"I'd love to."

"May I pick you up, say, at eight o'clock?"

"That would be perfect."

"I'll call you during the week to reconfirm."

"Okay."

He said goodbye and hung up, and she was left wondering if he meant they wouldn't talk to each other or see each other until he picked her up. Was that how far the role-playing would go? Or would they have a separate life, continuing what they'd started?

For now she would let him lead the relationship. She would go to The Tides for the weekend to visit Gram and Granddad, as planned; attend the Spring Fling at the country club; and make herself unavailable to John, letting absence do its work.

Which was crazy, since nothing long-term could come of this relationship, anyway. But for the month that Summer would be out of town, Scarlet would indulge herself with the man who should be most forbidden to her and make herself a memory.

Five

Since the tragic day when Scarlet and Summer were orphaned, Scarlet had never spent an entire weekend at The Tides without her sister. It was strange now to be in her own bedroom and know that Summer wasn't just a few feet away in hers, or sharing a room as they got ready for a special occasion. The tomblike quiet was eerie.

Scarlet took a final look in the mirror and gave herself the okay sign, something Summer would've done. Once upon a time, Gram would have come in to share in the fun, too, but her arthritis prevented her from climbing the stairs easily anymore. She and Granddad had moved downstairs. Why they hadn't installed an elevator was a mystery to Scarlet.

Her heels tapped softly as she descended the long marble staircase to the first floor. She looked forward to the evening, even though she was dateless. She would know many of the guests, however, and would surely be asked to dance.

She was glad she hadn't told John where she was going. He might have decided to show up, and she wasn't sure she could pretend not to notice him.

Scarlet headed toward the back of the house to the living room, beyond which was her grandparents' suite. As Scarlet neared, her grandmother came out her bedroom door, carrying herself with the grace of a queen, a far cry from the seamstress she'd been when Patrick had first met her in Ireland and swept her off her feet, bringing her to his home in America. Her face barely showed age or tragedy, even at seventy-five and having suffered the loss of several children through miscarriage or death.

"Aren't you enchanting, *colleen*," she said as Scarlet hugged her. "And dressed to stop lungs from pulling in air, I'm thinking. Your own creation?"

"Brand-new." Scarlet did a quick pirouette, showing off the snug violet-and-fuchsia sheath with the flounce that would swirl just above her knees when she danced. Three-inch heels brought her to six feet in height. She loved the additional height, which gave her a sense of power. "You're looking beautiful yourself, Gram."

Maeve wore a simple lavender beaded gown on her petite frame. Her makeup was applied deftly, a few freckles visible on her gorgeous Irish skin. She'd worn her white-and-auburn hair in an elegant updo for as long as Scarlet could remember, and it was no different now. As usual, too, a gold locket hung around her neck, rumored to hold a picture of her daughter Anna, her secondborn, who had died of cancer when she was seven. Scarlet wondered if the locket also contained a picture of her thirdborn, Stephen, Scarlet and Summer's father.

"Looking to turn a few heads, are you?" Patrick Elliott boomed from behind them.

In her heels Scarlet met her grandfather eye to eye, yet another reason she liked wearing them.

At seventy-seven Patrick was still a sight to behold. His fit body, thick gray hair and blue eyes continued to draw glances from women thirty years younger. "I'm hoping to, yes," Scarlet said.

"I was talking to your grandmother, missy." He tempered the comment with a slight smile at Scarlet, which turned tender when he looked at his wife and kissed her cheek. "You look lovely, *cushla macree.*"

Pulse of my heart. Scarlet had heard him call her grandmother that forever, had always found it hard to believe that this adoring husband was the same dictator who'd raised her and Summer. And as a businessman, he was ruthless—even, or more accurately *especially,* with his children, who ran four of his various enterprises.

"Are you taking your own car?" Patrick asked Scarlet. "I'm sure you'll want to stay longer than your grandmother and I."

"I'll ride with you. If I'm not ready to come home when you are, I'll get someone to drop me off."

"We'll send Frederick back for you," Gram said.

"Thanks, but it won't be necessary." Scarlet recognized she was being stubborn out of habit. Her grandparents' driver would be happy to make a second trip to pick her up. Still, she found it hard to alter the long-

established adversarial relationship with her grandfather. "I'll make my own way."

"Make sure your escort hasn't been drinking." He put
his hand under Maeve's arm as they moved toward the
door.

Scarlet brought up the rear, irritated that her grandfather assumed a man would bring her home. "I'll make
him take a Breathalyzer."

Maeve chuckled, which stopped Patrick from countering with something equally sarcastic. "So alike, you
two," Maeve said.

"Alike? Us?" Scarlet wasn't as stunned as she pretended.

"Yes, *colleen*. But enough of this. It's a night to cel-
ebrate the arrival of spring. New beginnings. Let's have
no more battles of wit, no matter how clever the words."

"Fine by me," Scarlet said.

Patrick said nothing, which was answer enough. He
would do whatever Maeve asked of him.

Scarlet stopped short of heaving a sigh. She and
Granddad had butted heads forever, with Gram and
Summer interceding when possible. Her grandfather
had never liked any of her boyfriends, even during her
first tender explorations into the dating world, and so
she had begun to bring home guys she was sure he
would despise—men without much motivation or am-
bition, men whose main interest in life was having fun,
not working. Nothing turned off Patrick Elliott more
than a man without a solid work ethic, especially since
he had built his own empire from nothing.

Scarlet was tired of the game, though, and tired of
being at odds with her grandfather, especially now. He

must be feeling less invincible these days or else he wouldn't have given his children the challenge that the next CEO of Elliott Publication Holdings would be the person who produced for their magazine the biggest individual financial success by year's end. His surprise announcement at a New Year's party that he would be retiring, and the game he'd begun by pitting the Elliott children against each other, had turned all their lives upside down—a typical Patrick Elliott move.

During the twenty-minute limo ride to the country club, the conversation turned to safe topics, setting a new, peaceful tone for the evening. The club ballroom was decorated for the Spring Fling as it always was, with spring-flower arrangements and tiny white lights everywhere, nothing overly original or creative. A sumptuous buffet would be laid out, bars set up in convenient places, with dancing to come later, a twenty-piece band providing music. Scarlet loved its predictability.

"You look like an exotic bloom," Gram said as they waved and nodded to friends and acquaintances. "Your talent for design is staggering."

"I learned from the best." Scarlet put an arm around her grandmother, remembering fondly the hours and hours they'd spent sewing.

"That's a fine compliment, indeed, but I never had the vision, just the practical skill. I always expected you'd go into that field instead of the magazine, especially with your degree in design." Her sideways glance probed.

"I've got time. And the magazine's a useful place to learn more," Scarlet said evasively, wondering if Granddad had overheard. He didn't indicate outwardly that he had; in fact, he seemed focused on something across the room. She followed his gaze, spying the couple she'd most wanted to avoid.

She leaned closer to her grandmother. "Bill and Greta Harlan are here. Have you seen them since Summer called off the engagement?"

"I called Greta. As you know, we weren't great friends before John and Summer decided to marry. If you're wondering whether everyone will be civil, the answer is yes. Especially here. Now then, be off and enjoy yourself."

"I'll join you for supper later."

"You're not to feel obligated. Have fun, *colleen*. I don't think you're having enough fun these days."

"I miss Summer."

"And you're a mite envious, perhaps?"

"Not at all." Scarlet waited for lightning to strike her at the lie, but the world stayed normal. She did envy that Summer could be public with her relationship—and with a man she could count on and keep, whereas Scarlet was setting herself up for heartbreak, one she could never talk about or get sympathy for when it ended. But she wasn't jealous of her sister's happiness.

Scarlet wandered around the festive room, stopping to talk, admiring baby pictures thrust in her face from old friends settling down. She'd attended a record number of weddings in the past few years.

Gram was right. She wasn't having enough fun. Maybe it was because Summer wasn't there, and she was Scarlet's best friend. Maybe because Scarlet lived in Manhattan most of the time, and the country club now seemed too laid-back and…rigid, even though that seemed contradictory. Rules, rules, rules. She'd grown up with them, ignored them, gotten into trouble when she did. There were fewer rules in the city, more action, more options.

After dinner the dancing began. She watched her grandparents take the floor for the first slow dance, their steps perfectly matched after so many years of dancing together. Scarlet smiled as she watched them—until she spotted John walking onto the dance floor.

The lightning she'd expected before struck her, although for entirely different reasons. Everything inside her came feverishly to life. He was the best-looking man in the room. And she'd made love with him. And he'd wanted her, bad.

Okay, so she *was* glad he'd shown up. Admitting she had a problem was half the battle, she thought, being honest with herself. Then she saw a petite blonde step into his arms. Who was she? They waltzed together like long-time partners, their steps perfectly attuned, his hand resting at the small of her back, his gaze on her. He said something and the blonde laughed. Scarlet hated her.

The music went upbeat, and her grandparents left the dance floor, but John and his partner didn't. Scarlet tapped her toe. Was he trying to make her jealous?

"Hey, Scarlet."

She focused on the man who'd approached invisibly through her green haze. "Mitch, hi. Long time."

Mitchell Devereaux was as handsome as he was shallow, which was a lot.

"Yeah. Wanna dance?"

She certainly didn't want to sit on the sidelines,

watching. She would ignore John and have fun, as Gram had ordered.

Scarlet didn't leave the dance floor after that, changing partners with each new song, dancing her heart out and keeping a casual eye on John, who also didn't sit out a dance until the music slowed again, although he finally changed partners. Over her own dancing partner's shoulder she watched John stroll away, get a drink from the bar then prop a shoulder against a pillar and scan the dance floor, stopping on her, catching her looking at him.

He lifted his glass slightly, his gaze intense. She could hardly believe she knew what he looked like naked, what his skin felt like, tasted like. How he kissed as if he were being sent to war, and how he made love as if she were the only woman on earth.

The song ended. She made an excuse to leave the dance floor and headed toward him, pulled by a force stronger than her own willpower. Discreetly she pointed to a side door. He pushed away from the pillar and headed there. She followed at a distance, but as she passed through the door she saw her grandfather, apparently already on the patio, approach him.

Almost caught, Scarlet darted behind a pillar topped by a plant large enough to hide her.

"I never expected it from you, John," Patrick said.

"Expected what?"

"Retaliation."

"It's business, Patrick. Nothing more."

Scarlet wished she could see them, analyze their body language. All she could do was listen. Granddad's voice cut through the darkness, sharp and lethal. John seemed unaffected.

"Gills and Marsh have bought ad space in *Charisma* since the magazine debuted," Patrick said. "Crystal Crème soda has been with *The Buzz* for five years."

"A lot of my clients have decided to experiment with other forms of advertising, to see what gets them the most bang for their buck. Product placement in movies and on television guarantees a bigger, wider audience, not only in initial viewing but in DVDs and reruns."

"With the target demographics?"

"We're choosing each situation carefully."

The sound of crickets filled a long silence.

"You must be angry with my granddaughter," Patrick finally said.

"I'm over it."

"I don't think you are."

Scarlet leaned closer, as her grandfather's voice had gone low and cool.

"What makes you say that?" John asked.

"The way you were watching Scarlet a few minutes ago…. That wasn't the expression of someone who was 'over it.'"

"You're wrong. But even if I hadn't stopped caring about Summer, I wouldn't take it out on my clients— or Scarlet. Or you."

Another silence ensued. John didn't take the bait. Scarlet was grateful her grandfather hadn't realized John's expression was one of lust, not anger.

"Don't know what got into that girl," Patrick said at last. "She always had such a good head on her shoulders. Now she's run off with that…that singer. Left her job."

Exasperation coated the words. John still said nothing.

"I'm going to keep a close eye on all your accounts, John. Might have to do a little wooing of my own."

Scarlet smiled at the word and figured John had, too.

"They pay me for sound advice," John said.

"We'll see how sound it is."

"It's a new day in advertising, Patrick. Time for changes."

"Maybe." He took a couple of steps then stopped.

Scarlet had to duck a little.

"I should've called you and apologized," Patrick said. "Thought about it. Just didn't do it."

"No need to, but thanks. It was between Summer and me."

"So it was. Good night."

"Good night, sir."

Scarlet eased farther around the pillar so her grandfather wouldn't see her as he passed by.

"You can come out," John said after a few seconds. "He's inside."

She moseyed over. "That was close."

"I'm surprised you risked being seen with me in the first place, Scarlet."

"That wouldn't be a scandal, just a reason for people to talk a little. Are you enjoying yourself?"

"Not particularly."

"You could've asked me to dance, you know."

He straightened. "You had a partner for every dance. I shouldn't cut in, should I?"

"Maybe."

His gaze intensified. "Consider this tonight's Woo U lesson. Yes or no?"

"Each situation has to be judged individually."

"I judged. I chose not to."

"Okay." Because he was right and there was nothing more to say, she changed the subject, twining her fingers so that she wouldn't touch him, though she *really* wanted to. "*Was* it strictly business, John? What my grandfather asked you about?"

"Yes."

"You would've done the same thing, switched the business, if you and Summer were still engaged?"

He hesitated no longer than a breath, and his gaze never wavered. "Yes."

She wondered if he'd paused because he had to justify his answer to himself first.

"Wanna blow this joint?" he asked, surprising her.

"More than I can tell you. But impossible, as you know, at least together. I'd better go." She started to turn.

"Scarlet?"

His husky voice would've stopped her, no matter what he said next. "What?"

"I was jealous of every guy you danced with tonight, every guy who touched you and got to be so close to you."

Desire flooded her body…rushing…pounding…pulsating. His gaze drifted down her. Her nipples drew taut. She wasn't used to having a man want her so passionately, so…violently. It fascinated her, both that he wanted her that much and that she liked his Neanderthal reaction. She'd never tolerated jealousy before, but the flare of heat low in her body told her *his* jealousy meant something.

"You don't think I felt the same?" she asked. "I have to go." She wouldn't risk staying any longer with him, having someone see their attraction instead of just acquaintances having a conversation, or whatever defined the parameters of their relationship now in the public eye.

He said nothing. He was good at that.

She didn't see him return to the dance, and was torn between gratitude and disappointment as Mitch again invited her to dance. She saw her grandparents come onto the floor, as well, as Glenn Miller's "Moonlight Serenade" played, Gram's favorite.

A few seconds later, John tapped Mitch's shoulder. Mitch looked at Scarlet. "You don't have to."

"It's fine." Her heart thundered as John's arms came around her. Several inches of space separated their bodies.

"What are you doing?" she whispered, pasting on a smile.

"Passing another Woo U course."

"I can't believe you did that."

"Then you don't know me."

She didn't. She loved him, but she didn't know him. Not really. But everything she learned about him only deepened her feelings.

"Scarlet, there's no reason we can't be civilized in the world's eyes. So, there'll be a little talk. It'd mostly be about me and that I must still be pining for Summer."

"Are you?"

"No."

It was one of the most awkward moments of her life. She glanced at her grandparents. Gram lifted her brows. Granddad kept a carefully blank expression.

And yet through all the awkwardness, all the awareness of eyes focused on them, all the annoyance at being the center of attention when she'd tried so hard to stop doing that, she loved that he'd done it. Loved that he was that self-confident and daring. She never would've guessed it of him.

At the end of the dance the club manager approached Scarlet. "You have a phone call, Miss Elliott."

"From whom?"

"I wouldn't know. If you'll follow me, please."

She excused herself from John, grateful that the potentially awkward moment of moving off the dance floor and away from each other had been solved by a mysterious phone call.

She and the manager went down a long hallway to a door marked Conference Room. He opened the door then walked away. Scarlet peered in. A phone sat on the conference table but no light blinked. Uneasy, she took a step back.

"Careful," came a whisper in her ear. John. He moved her inside the room, shut the door and locked it, the sound echoing like a prelude to gothic seduction.

He slid a hand along the wall beside her, then the lights went out, plunging them into darkness. Music drifted faintly through the closed door.

"You dance like you make love," he said, dragging a finger along her jaw, across her mouth.

"How's that?" Breathless, she parted her lips.

"Primal. Like a creature of the earth. With passion and abandon." He slipped his arms around her waist. "Dance with me. A real dance."

"Dance" was a relative term. They barely moved. It was just an excuse to align their bodies, and since in her heels she was as tall as he, their bodies aligned perfectly.

"You're quiet," Scarlet murmured after a while.

"Some of us are capable of it."

She nipped his earlobe, and he laughed softly. She'd needed this moment alone with him. Needed to touch him. The music stopped, but they kept moving, pressed together, their clothing the only barrier, and even that wasn't much. He curved his hands over her rear and lifted her slightly, changing the point of contact. Perfume and aftershave mingled with the urgent scent of desire. His need was evident in the tautness of his body and the hard ridge pressed to her abdomen. His breath felt hot and unsteady against her temple.

Scarlet tried to resist. She couldn't abandon herself to him, all too aware of where they were and the possibility of discovery. She wouldn't do that to her grandparents or Summer. Or herself.

But she had a hard time not letting go, giving in, enjoying....

His hand slipped over her breast just as his mouth took hers in a long, hot kiss, a merging of breath and need and unchecked lust. They were always in such a hurry with each other.

He moved her back until her thighs hit the table. She realized what he intended and pushed at his chest.

"We can't do this here."

He trailed her low V neckline with his tongue, leaving a damp, shivery trail. "I'm familiar with the long list of rules this club has," he said. "Nowhere does it say there can't be sex in the conference room. In fact, I would hazard a guess that this room has seen plenty of action."

"Stop." She slipped away from him and found her way to the door, then fumbled for the light switch, turning it on. "I mean it. We can't do this here." She blamed herself for letting things get out of hand. The speed at which they'd landed in bed before this— twice—would have led any man to think he could have what he wanted, whenever he wanted it.

He shoved his hands through his hair. "You're hard to figure out," he said, then blew out a breath.

"I know. I'm sorry." *But I love you, and that's why I took those chances the other times. I needed a memory of you.*

"You don't really live up to your reputation, do you?" he said, half sitting on the table, his arms crossed.

"Do you want me to?"

After a few long seconds he shook his head.

She thought about her grandfather, how much she'd disappointed him. As a teenager she'd desperately wanted his attention, and he'd been totally focused on his business, but his disapproval of her dates meant he would at least communicate with her, if only to berate her. She was such a cliché, she thought.

"I always found the 'wild-child' tales interesting," John continued, "because there was no hard evidence you were easy, just speculation, based on who you dated—and maybe how you dress in look-at-me outfits and move like a whirlwind, as if you always know where you're going and who you are, which is very sexy. I'd say you pretty much made everyone wonder."

"I'm not the one who arranged this tryst."

"I didn't mean to offend you, Scarlet. I thought you would want it as much as I did."

"Believe it or not, sometimes I think about other people before my own needs."

His gaze locked with hers. He studied her for a long,

quiet moment, then he nodded slowly and stood. He ran a hand down her arm as he passed by.

"Good night," he said. "Thank you for the dance."

After the door closed quietly behind him she stood motionless, waiting for her world to return to normal.

She'd misread him, pure and simple. And maybe he'd misread her. It was her manufactured reputation that had driven him to take such a chance as to want to have sex with her on a conference room table with hundreds of people—her grandparents included—nearby.

Maybe he got a rush out of such clandestine moments.

She didn't. She'd only gotten a rush out of *him*.

So where did that leave them now?

Six

On the Wednesday after the country club incident, John arrived a few minutes early for a three o'clock meeting with Finola Elliott at *Charisma* magazine. He wasn't made to wait in the lobby but was escorted immediately to Fin's office by an auburn-haired young woman named Jessie, who kept up a running commentary as they wove through the maze of cubicles. He learned she'd been raised in Colorado, was an unpaid intern and a roommate of a *Charisma* proofreader, Lanie Sinclair. And by the way Jessie eyed him curiously, he guessed she knew he'd been engaged to Summer.

He wished he could ask her which cubicle was Scarlet's. If he could just look into her eyes, he'd know where things stood between them. They hadn't spoken since the disaster at the club. In three days they were supposed to go on their first Woo U date.

Or were they?

Maybe his lesson had been only in how to ask a woman out, not the actual follow-through. Another question he needed answered.

Who would break the stalemate? Or had they already burned out? He wasn't ready to end it. He wanted the whole month until Summer returned. Every last minute. And he wanted some of that in bed.

John wasn't taken into Fin's office but to the conference room attached to it. Several people were seated at the oval mahogany table—the editor in chief, Fin; her executive editor, Cade McMann; Bridget Elliott, the photo editor…and Scarlet.

He'd never been to a meeting with Scarlet in attendance before. Why would an assistant fashion editor be there?

John shook hands with Fin, Cade and Bridget. He met Scarlet's gaze directly and nodded. She raised her brows. No clue there as to how she felt.

"I'm not going to beat around the bush, John," Fin said. "I'm sure you've heard about the competition my father instituted."

"I'm aware of the details." Having just seen Maeve over the weekend, John realized how much Fin looked like her mother, although she had Patrick's head—and drive—for business.

"I intend to win." She leaned toward him, her body rigid. "But I can't if you keep pulling ad revenue from my profits."

"I'm responding to what my clients' needs are, Fin."

"We came up with an idea we'd like to toss out at you. Go ahead, Scarlet."

Scarlet picked up a remote control. She gave him a quick look, all business, which might have worked had she been wearing a gray, pin-striped, baggy suit and her hair in a bun. Maybe. As it was, her shiny hair curled softly over her shoulders, and she wore a deep purple dress that clung to every shapely inch of her. His mind wandered....

She brought up an image on the big-screen monitor on the wall. "Picture this as a feature article. We might call it 'Trends,' or something like that," Scarlet said. "Ten to twelve photos of the hottest trends for each season, as we generally do. But this is an example of how we would incorporate your clients' products."

A hip blond model was seated at a bar in what looked to be a neighborhood pub. She wore an outfit meant to draw the magazine reader's eye, but in her hand was a bottle of Crystal Crème soda. The juxtaposition of a soft drink being served at a bar would make the reader pay even more attention, he decided. Very clever.

"Product placement," Scarlet said unnecessarily. "Here are a few more."

Images flashed across the screen, each photo the superb quality that *Charisma* was known for, and each including a product of one of his clients, generally a food or drink item, easily integrated into the scene.

Cade pushed a folder toward John. "Price guides. You'll find it cheaper than a full-page ad, of course, but a fair price, we think, for the value."

Scarlet handed him a manila envelope. "Here's a CD of each sample so you can pitch your clients with visuals. These are mock-ups, obviously. We'd have to work closely together, matching our focus for the article with your product for the layout. Some products will lend themselves easily, but some won't. Some of these products have never been advertised in *Charisma,* like Crystal Crème. We think it opens a lot of new doors."

"You know that once you start down this path, you won't be able to go back," John said, skimming the price sheets. "And you'll be accused of selling out."

"We've talked it over," Cade answered. "Analyzed it. Had a few hearty debates, too. It's no different from a television program or movie showcasing products."

"It's not as if it's something new in the business," John said. "But it *is* new for you. Something you've resisted because of the ethics involved."

"It's a new day," Scarlet said. "A time for change."

She'd parroted what she'd overheard him say to Patrick the past weekend.

"We ask one thing, John," Fin said. "We want an exclusive. You don't go to the other EPH magazines—or anyone else—asking for the same thing. Let us run with it first."

John nodded. "Unless they ask. I can't pass up reasonable business, either, Fin. And I want an exclusive, as well. You don't offer this opportunity to anyone else for a few months, either."

"Fair enough," Fin said. "I've asked Scarlet to be your liaison on this project. Does that work for you?"

He didn't dare look at Scarlet. "Sure."

"She came up with a list of your clients whose products might be suitable for us."

"That's very competent of her."

A momentary silence hung over the room, then Fin

said coolly, "We're pleased we found a way to keep your business at *Charisma*."

"So am I." And now he and Scarlet would work together as well as play together, if that was what they could call it. But this business relationship would extend beyond the month.

"If you have time to stay and talk with her now, we would appreciate it."

"I do."

"Good." Finola rose, as did Cade and Bridget. "We'll be in touch."

The room emptied except for Scarlet and John, who sat across the wide table from each other.

"Your concept?" he asked her.

"Does it matter?"

"Just curious. I couldn't figure out why an assistant fashion editor was in on an ad meeting. If you came up with the idea, it makes sense that you would be here. Seems to me, though, that you'd like to take credit for something so daring for *Charisma*."

Scarlet sat back in her chair, her arms crossed. "Fin's a great boss. She's turned us into a team where credit *and* blame are shared."

"I've known her for a few years. This is the most on edge I've seen her."

"The competition." Scarlet shrugged. "Everyone's feeling the pressure."

"You think she should be the one to win? The one to become CEO of EPH, over your uncles?"

"I don't work for them." She smiled sweetly. "Here's the list." She skated it across the table.

He caught it, stood and walked around the table, not

taking his eyes off her. She watched him, as well. He sat beside her, close enough that her perfume drifted across the space between them. Her signature scent aroused him instantly.

"Are we still on for Saturday night?" he asked.

The door opened. Jessie shouldered her way in, carrying a tray with bottled water and glasses of ice. "Cade said I should sit in on your meeting."

"Great," Scarlet said with a little too much enthusiasm.

Saved by the intern. John could see the thought flash through Scarlet's mind.

And because he wasn't going to take no for an answer, he decided to be creative himself.

John had been right about one thing, Scarlet thought a half hour later as they left the conference room and headed to her cubicle. She *did* want credit for her idea to keep his business at *Charisma*. Not for the glory— she was a team player—but she wished her grandfather knew what she'd come up with. She wanted him to see that she was valuable to the magazine, not just an Elliott being given a position because of the family name.

As long as she was being honest with herself, she admitted she wanted John to know, too, because she needed him to acknowledge her abilities. It was unlike her to crave approval. What did that say about her? A sign of a new maturity…or insecurity? She wished Summer was home so they could talk about it, at least the part about Granddad. But their phone conversations, frequent but short, never allowed time for deep discussion, plus Summer was living a dream. Scarlet didn't want to wake her with reality yet.

Scarlet knew John was right behind her as they reached her cubicle, but his footsteps were almost silent. Sneaky. He was sneaky in a lot of ways. Good ways, interesting ways, like his card with the flowers that had only his phone number printed on it. Like luring her to the conference room at the Spring Fling. Like disguising his incredible body with boring suits. Outwardly he needed some flair to match what he was inside, which was fascinating.

The orchids he'd sent were still fresh, the vase overflowing with the wondrous blooms. She saw his gaze land on them.

She thumbed through a stack of papers on her desk, pulling out the one she wanted to give him.

"Thanks," he said. He stuffed the sheet into his briefcase. "I'll be in touch as I meet with each client."

He left. Just like that. Without finalizing plans for Saturday night, even though he'd asked her before.

An assortment of possibilities about how she could do him bodily harm ran through her head. Had he forgotten or was he playing a game with her? Maybe he was unhappy that they would be working together on the same project for an indefinite period of time.

Any other man might—

She stopped. Sat down. Set her elbows on her desk and rested her chin in her hands. John wasn't like any other man. And that was the problem.

She was used to leading a relationship, had thought *she* was letting *him* lead. But the fact of the matter was, he wasn't...leadable.

At five o'clock she headed to the elevator bank, grateful she wasn't an executive, whose work hours often stretched long into the night, even more so since Granddad had fired the starting gun on the competition. She was worried about Aunt Finny, who was way too tense, and determined to win, and was spending far too much time in the office these days.

"Scarlet!" Jessie ran up to her at the elevator, holding tight to a red helium-filled balloon. "This just came. There wasn't a card, but the delivery guy said it was for you."

Scarlet spied a piece of paper inside the balloon. She had no doubt who'd sent it.

But what did the note say?

"Thanks," she said to Jessie, leaving her curiosity unsatisfied as Scarlet stepped into the waiting elevator. "See you tomorrow."

She strode down Park Avenue, the string wrapped securely around her hand, the balloon hovering just above her head. She smiled as she walked. People smiled back. It was a drizzly spring day, but it was beautiful.

The man learned fast, she thought. He could've talked to her while they were in her cubicle, or called her after he'd returned to his office. Instead he sent her a balloon. How imaginative. Maybe it held a little apology for last Saturday night, as well as a reminder of the upcoming Saturday night.

She hailed a cab, lucky to find one unoccupied. Then at the town house she swung open the gate and headed for the door to the underground pool and garage to get to her private entrance. The sound of someone knocking on a window caught her attention. She spied her grandmother waving at her, motioning her to come through the front door.

Gram rarely came into the city anymore unless she was going on a shopping binge, in which case she made arrangements to shop with Scarlet in tow. They always made a day of it.

Curious why Gram hadn't alerted Scarlet that she was coming, Scarlet climbed the front stairs and walked into the entry, where a grand piano held center stage. When someone played, the sound reverberated through the entire three-story house.

"What are you doing here?" she asked her grandmother as they hugged.

"We have tickets for the opera. We came early so that Patrick could go into the office." She smiled at the balloon. "It's a special occasion, then, is it?"

"What? Oh, someone was passing them out. They're advertising something."

Maeve's brows lifted. "And you carried it all the way home?"

Scarlet shrugged, trying to look innocent. "It suited my mood."

"Why don't you pop it and see what's inside?"

"I, um, don't really care what's inside. I'd like to enjoy the balloon for a while."

Gram's eyes held a secret smile. "If you don't want to share the note, just say so, *colleen*. I respect your privacy."

Then for no fathomable reason the balloon popped on its own and the note went flying, landing faceup at Maeve's feet. Scarlet grabbed it before her grandmother could bend down, then held it up to read.

I look forward to Saturday night. Pick you up at eight.

Scarlet somehow managed not to sigh her relief at the

G-rated note, unsure whether her grandmother had had time to read it or not.

"So, you have a date tonight, then," Gram said, her eyes twinkling.

Scarlet looked at the note again. "No. Saturday."

Maeve pointed to it. "I think you've got a different message on the other side."

With dread Scarlet turned the note over. *Tonight. Nine. Be prepared for some lessons of your own.*

Gram laughed, softly at first, then with utter amusement at Scarlet's embarrassment.

"A healthy love life is a good thing. Is it anyone I know, then?"

Scarlet's face heated to broil. "Gram, please."

"Someone your granddad would approve of, for a change?"

She wished she could answer yes. Wished it with all her heart. But no one would be happy with her choice of John Harlan. No one.

Her grandmother patted her on the arm. "I won't tell Patrick, if that's your worry."

"I'm just not ready to talk about it."

"Sure, then, I'll leave it alone for now. Oh. We'll be taking the helicopter back to The Tides tonight, so you don't have to be worrying about us seeing your young man in the morning."

Like there was any way she would let John come over tonight, knowing that Patrick could change his mind and be there in the morning.

"Have a wonderful time at the opera," she said to her impish grandmother.

"I don't suppose you'll be visiting us this weekend?"

Scarlet laughed. "Good night." She headed to the indoor staircase, appreciating, as she always did, the calm, tasteful decor of the town house, decorated so similarly to The Tides. Maeve Elliott knew how to bring peace to a place—and a person.

When she reached her floor, she went straight into her room and dialed John's number.

"You got my balloon?" he asked, his voice full of sexy promise.

"My grandmother got your balloon."

"What?"

Good. At least she'd shocked him in return. "I was reading your lovely note about Saturday, while she was reading your more direct note on the other side."

The sharp, succinct curse that came next made her relax, although she didn't know why.

"What did she say?" he asked.

"That you could spend the night."

A long pause, then, "I beg your pardon?"

"You didn't sign your name to the note, so she doesn't know it's you specifically, but she made it clear that my young man could spend the night. She and Granddad are taking the copter home tonight."

A pause ensued. "I'm not willing to risk that," he said.

"Neither am I."

"Are you disappointed?"

She waited a couple of beats to answer him, not because she didn't know the answer but because she wasn't sure she wanted him to know exactly how disappointed she was.

"I'm going to take that as a yes. Saturday night is still a go, though, right?"

"Of course."

"Scarlet? About Saturday night… Is that to be a Woo U date, like a real first date?"

"You mean with no fringe benefits?"

"I'm just trying to know what to expect. Having two different—and opposite—relationships doesn't make things simple."

"It's a first date," she said. "We've already straightened out a few errors you've made in the past. Let's see if anything else needs fixing."

"All right."

She couldn't tell if he was disappointed, but she could guess. She didn't know how well she could stick to her own rules herself. She was still revved up from Saturday night at the country club. Just sitting next to him at the meeting today had made her wish they could find a dark corner somewhere and put an end to the aching need.

"Good night, John," she said as cheerfully as possible.

"'Night."

Scarlet changed into casual pants and a top, grabbed a leftover chicken Caesar salad from the refrigerator, then settled on the sofa with her sketch pad. She'd been unusually creative lately, ideas flowing so easily that she had already filled one pad and was halfway through another, in barely a month's time.

A psychologist would say she was sublimating—diverting her forbidden desire for John into a socially acceptable substitute, like designing an entire clothing line. After more than an hour she set aside her pad and wandered to the living-room window. People walked along the sidewalk, going to or coming home from dinner, probably. Singles moved along in haste. Couples strolled.

When was the last time she'd been on a date? Gone out to dinner with someone other than Summer or a girlfriend? Sometime during the past year she'd given up trying to irritate her grandfather by dating men he wouldn't approve of. She'd been asked out during that time, but had made excuses not to go.

Looking back, she realized she'd stopped dating when John and Summer had started getting serious, and Scarlet had begun falling in love with John. She'd spent a lot of time at home, sewing. Summer had been worried about her, had often invited her to come along with her and John. Scarlet had made so many excuses she'd run out of creative ideas.

The irony, of course, was that her grandfather would approve of John—if he hadn't once been engaged to Summer. Patrick wouldn't tolerate scandal. He'd even forced Aunt Finny at age fifteen to give up her baby born out of wedlock, in order to save public face. Scarlet figured Fin was fighting so hard to win Patrick's corporate game because she'd harbored so much resentment for him these twenty-plus years since having her baby taken away.

Scarlet didn't want to become like Fin. She wanted to make peace with Patrick. But there was no way she could make peace by pursuing John for anything beyond this month of stolen nights. People would talk too much, especially this soon after the breakup.

She wished she were brave enough to end the relationship now, but she wasn't. Only a couple more weeks, then the choice would be taken from her.

The phone rang, slicing into her thoughts, for which she was grateful.

"What do you think about using Une Nuit as a locale for a shoot?" John asked without saying hello. "Models seated at a table, looking at a menu, the name of the restaurant right there for the world to see."

"I think it could be considered a conflict of interest, since my cousin Bryan owns the place. Is he a client of yours now?"

"Brand-new."

"I thought Bryan liked to fly low under the radar. And last I heard he had reservations booked until the twelfth of never."

"I can't tell you what his plans are."

"Can't or don't know?"

"Take your pick."

She smiled. She liked a man who could keep confidences. "So, you're spending the evening working?"

"It was that or stand in a cold shower all night."

She burrowed into the sofa cushions, tucking the phone closer. "Were you serious in your note about having something to teach me?"

"That's for me to know and you to find out."

How in the world had Summer given up this man? Scarlet wondered for the thousandth time. He was quick-witted, funny, smart and sexy. What more could a woman want?

"Want to reschedule tonight's plan for Friday?" he asked.

"Can't. I have a meet and greet at Michael Thor's new studio," Scarlet said.

"It can't last all night."

"I promised Jessie I'd take her by Une Nuit afterward. I'm really sorry."

A beat passed. "So, that leaves us back at our Saturday night Woo U date," he said.

"Good thing you asked early," she said pertly, glad when he laughed. "John?"

"What?"

"I've been thinking." She waited for him to come back with some clever insult, but there was only silence. Maybe he heard the tension in her voice. "I'm not sure we should be doing more than just the Woo U stuff."

"Meaning?"

"We were lucky my grandparents didn't catch us tonight. Maybe that's a sign we shouldn't spend all that much time together."

"You believe in signs? Omens? Fate?" he asked.

"When it's convenient…or logical."

"Before we make such a big decision, why don't we sleep on it? We'll talk about it on Saturday. After the date ends."

Because she wanted to avoid the discussion herself, she said, "Works for me. Good night, John."

"Sweet dreams, Scarlet."

The way he said the words turned her to mush. She knew he had to be disappointed in her decision, yet he'd said his own good-night with tenderness in his voice, not impatience or irritation. Personally, she would've been irritated if he'd come to the same determination that she had.

She liked that she kept learning something new about him.

After a minute she glanced at the clock. She could change her mind right now—grab a cab and surprise him. He was at home and alone. He would satisfy her deprived needs….

Instead she took a warm bath and went to bed, in search of those elusive sweet dreams.

John printed the results of his evening at the computer, stacked the papers and put them in his briefcase. He started to pour himself a Glenfiddich, hesitated then went ahead and splashed some in a glass. The smooth, pricey scotch could've easily reminded him of the day Summer broke their engagement, but instead he chose to associate it with his first night with Scarlet.

He carried the glass with him to look out his window. It had started to rain sometime in the past hour. He turned off all the lights and stood, sipping and watching and remembering. The way she'd watched him undress. Her red bra and thong. The incredible sounds she made, flattering and arousing. Then the way she rushed away, leaving her coat behind. He'd sat on his bed, holding it to his nose, breathing in her scent for a long time after she was gone.

He hadn't expected to ever see her again, at least not like that. He'd been wrong.

And somehow he'd gotten himself into a position where they would spend hours together on Saturday without hope of ending up in bed. Maybe never sleep together again.

He really wondered whether he'd fried a whole lot of brain cells since he'd first slept with her. He knew he was infatuated, because she was rarely out of his mind. Even now he'd gone hard just thinking about her, a condition he hadn't experienced with this much uncontrolled regularity since he was a teenager.

It couldn't be more than lust. He refused to have his

heart broken by another Elliott woman. Or even have his life turned upside down.

But he wanted her….

To hell with it. He set his empty glass on the bar, grabbed his coat and keys and went out the door. He could sneak out of her house long before anyone was up to see him, convince her not to give up the sexual relationship.

But when the elevator doors opened he stared at the empty car until the doors closed. He returned to his apartment. His huge, quiet apartment. And went to bed alone.

Seven

Une Nuit buzzed no matter what night of the week, but this was Friday, and the crowd was different on Friday. Younger, even hipper, if that was possible. A visual sea of beautiful people dressed in New York's color of choice—black—enjoying the daring French/Asian fusion cuisine that was always being written up in the media, thus keeping the very trendy restaurant *the* place to be.

With Jessie in tow, Scarlet wove through the bar crowd at the front of the restaurant, looking for her cousin Bryan. While he might join them at dinner briefly, he generally wandered around the rest of the time, a hands-on owner.

She'd almost reached the maître d's podium when she came across Stash Martin, a wickedly handsome

Frenchman in his early thirties. As manager of Une Nuit, he was as much a fixture as Bryan.

"Scarlet, welcome," he said. They exchanged kisses on both cheeks.

"Crazy," she said, grinning, looking around.

"But quite typical. If you are looking for Bryan, he is not here. He is out of town. Again."

"Where does he go?" she asked rhetorically then introduced Stash to Jessie, who was wide-eyed at the scene. Bryan had always been an adventurer, even as he seemed to love his restaurant. He came and went a lot, but his business thrived because he had a staff he could count on.

"You would like a table, eh?" Stash asked.

"Any family members here?"

"Not a one. The Elliott table is free."

"What do you think?" Scarlet asked Jessie. "Table or the bar? How hungry are you?"

"Not very. The bar is fine."

"Wait here a moment," Stash said, then he approached the maître d'.

Scarlet had talked Jessie into borrowing an outfit from the closet of designer clothing at the magazine, but she hadn't been able to talk Jessie into letting her hair loose from the braid she always wore. The black leather pants and turtleneck did give her a different look, a fashionable one. Even Scarlet, usually a standout because of the colorful outfits she often wore, was wearing black—a miniskirt, boots and belted leather jacket. Her hair was pulled up into an untidy knot. She considered the look as just another aspect of her personality.

Stash returned then pointed to a couple sitting at the very center of the long, black lacquered bar. "Stand behind them. They'll be called in to dinner as soon as you make your way over there."

Scarlet flashed him a smile. "You're the best."

He lifted Scarlet's hand to kiss, and she fluttered her lashes playfully.

"When are you going to sleep with me and get me out of your system, *ma chérie?*" he asked, as he always did.

"Soon," she answered, as she always did.

A few minutes later she and Jessie were seated at the bar, waiting for their drinks.

"I've never seen anything like this," Jessie said in awe. "It's like a movie. Red and black and sexy. And I love the copper-topped tables."

"Maybe we'll order something to eat later, so that you can taste how incredible their food is." She smiled at the bartender when he placed an apple martini in front of her, then lifted her glass to Jessie. "To adventures in the big city."

"I wish I could afford more of them. Someday. When I have a paying job. Every penny of my savings is budgeted. Thanks so much for this treat."

"Keep performing well at *Charisma,* and you could be offered a paying job at the end of your internship." She sipped her drink then looked around, making eye contact with a man at the end of the bar, who toasted her. She smiled but looked away, then realized she shouldn't put up roadblocks, since Jessie might be interested. She decided to give him another chance, but Jessie's words stopped her.

"There's that man from the ad agency, John Harlan."

Surprise pelted Scarlet from all sides. "Where?"

"At a table behind you, in the corner."

She wasn't sure she wanted to turn around. If he was with a woman, she didn't want to know.

"He's looking right at you. I think he knows I'm telling you he's there," Jessie said in an emphatic whisper.

"Hmm." She took a long sip of her drink. He was courteous and would probably approach them at some point, especially since he and Jessie had taken note of each other. Scarlet would wait for him to initiate contact. Until then she could ignore the possibilities of whom he was with.

Maybe that blonde from the country club dance. She never had asked who that was.

"Is it true he was engaged to your sister?" Jessie asked.

Scarlet sighed. "They were engaged on Valentine's Day, but Summer called it off a couple of weeks later, just about the time you were hired."

"It must be weird for him, seeing you. Working with you, her identical twin."

Tell me about it. She'd wondered at the beginning if she was only a substitute for her sister, a way to get Summer out of his mind, but she didn't think that was true now. They had their own relationship. And while it was fun at times, she was always aware of the impending and necessary conclusion. They couldn't even just date and see where things might go. Even if Summer—and their grandfather—could somehow accept it, because of Scarlet's reputation, many people might assume that Scarlet had interfered somehow, even before Zeke Woodlow had appeared on the scene. It wasn't worth the grief.

Or was it?

The man from the end of the bar approached, saving Scarlet from coming up with an answer. Late twenties,

Scarlet decided. A little taller than she, blond and blue-eyed. He didn't look overly sophisticated or jaded, which meant he might work as a flirtation for the still-naive Jessie. Diverting her attention from watching John was a good idea.

"I'll bet you're sisters," the man said.

Scarlet met Jessie's gaze. She looked startled, but Scarlet smiled. "Coworkers," she said.

"I'm Rich."

"Money doesn't matter to me," Jessie said sincerely.

Scarlet grinned. "I think he means his name is Rich. That's Jessie. I'm Scarlet."

"I know who you are," Rich said to Scarlet, his hand resting on the back of her bar stool, almost touching her. "I saw your picture in the newspaper with Zeke Woodlow."

Scarlet angled closer to the bar. "That was an impersonator," she said, trying to make light of it. It had actually been Summer, dressed in Scarlet's clothes, made to look like a groupie. Scarlet held up her empty glass to the bartender.

"I'll get that," Rich said to the man.

"No, thank you." She decided she didn't want this guy around, after all. She caught Stash's eye, then tipped her head slightly toward Rich. Stash headed her way.

"Mon petit choux," he said, nudging Rich out of the way to kiss her, a little longer than was necessary for the ruse, Scarlet thought, wondering what John was thinking of the scene. "I apologize for keeping you waiting, *ma chérie,*" Stash continued, nuzzling her neck.

"Don't do it again." She leaned into him as he slipped an arm around her shoulders.

Rich was resourceful, however, and undeterred. He turned his attention on Jessie. "May I buy you a drink, um, Jenny?"

Jessie used her little straw to swirl her ice, then she slipped the straw in her mouth and pulled it out slowly, getting his attention. "You know, Rich, I believe my daddy would get a kick out of you."

He looked ready to swagger. "He would?"

"In fact, he has a saying that would fit you to a T. He'd say, 'That poor Rich. He's got nothin' under his hat but hair.'"

Scarlet had to set her drink down before the contents sloshed over the sides. Jessie's handling of Rich showed she wasn't quite as naive as she sometimes seemed.

"Bitch," he said, low and furious. "You—"

Stash moved but was blocked by John, who snatched the glass out of Rich's hand and thumped it on the bar next to Scarlet's. "Time to find a new watering hole, partner," John said, clamping a hand on his shoulder.

Rich glowered, but he left without comment, just a surly look.

"Are you okay?" John asked Jessie.

"I'm fine. Actually, it was kinda fun." She grinned.

Scarlet waited for him to turn his attention on her, but he said good-night and left. She watched him walk out the door, cross in front of the window and disappear. Only then did she look toward the corner where he'd been seated. Three women sat there.

"He had been alone," Stash whispered in her ear.

Scarlet tried to calm her nerves. She didn't know what to think about John. Was he mad? Jealous of Stash? Hurt?

She decided to change her outward mood since even Stash had picked up on something he shouldn't. "Thanks for the rescue. But, *mon petit choux?*"

"My little cabbage." His eyes twinkled. Jessie laughed.

"I know what it means."

"It is an endearment." He lifted a loose strand of hair over her ear. "Perhaps you ladies have had enough excitement and would like to have dinner now. I have kept the table for you."

Scarlet decided if she didn't take some time to think about John and how to handle what had just happened, she would probably do the wrong thing—like go after him. "I've worked up an appetite. How about you?" she asked Jessie.

"I could use a big ol' rib eye myself. There's nothing like dispatching a preening bull to give me an appetite."

Scarlet smiled. She was glad they'd gone out together. Glad she'd gotten to know Jessie better. "Would your father really have said something like that?"

"Oh, yeah. He's full of 'em."

"What does he do?" Stash asked as they reached their table.

"He's a cattle rancher."

"Do you rope and ride?"

"About as easily as breathing," she said.

His brows raised. "I have never before met a cowgirl." He asked a passing server to bring two menus.

"I'm going to use the restroom first," Jessie said to Scarlet then headed toward the back of the restaurant.

Scarlet hoped Stash wasn't going to comment on John's behavior, but she should've realized she wouldn't be that lucky.

"So. Your sister's fiancé."

"Ex-fiancé."

"And you."

"No. Just in the same place at the same time."

"T'es menteuse, toi."

"I'm not a liar." Technically, they weren't together. They were just enjoying each other's company briefly.

"He did not take his eyes off you from the moment he saw you."

She wished she had a menu to hide behind. "I have no control over John's actions."

He only smiled. "Bryan would want me to tell you your meal is on the house."

"He's my favorite cousin," Scarlet said sweetly.

Stash grinned and walked away.

Much later Scarlet and Jessie shared a cab home. Scarlet lived only a few blocks from Une Nuit and was dropped off first. Jessie continued on after thanking Scarlet profusely for the amazing night.

Scarlet headed up her stairs, questions running through her head. Should she call John? *Was* he angry? Was it better just to leave it alone for now?

She turned the landing of the third floor and spotted John leaning against the wall by her door. She slowed, studying his face, trying to guess his mood. She wanted to see him flash those dimples, but she didn't think there was much chance of that. He looked…single-minded.

He didn't move an inch when she approached. Her shoulder brushed his chest as she put her key in the lock. "What would you have done if I'd brought someone up with me?" she asked mildly, her heart pounding.

"Discouraged him from going inside."

Scarlet opened the door and went in, leaving the door open but not inviting him. He came inside and shut the door.

She tossed her purse on an entry table then crossed her arms. "What do you want, John?"

"You know the answer to that."

"Short of *that,* what else?" The game, the words, excited her. She sensed he knew it, too.

"You ignored me."

"You ignored me, too," she said. It had confused her, angered her, that he'd spoken to Jessie at the bar but not her.

"You were cozy with Stash. I didn't want to interfere."

"Stash and I flirt with each other. It's nothing."

"I'm not telling you what to do or not to do. We don't have an exclusive relationship."

That hurt. Even if it lasted only the month, she'd thought it was exclusive.

"Well, fine, then. Because I don't explain myself to anyone." She turned away, not having a clue what to do next, just that she couldn't look at him.

"Look," he said, coming closer, touching her shoulder.

She pulled away.

"This is not going the way I envisioned," he said, frustration in his voice. "I just wanted to clear the air before tomorrow night. I don't think I could have even a pretend date with you with tonight hanging over us."

"What is 'tonight' to you? Why are you angry?"

"You think it was easy watching you flirt with that jerk at the bar, then again with Stash? And you knew I was there. I know Jessie told you. Were you trying to make me jealous?"

She spun around. "The jerk came up on his own," she said, breaking her own rule about not explaining herself. "I sort of encouraged him because I thought he might work for Jessie. Then he showed his true, sleazy colors and I beckoned Stash to come over. I flirted with Stash so that there wouldn't be a scene, but the jerk was also stupid and things got out of hand, anyway. Stash is a friend. That's *all*."

"You could've beckoned *me*," John said quietly.

He was hurt? That was what his problem was? She closed her eyes for a moment. Since he was being honest with her, she could do the same. "I hadn't turned around at the bar. I didn't know if you were on a date. I didn't want to know."

"I would've come to your rescue regardless."

"Your date would've been unhappy about that."

He set his hands on her shoulders. "Why would I have taken a date to Une Nuit? You told me you were going to be there. Why would I do that to you?" He didn't wait for answer. "What kind of man do you usually go out with that you would think me capable of such rudeness?"

"Obviously a different kind of man. I'm working on changing that, however."

She saw him relax.

"I don't intentionally hurt people, Scarlet. I *am* civilized."

Maybe on the surface he was. He'd been raised well, raised to be civilized. But at moments like tonight and during their private tryst in the country club conference room, he wasn't completely civilized. She liked that about him. She loved that about him. She'd fallen in love months ago with the kind man who'd been so good to Summer, but now she'd fallen deeply, hopelessly in love with this fascinating man who was more primal than she'd expected, more intriguing, more complex. She liked that he'd been waiting for her when she got home, wanting to clear the air, even if the answers to his questions weren't what he wanted to hear. She liked that he faced things head-on.

She laid her hands on his chest and looked him in the eyes. Words didn't come, however. After the longest thirty seconds of her life, he lifted his hands and pulled out her hair clip, letting her hair fall around her face, then combed it with his fingers. He cupped her head, moved toward her. She suddenly wished she'd kicked off her shoes so that she could rise up on tiptoe to meet him. The idea made her smile.

"What?" he asked.

"You make me feel so…female."

One side of his mouth lifted. "Is that a good thing?"

"No one has made me feel like that before."

"Again, is that a good thing?"

"Yes."

"How have you felt before?"

"I don't know. Equal. Or sometimes even dominant." She didn't want to tell him more, didn't want to give him ammunition for teasing her. She just knew she felt different with him.

"You've been plenty dominant with me." He was still holding her head, keeping her close. His breath dusted her face. His beautiful dark brown eyes were filled with tenderness and need.

She smiled wider. "Not in comparison."

"Ah." He brushed his lips over hers once, twice, once more. "You make me feel different, too."

His mouth finally settled on hers, his tongue seeking hers. She wound her arms around him.

So much for resisting each other.

With a sigh she gave in to her needs, not attempting to stop the urgent sounds that rose from within her, which seemed to arouse him more. He pulled her close, slid a hand over her rear, tugging her against him, letting her feel his need. She moved her hips against him, and his kisses turned almost violent. He fisted her hair and tipped her head back, ran his tongue down her neck, his fingers frantically opening the belts and buckles on her jacket then shoving the jacket off her, hearing it land with a quiet thud. She was starved for him, had never wanted like this before, as if she could die if she didn't have him inside her immediately.

He fumbled with her zipper, then her skirt joined her jacket, leaving her in a sheer black bra, thong and boots. Her nipples were so hard, they hurt.

He took a step back to unbutton his shirt, dragged the tails free.

"When I'm ninety I will remember this," he said, low and harsh.

She hooked her hand in his waistband and brought him closer, wanting him, needing him. She knelt before him, pressed her mouth to his fly, his hard need flattering and exciting. She reached for his belt buckle—

The phone rang.

"The answering machine will get it," she murmured, placing both hands on him, watching his head fall back as she traced the length and breadth of him through the fabric.

Second ring.

He dragged her up, flicked open her bra and sent it flying.

Third ring.

He cupped her breasts, thumbed her nipples, sucked one into his mouth.

Fourth ring.

"We're not home. Leave a message," came Scarlet's own voice from the nearby machine.

"Hi, it's me!"

Summer.

John became like a statue.

"You must be out having fun. Maybe I'll call your cell after this. Haven't talked to you for a couple of days, and I'm missing you. Although not too much," she added with a laugh. "Scar, I can't tell you how happy I am. How incredible Zeke is. You've got to fall madly, passionately in love. You do. It's…it's indescribable."

John straightened, stepped away. He shoved his shirt into his pants. His eyes met Scarlet's. She felt naked, clear to her soul. She couldn't read his thoughts. He guarded his expression.

"Zeke, stop. I'm talking to my sister."

In the background came the rumble of a deep voice, but the words weren't clear.

John scooped up Scarlet's jacket. She turned around, letting him help her put it on. She tugged the edges together before she faced him again.

"I guess I won't call you on your cell, after all. I have something else—" Summer laughed "—to do at the moment. I'll catch you later. Bye. I miss you."

Scarlet didn't know what to say. She couldn't joke

about it—it wasn't the least bit funny. And making light of it wouldn't sit well with either of them.

As a reminder of the predetermined parameters of their risky relationship, it had a powerful effect. Resistance was the key. This time they needed to try harder.

Maybe her disappointment and fears were in her eyes, though, because John laid a hand tenderly along her face. She covered it with her own.

"Tomorrow night?" he asked.

She nodded. She wasn't going to miss any opportunity to see him, be with him.

He left with no kiss, no hug. Just a long, thorough, final look at her in her jacket, thong and boots.

For the first time in her life, she wished she didn't have a sister.

Eight

Saturday refused to pass by with any kind of speed. Scarlet picked out what she would wear on her Woo U date, pressed it, chose jewelry, then looked at the clock. Noon. She had hours and hours to fill. Normally she would spend her free time sewing, but not now. She was too keyed up, plus today was glorious, clear and crisp. She decided to walk the three miles to the EPH building and work out in the company gym.

At the gym Scarlet pushed herself until every muscle burned, then she showered, wrapped up in a towel and settled in the sauna. She wished she could say that she'd been able to block John from her thoughts, but she kept seeing the look on his face—or the nonlook—as Summer talked to the answering machine, and how quickly he'd left.

Not that she would've wanted to make love after that, either, but—

No *but*. There was nothing either of them could've done differently. Fate had intervened. For a moment— just a moment—she'd even thought they might have a chance for a future together.

The sauna door opened, and Fin came in. She was entitled to use the private executive section but hadn't chosen to. The four siblings being put through the wringer for the CEO job were straining to keep their familial ties, but it was more of a competition now than a family unit.

"Good workout?" Fin asked as she sat a few feet from Scarlet.

"I pushed myself hard. I needed it. Hadn't been here for a couple of weeks. I'm sure I'll pay for it tomorrow, though."

"I just had a massage from Magda. See if you can catch her before she leaves."

Scarlet stuck her head out the door, caught an employee passing by and made her request then sat again.

"I'm glad to see you taking care of yourself," Scarlet said to her aunt. "I worry about you. Everyone's worried about you."

"It's only a year out of my life. I'll manage. After I win, I'll take some time off." She leaned her head back and closed her eyes.

"Did you go home last night or sleep on the couch in your office?"

"Office," she said lazily. "Everything going okay with the new project?"

"Everything's great."

"It's comfortable working with John?"

"It's fine." Scarlet didn't want to get into it with Fin. "It's business."

"And how's the new intern working out?"

"Good. Jessie's got the eye, Fin. I think you should seriously consider keeping her on. She'll land someplace. Might as well be with us rather than with a competitor."

The door opened. "Ms. Elliott, Magda says if you can come now, she can give you forty-five minutes."

"Tell her I'll be right there, please."

She scooted close to her aunt and tapped her arm, making her open her eyes. "We all want you to win, Aunt Finny. But we all want you healthy when you do."

"I'll be fine. Go."

Scarlet made sure an attendant knew not to let Fin stay in there for more than fifteen minutes. She would undoubtedly sleep, and could easily end up in the sauna for hours without anyone knowing.

An hour later, exercised, steamed and massaged, Scarlet headed for the elevator, feeling utterly relaxed. She would go shoe shopping, she decided. It would help her pass the time.

"Ms. Elliott," said a gym attendant, running to catch up and sounding frantic as Scarlet waited for the elevator. "Your grandfather would like to see you."

To her credit, Scarlet didn't groan, but thanked the young man and hit the up button. If she hadn't taken time to indulge herself with a massage she would've been long gone by now. She sighed at her bad timing.

Scarlet had been to the twenty-third floor surprisingly few times in her life, and not at all since she'd been working at *Charisma*. Her grandfather's office was furnished in an old European style, like The Tides and the

Manhattan town house, with antiques that he and Gram had collected on their travels. The familiarity should've helped to make her feel comfortable, but it never had, not when the man himself was present.

Had Gram told him about the note in the balloon? She'd said she wouldn't, but...

Mrs. Bitton, his assistant/watchdog, wasn't at her desk, and the door to his inner office was open. She peeked in.

He was on the phone and waved her in.

"I will be there in time," he said gently into the telephone. "And I'm not working too hard, *cushla macree*. In fact, Scarlet just stopped by, so I'm going to visit with her for a while, then I'll head home."

Scarlet shook her head at his ability to twist things for his own purposes. As if she would just stop by on her own. Ha!

She wandered to the opposite wall to study a painting of her grandmother as a young bride. Most of the Elliott women took after her in one way or another. In this pose, Scarlet could see Fin's heritage directly.

"Prettiest woman on earth," her grandfather said, coming up beside her.

"Inside and out," Scarlet said.

"Why she's put up with me all these years only God knows."

Her instinct was to agree with him. Because of that, she didn't.

"No comment, missy?"

She smiled and shrugged. He invited her to sit in one of the wingback chairs in front of his desk. Surprisingly, he sat in the other instead of taking his position of authority behind the desk.

Hmm. He must not want to intimidate her this time. What was going on?

"Would you like something to drink?" he asked.

Curiouser and curiouser. "I'm fine, thanks. What's up, Granddad?"

"Are you dating anyone in particular these days?"

She went on full alert. "Why?"

"Just making conversation."

"Since when?" The words slipped out before she could stop them. She regretted being sarcastic, but his question worried her. Did he know about John? No. He would've been direct if he knew.

His lips compressed. "Can't I be interested in your life?"

"So, you're just making conversation? You really don't care if or who I'm dating, right?"

"Of course I do." He shifted in his chair, obviously uncomfortable.

"What if I told you I was dating, oh, say, John Harlan?" Was she stupid or brave to test him? she wondered.

"I would know you were just being obstinate about answering."

"Why?"

"You would never betray your sister like that."

Betray. Of all the reasons she'd come up with for why she couldn't see John beyond this month, it had never entered her mind that she would be betraying Summer. Summer had given up John. Period. Scarlet hadn't stolen him. But Granddad would see it as a betrayal, probably because it would be like shoving Summer's nose in her mistake, a reminder of how much she'd hurt another human being.

"Nor would John go out with you," he added. "Don't even joke about such a thing. Although I was surprised to see you dance with him."

Scarlet couldn't find words to reply.

"Okay, I can take a hint," he said after a few seconds. "No personal questions. I called you up here because I've been hearing good things about the job you're doing. Competent and creative, that's what people are saying. I wanted you to know I'm proud of you."

Scarlet was stunned into further silence. She couldn't remember her grandfather ever doling out compliments to her. "Thank you," she managed to say, fighting back the sting of tears.

"I'm looking to you now, Scarlet. Summer has gone off to live in sin with that rock star. Even if she does come back to work, she'll probably have babies soon. I think you'll stick around. You're not one to romanticize."

He shocked her anew, this time in a way that ticked her off. Did he think he was complimenting her by saying such a thing? "Meaning?" she asked.

"I think you're part of the future of EPH. Like your aunt, you'll devote yourself to your work."

Considering that Fin was driving herself to an early grave, Scarlet didn't consider her aunt's devotion something to strive for.

Then there was the other issue, how Scarlet wanted to be a designer, not an editor. How long would she have to pay family dues before she could do what she wanted? How much did she owe her grandfather for raising her after her parents had died?

"You're not usually so reluctant to argue with me, missy."

"Maybe I'm growing up."

"That's a welcome possibility."

She kept her expression serious. "It couldn't be because you're getting feeble, and I'm being careful not to cause you to have a heart attack or something."

His fists landed on his thighs. "Feeble?" he roared.

She drew a deep breath, exhaled slowly. Now this was the Granddad she knew and understood. She decided to take advantage of his bluster to kiss his cheek and leave while she had the upper hand. "Let's do this again sometime, Gramps."

She heard him chuckle as she walked through the door. It made her smile—until she got into the elevator and remembered his comment about betraying Summer. Summer wouldn't see it as a betrayal, but she would surely be uncomfortable. Adults made choices in life. Scarlet could choose to make things easy on her sister or difficult.

Without question, Scarlet would always make things easy for Summer—even to the point of denying herself love and passion, something Summer had found, and wanted Scarlet to find.

But probably not with John Harlan.

John knocked on Scarlet's door at precisely eight o'clock. He was nervous—seventeen-years-old, first-prom-date nervous. Which was stupid, since he'd already slept with her. How could he be tense about seeing her, making conversation now?

Because he had to act like he *hadn't* slept with her. Hadn't seen her incredible body in its natural state. Hadn't seen her face as an orgasm overtook her. Hadn't felt her hands and mouth all over him, hot and curious....

Okay. That line of thought had to be stopped right now, or else when she opened her front door she would see a bulge in his pants and he'd get his hand slapped with a ruler or something. The thought made him smile. Sister Scarlet. *There* was an image.

He saw the doorknob turn and tried to get himself into character. First date… First date.

"Hello, John," she said, looking soft and sweet in her buttoned-to-the-neck, electric-blue dress, her hair piled on top of her head but still looking touchable.

"Hi." He handed her a single white rose wrapped in green florist's paper and tied with a satin ribbon. He watched her bury her nose in it and smile. She looked nervous, too, he decided. It relaxed him.

"Thank you," she said. "It's lovely."

"Are you ready to go?" he asked.

"Let me put this in water and get my wrap. Come in."

He almost told her not to bother putting the rose in water, then decided not to spoil the surprise he had for her later.

She was Scarlet but not Scarlet, he thought, as she disappeared into her tiny kitchen. Her dress wasn't as daring as she generally wore, except that long line of buttons begged to be undone. Her jewelry was understated, and not as musical as usual. A couple of bangle bracelets that made a little noise, diamond studs instead of intertwining hoops in her ears, but that was all.

"I'm ready," she said, slipping a silvery wrap around her shoulders.

Should he tell her she looked beautiful? Was that kind of compliment encouraged at this point? Man, he felt like a kid.

"You changed your perfume," he said instead. It wasn't her usual citrusy scent, but tempting nonetheless. He couldn't put a name to the fragrance. Not flowery. Not powdery. He'd smelled them all in his years of dating. Scarlet's was just arousing.

She smiled. He guessed it was a good thing, noticing a detail like that.

He rested his fingertips lightly against her lower back as they left her apartment. It was going to drive him crazy not being able to touch her more than that all night. But he planned to kiss her good-night at her door later, a decent kiss, not a polite, end-of-evening peck. He didn't care if it messed up the Woo U curriculum at that point.

While in the car, they didn't speak beyond routine chitchat about the traffic and weather. The awkwardness of knowing what they did about each other, and pretending not to, tied his tongue. Hers, too, he guessed.

He pulled into his underground parking garage, a luxury he paid a huge premium for.

"This is your apartment building," she said, sitting up straighter.

"Yes. I hope you like paella."

After a long, uncomfortable pause she gave him a tentative smile. "It's one of my favorites."

They rode the elevator in a silence that wasn't completely awkward, but unusual for them. He opened his apartment door and took in the scene, trying to see it through her eyes—the table set for a romantic dinner for two. The fireplace ready to light. Candles waiting to be lit. The scent of paella lingering, being kept warm in the kitchen.

"What a wonderful view," she said as if seeing it for the first time. She moved to the window.

It gave him time to turn on the stereo, set to play a classical guitar CD to match the dinner theme. He lit the candles, then the fire. He went into the kitchen to pour them some wine. By the time he returned she'd moved to the fireplace.

"Thank you," she said, accepting a glass.

He touched the rim of his glass to hers. "To the lady in blue. Welcome to my home."

She didn't make eye contact as she sipped. What was going on? Something was obviously wrong, but what?

"Have a seat." He indicated the couch facing the fire. "How was your day?" he asked when they were settled.

"Busy. I walked to the office so I could use the gym. Talked to Fin and my grandfather there for a little while. Went shopping. How about you?"

He'd spent the entire day getting ready for this date, worrying about things he'd never worried about before. "I spent the day awaiting the night."

Everything about her relaxed—her expression, her shoulders, her spine. Had she just been nervous? She couldn't possibly be more nervous than he.

Still the evening dragged. Where was the vibrant Scarlet he knew? Oh, she smiled, even laughed, and touched his hand across the dinner table with her fingertips, but their conversation was less than dazzling. He plied her with work anecdotes and celebrity stories, but she kept her distance. He told her that the vase of eleven roses on the table was for her, to add to the one he'd given her earlier. She thanked him sweetly.

He had no idea how to fix what seemed to be wrong.

When she excused herself to use the bathroom he pushed back from the table, moved to a cabinet and poured two brandies. To hell with Woo U. He wanted Scarlet back.

He heard a slight noise and turned. Scarlet stood a few feet from him—and it was definitely Scarlet. There was fire in her eyes, a flush of color in her face. She'd taken down her hair. She looked like every fantasy he'd ever had of her.

He started to pass her a snifter of brandy, but she held up a hand.

"I'm sorry, but this just isn't working, John."

Nine

Scarlet saw him retreat, his expression distant and self-protective. She hurried to assure him.

"No. Wait." She blew out a breath. "I shouldn't have said it that way. I meant that this…dating thing isn't working for me."

She'd tried all evening to just be his date, but she knew too much about him, wanted him too much. Loved him. And what was she doing, turning him into a better date for other women, anyway? How ridiculous was that?

He set the glasses on the table and took her hands. "Why didn't you say so earlier? I thought I'd really screwed something up."

"Well, actually, you had, but that wasn't the problem."

His brows drew together. "What'd I do wrong?"

"You brought me to your apartment on a first date."

"Where was I supposed to take you? We can't be seen in public."

"You could've gotten creative. You could've thought of someplace to go, something to do where no one would know us. We're not *that* recognizable."

"You're right," he said after a moment. "Bringing you here, especially when we already had memories here…"

"Exactly." She laid her hand against his chest and looked into his eyes. "But that's minor. Truly. Let's be honest. The real issue is that we both know that Woo U was only a ploy to keep us in proximity, an excuse and nothing more so that we could…"

"Sleep together."

She nodded. "We only have two more weeks until… Until. I don't want to waste that time going on 'dates.'"

He scooped her into his arms. She knew where his bedroom was, knew he was headed there. She kicked off her shoes along the way. He said nothing. Maybe he couldn't. She wasn't sure she could, either, she wanted him so much.

It had been nine days since they'd slept together. During that time they'd aroused each other to fever pitch twice—last night and at the country club the week before. This wasn't going to be slow or tender, and she didn't care. Except that sometime she wanted slow and tender.

He didn't wait for her to undress, didn't undress himself. In the bathroom she'd taken off her underwear. When he discovered that, he shoved his pants and briefs out of the way, and drove into her, filling her so suddenly and completely that she cried out.

"I'm sorry. I didn't—"

"It's fine. It's good," she interrupted in a rush. "I was more than ready. You feel wonderful. Incredible." She arched toward him as he moved, finding a strong, hard rhythm. Demand became need. Need didn't want to wait another second. Was that her making that noise? His mouth covered hers, open, wet. He changed the angle of the kiss, groaned into her mouth. She grabbed his hair as the climax hit her, no gentle buildup but a thunderous explosion, matched by him in sound and intensity. Life stood still. Life went on. Life suddenly had direction.

The two other times they'd been together were good. This was phenomenal.

This would never be matched by anyone, anywhere, anytime. She wasn't given to exaggeration, so she believed her own prophecy.

She wrapped her arms around him as he sprawled over her, taking off some of his weight with his elbows, but mostly lying on her like a warm, heavy quilt.

"That was quick," he said, his mouth near her ear.

"And good."

"And good," he agreed, rolling to his side, keeping her in his arms.

She snuggled close, savored the way he stroked her hair. The pent-up tension dissipated. He felt like home.

"Hungry?" he asked.

"Not yet."

"Want to sleep?"

"Hmm." She burrowed closer.

"Let's get undressed first."

She left her eyes closed as he unbuttoned her dress and slipped it off her. She didn't even have the energy to watch him undress. He pulled a quilt over them, wrapped her in his arms, ran his hands up and down her back, then over her rear, along her thighs. When he gently stroked her breasts, she wriggled.

"Relax," he whispered as her nipples puckered. "I just want to touch you. Go to sleep."

She laughed drowsily. "Sure."

He propped himself on an elbow, continuing his exploration. She opened her eyes.

"Spend the night, Scarlet."

"Okay."

His hand stilled for a moment, then journeyed on. A while later, his generosity accepted and enjoyed, she fell asleep in his arms.

He could get used to this, John decided, sitting next to Scarlet. They'd dozed for half an hour, showered together, then decided to have ice cream by candlelight in the kitchen. She was dressed in his robe. He'd pulled on boxers and a T-shirt.

"I would've guessed you didn't even own a T-shirt," she said, spoon in hand. Candlelight flickered across her face. "You look younger."

"Since when is twenty-nine old?"

"Since you dress like you're fifty."

"I do?" He set down his bowl. "In what way?"

"Your suits are boring. And your shirts. And your ties."

He felt too relaxed to take offense. "I think anything compared to your clothing probably seems boring."

"It's an observation, not a comparison."

"I've never felt a need to keep up with the trends."

"You should. You're supposed to be selling cutting

edge, whether it's products or people. You should look like it."

He'd never considered that. "What should I do?"

Even though she didn't rub her hands together, it seemed like she did. "Let me help you choose some new things."

"Put myself in your hands?" The image that came to mind had nothing to do with clothes, but rather the lack of them.

She set down her bowl carefully then moved over to straddle his lap. He was learning just how complicated she was. He'd always expected her to be a sensual, sexual woman, although he'd based that opinion on her reputation more than anything tangible. But he saw shyness at times, too, which surprised him.

This wasn't one of those moments. When it came to sex, she was bold and demanding, but not domineering. A partner in every sense.

"What are you thinking about?" she asked, planting little kisses all along his jaw. "You're so serious."

"Everything that should be at attention is at attention," he countered, with a smile. He had no interest in starting a conversation at the moment.

She dragged her fingers down his cheeks. "I don't get to see these dimples often enough."

"When a clock is ticking on a relationship, there's not much to laugh at." He surprised himself admitting such a thing out loud.

She kissed him, tenderly, chastely. "Let's go to bed."

They blew out the candles, set their bowls in the sink, turned out the lights. In his bedroom they got naked, slipped under the covers and held each other close.

"This is just about sex, John," she said finally. "We can't have more than that."

"I know."

After they made love, she fell asleep. He studied his ceiling for hours, as if the answers to his problems might be written there.

All he saw was that it looked very much as if an Elliott woman would break his heart, after all.

In the morning, her head on a pillow next to John's, Scarlet watched him sleep, his hair mussed, his beard shadowy. She'd slept until nine, not waking once. She couldn't remember a night when she'd slept so well.

Her eyes stung. Anything in life she'd wanted badly enough, she'd gotten, had worked hard enough to get. But no matter what she did in this relationship, she couldn't win.

Betray. Her grandfather's word echoed in her mind.

She eased out of bed, donned John's robe and headed to the kitchen. She hunted for coffee and filters, then fixed a whole pot, not knowing how much he drank in the morning, or if he drank it at all.

At the front door she looked out the peephole to make sure the coast was clear, then grabbed the Sunday *Times* from the hallway. She finished up the dishes from the night before and checked out his refrigerator for possible breakfast food, finding eggs, cheese and English muffins.

At about ten o'clock she heard water run in the bathroom. Curled up on the sofa, she was enjoying her second cup of coffee and the *Times* travel section. A few minutes later he emerged, unshaven but with his hair combed. He'd put on the T-shirt and boxers from the night before. She'd been afraid he would come out in khakis and a preppy sweater or something, dressed for the day.

He stopped in the doorway. A slow smile came over him. "Good morning. How'd you sleep?"

"On my side, mostly."

His smile widened.

"I slept really well," she said, moving her legs so that he could sit beside her, facing her. "And you?"

She offered her mug. He took it, then leaned over and kissed her, deeper than a peck but not an invitation to more. He sipped from the mug, resting his hand on her thigh, rubbing it through the fabric.

"I slept great, thanks. So, what do you usually do on Sundays?"

"If I'm at The Tides I go to church with Gram and Granddad. If I'm in town, I'm pretty lazy. Read the paper. Go for a walk. Have a late breakfast somewhere. Do some sketching and sewing. How about you?" There was so much she had yet to discover about him. She knew his body. She knew his scent, his touch, his laugh. But nothing about his routines, his likes and dislikes. His passions.

"I don't think any two Sundays are the same for me. I play racquetball sometimes, or golf, depending on the season. Visit my parents sometimes. Work at home or even in the office occasionally. Go for a drive. Would you like to go for a drive?"

She wished she could say yes. "Probably not a good idea, John."

His hesitation was barely noticeable. "Right. Well, breakfast, then. I'm pretty sure I have the makings for omelets."

"Do you cook?"

"A little. You?"

"Salads and eggs. And I reheat brilliantly."

"Took a master course in that, did you?"

She recognized the conversation for what it was—avoidance. They were painted into a corner. Don't get too close, learn too much, enjoy too thoroughly. Sex and inane conversation were apparently all they could have. They had to otherwise resist.

"Maybe I should shower," she said. "Then we can fix breakfast together. Then I'll go home."

We can't spend the whole day with each other. The words hung over them as if in neon lights.

"How about we shower together?" he asked, standing, holding out a hand.

Later, she argued against him driving her home. She could take a cab. He didn't think she should be seen wearing what was obviously an evening dress at noon. On the drive to her house he held her hand. She didn't pull away.

"Can we get together during the week?" he asked as they neared her house.

"Definitely. Let's talk later and compare calendars. It'd have to be at your place," she added. "Granddad seems to like being unpredictable these days. I never know when he's coming to town."

"Okay."

They had shared a long goodbye kiss before leaving his apartment, yet she hungered for another.

"Did you expect it would be this complicated?" he asked when they pulled up around the corner from her house.

She nodded. "I'm pretty realistic about most things in life."

"Are you having regrets, Scarlet?"

"None." *Yet.*

"Can I ask a favor of you?"

Her heart fluttered a little.

"If I can arrange a private consultation with my tailor, would you come along and help me choose some new things for my wardrobe?"

"Will you promise not to argue about my choices?"

"No."

She laughed. "Well, okay. That's fair."

"I'll call you later."

The long day loomed before her. She almost wished she'd taken the chance and gone on a drive with him. "Have a good day," she said, then looked around, not seeing anyone she knew. She opened the door.

He just watched her, apparently as tongue-tied as she by the necessarily banal conversation, then he drove off. She walked around the corner. Someone was sitting on her doorstep. She could see fabric through the railings but that was all. Then the person stood, not looking in her direction, as if giving up.

"Aunt Finny." Relieved it wasn't…well, almost anyone else, she waited as Fin met her on the sidewalk.

"I wish I looked that good without makeup," Fin said.

"Oh, right, like you're some old crone. You're only thirteen years older than me."

"That's a lot of years in prime-woman age. I hope you had a good night?"

Scarlet grinned. "I'm relaxed."

"Ah. Lucky you."

"Come inside," Scarlet said, heading to her private entrance. "What are you doing here?"

"Taking your advice. I went for a walk in the park. I've been calling you off and on to see if you wanted to have brunch with me."

"Why didn't you call my cell?"

"I did. It's turned off."

"Oh. Sorry." Probably not turned off but a dead battery, Scarlet decided. "Well, I had a late breakfast, but I'll be happy to keep you company. Did you see Granddad yesterday? He called me up to his office."

"I got the same order, but I had a message sent to him that I'd already left."

"I should've thought of that," Scarlet said, unlocking her apartment door. "I'm trying to figure out who's talking to him about me."

"What do you mean?"

"He said he'd been hearing good things about me. Called me creative and competent. How does he know that?"

Fin frowned. "I haven't talked to him about you."

"You think we have a mole? Someone who reports to him about the goings-on at *Charisma?*"

"Maybe."

Scarlet started to press the message button on her answering machine, then decided against it. Later, maybe. In private. She'd learned her lesson there. "Who could it be? And why is it necessary? Granddad has access to all financial information. Since he's only worried about fiscal profit to declare the winner of this contest, why would he need someone reporting behind the scenes?"

"A very good question." Fin paced the living room.

"I'm going to change. Make yourself at home." Scarlet hurried. She changed into jeans, a T-shirt and a leather jacket, then pulled her hair into a ponytail, added a little mascara and lipstick and was done. She could smell John's soap on her skin, and her body ached comfortably. One area where the man had above average creativity—and flexibility—was in bed. The aftereffects lingered.

"Do you want to go to Une Nuit?" Scarlet asked Fin as they left the house.

"I don't want to go to any family-run operation."

Scarlet smiled. "Hot dog and soda in the park?"

"Sure. Why not?"

A few hours later Scarlet dragged herself home. They'd listed every employee, trying to come up with the name of the snitch. She wished she hadn't said anything to Fin, who didn't need something else to obsess about.

Scarlet made a promise to herself that she would never let her job consume her life as Fin had—easy for Scarlet to say, she supposed, at this point. Maybe when things ended with John, she would dive into her work, too, and not come up for air for a long time.

She hit the message button as she passed by the answering machine, listened from her bedroom to a message from Summer saying she would call Scarlet's cell, four hang-ups, then one from her grandfather.

"Your grandmother and I are coming to the city for the week. She thought I needed to warn you, for some reason."

Scarlet could almost see him rolling his eyes.

"So, here's your warning, missy. We'll be arriving around four. Plan on dinner with us."

Another command performance. Scarlet looked at her watch. Almost four. She needed to call John, let him know….

Why? How would it matter to him?

You just want to talk to him.

Right. And wrong. She had a legitimate reason. They needed to coordinate schedules and see when she could help him with his wardrobe. And she'd expected to spend the night with him at least once. Now they needed a new plan. She couldn't stay away overnight with her grandparents there.

With that rationale in her head she picked up her phone. His number was still on the speed dial.

She hesitated. Why hadn't Summer removed his number? Would a psychiatrist say she was keeping her options open in case things didn't work out with Zeke? Even though she and Zeke were engaged, she'd been engaged before, to John, and that hadn't worked. Maybe Summer was having a life crisis—

Scarlet shook her head. Summer was different with Zeke. Openly happy. Relaxed. Excited. All the things she hadn't been with John, or even before John. Nothing was going to change there, even if Summer changed her mind. And John wouldn't want her back, anyway. Would he? No. Of course not.

She dialed his number, got his machine, but didn't leave a message. She didn't know his cell number.

The intercom buzzed from downstairs. Her grandparents had arrived.

Time to put on a happy face.

Ten

A few days later John stood by while Scarlet pulled item after item from his closet to make room for his just-delivered new clothes and shoes—although he suspected her reason had more to do with removing the temptation of his ever wearing his old stuff again. His new tux and five suits wouldn't be ready for a couple of weeks, but everything else they'd bought could be put away—shirts, ties, jeans, leather jacket, T-shirts, boots, shoes, other casual clothing.

His credit card statement now seemed in line with the national debt, but he had to admit he liked the new look, not flashy but up-to-date.

Not that he hadn't argued with her, starting with her wanting him to use a friend she'd gone to design school with instead of the tailor he'd used all his life, his father's tailor. Somehow—he still wasn't exactly sure how—she'd convinced him to give her guy a try, then decisions were made all around him for a while before he asserted himself with veto privileges and started offering his own opinions. He was happy with the end result, particularly after he finished trying on clothes, when Scarlet locked the dressing room door and they made love, their need to be quiet somehow intensifying everything—scents, sights, the silken feel of her skin, the force of his orgasm.

Or maybe it was the four walls of mirrors that had done that, especially as she'd stripped for him, and he'd had a view of her everywhere he looked, and from every angle.

He went hard at the memory.

"When do you have to be back at work?" he asked her now, coming up behind her in the closet, his hands on her hips, keeping her rear snugly against him.

"Same as usual. One-thirty."

It was the third time this week they'd met at his apartment at noon, and it was only Thursday. They'd also had two meetings at her office about product placements, plus that evening at the tailor's before she had to go home to have dinner with her grandparents. She had to attend the symphony with them tonight, then they were returning to The Tides tomorrow, just in time for the weekend.

Tick tock. His time with Scarlet was slipping away.

They didn't talk about the inevitable end anymore, apparently deciding separately not to bring it up. Sometime soon they would have to, though. Only twelve days until Summer's return.

He'd had lunch delivered before he and Scarlet arrived—corned-beef sandwiches and coleslaw. They sat at his kitchen counter to eat.

Scarlet held a dill pickle aloft. "Make sure you bag your old clothes and leave them with your doorman tomorrow. They'll be picked up around ten o'clock."

He was grateful he didn't have his new suits yet so he didn't have to donate his old ones. They were good suits, with life left.

"And when your new suits are ready, you'll give your old ones away," she added, using her pickle as a pointer.

"Who appointed you queen of my closet?"

She grinned. "Trust me. Once you've worn the new suits and gotten a hundred compliments in five days, you won't miss the old ones a bit."

"If you say so." He had no intention of getting rid of them, but she didn't have to know that. He was taking back a few of the things she'd tossed onto his closet floor today, too.

"Do you have plans for the weekend?" he asked. They rarely planned ahead, usually not even a day, as if they were afraid to. Afraid that they would plan then something would prevent it, which would be worse than not making plans at all.

"I have to make an appearance at JoJo Dawson's party Friday night," she said, "which starts at eight. How about you?"

"I have to be seen at Shari Alexander's opening at the Liz Barnard Gallery."

She frowned. "I didn't get an invitation to that."

"Maybe because at the last opening, you stole Liz's boyfriend."

She met his gaze directly then studied her sandwich for a few seconds as she held it near her face. "I didn't know he was hers. He sure didn't act like he belonged to anyone.

Not to mention he's twenty years younger than she is. Anyway, I wasn't doing anything but flirting a little, *after* he made moves on me. Besides, he was too fussy."

"Fussy?"

"And full of himself."

He wasn't sure what she meant, except they weren't compliments. "I take it I'm not fussy."

She almost snorted. "Hardly."

He wanted her to explain what she meant, but left it alone. They only had a few minutes left before they had to return to their offices. "Want to get together after our respective appearances tomorrow night?"

"Sure." She picked up their plates and carried them to the sink.

He stuck his hand in his pocket, toying with the item he'd dropped in there earlier. After a few seconds, he pulled it out and passed it to her. "In case you're done before I am tomorrow night."

She stared at the gleaming object while she dried her hands, which seemed to take an extraordinarily long time. Then she folded the towel precisely into thirds and hung it on the oven door handle.

"It's a key, Scarlet, not a branding iron."

She took it from him without comment as she edged around him, heading toward the living room. He would love to know what was going on in that head of hers.

"I'll see you tomorrow night," he said as she opened the front door. He wanted her to come back and kiss him goodbye. He stuffed his hands in his pockets, waiting.

She stopped at the door. Her expression seemed to say she wanted to give back the key. A key was symbolic of a relationship deepening in trust and intent, a sign there was a future. It wasn't true here, which obviously confused her, and apparently upset her.

"It's just a key," he repeated to her. "I'm trying to make things more convenient for both of us."

"You keep on thinking that, John, if it makes it easier for you," she said, then she left, closing the door quietly.

So, he really didn't have a clue about how her mind worked. She hadn't been focusing on the same issue at all.

But she was wrong about one thing.

Nothing was making this relationship easier. Absolutely nothing.

Although Scarlet had been taken—dragged—to the symphony and the opera since childhood, she'd never developed an ear for it, nor could she easily distinguish one composer from another. Except for Wagner, that is, especially his *Tristan und Isolde*. Selections from it were on the program tonight.

Still, she would've rather been at a jazz festival or enjoying the pounding beat of a rock concert.

Just before the lights went down she spotted her aunt Finny sitting a few rows ahead with Georges Caron, a French designer old enough to be her father. From their vantage point her real father and mother had a perfect view of their emotionally estranged daughter. Scarlet didn't catch her grandfather looking, but Gram's gaze returned again and again. Scarlet wondered if Fin would ever forgive her parents for forcing her to give up her baby long ago. She'd rarely spoken to them through the years, *Charisma* having become her baby.

On the other hand, Scarlet was glad to see Fin out and about, a rarity for her. Undoubtedly it was a work night for her, an attempt to woo Georges Caron into giving *Charisma* exclusive coverage of his next collection or something. At least it got her out of the office.

Woo. The word stuck in Scarlet's head, along with the other dilemmas crammed in there like a Pandora's box. John had given her a key to his apartment. He was falling for her, beyond sex, beyond their stated intent at the beginning of their relationship. She knew she had to give him up at the end of the month, because of Summer and family image and other things that separately didn't matter a whole lot, but together made it impossible for them to be together.

So…her big dilemma now was whether to end things early with him, before he got hurt, too. She would suffer at the loss of him, but she'd gone into the relationship with her eyes open to that potential. He hadn't. He'd thought it would be a purely sexual relationship, that his heart wouldn't be in danger. She sensed that was changing. Maybe he wasn't in love with her, but he liked her a lot. They had become friends as well as lovers.

It was a dangerous situation for both of them. How had he put it at the beginning—a game with potentially disastrous outcomes? She'd been led by her heart. His mind had presented a more realistic view of the future—then, anyway.

Could she give him up before she had to?

Applause erupted around her as the lights came up. Intermission already?

Georges stopped beside her grandfather's aisle seat and chatted for a moment. Fin stood behind him, expressionless. She wouldn't make eye contact with Gram. Scarlet hated that most.

The Frenchman moved on. It appeared Fin would, too, then she stopped next to her father and in a low voice said, "If there's something you want to know, just ask me. Don't recruit spies."

"I don't know what you mean," he said calmly.

"Liar," Fin fired back before she went to catch up with her escort.

Gram's hands were clenched. Scarlet laid a hand on hers, but her grandmother couldn't even smile.

"Want to attempt the line at the ladies' room, Gram?"

She shook her head. "I see an old friend. I'll go off and visit for a few minutes. Stretch the kinks out, then."

After she left, her grandfather turned to Scarlet. "Do you know what Finola was talking about?"

"Yes. Don't you?"

He looked away, saying nothing. Scarlet didn't know whether he was telling the truth or bluffing.

Scarlet wished John was beside her, holding her hand, defusing the situation. He was diplomatic. He would know how to change the mood. She was too emotionally involved and didn't dare get into it. Instead no one spoke the rest of the evening beyond necessary, polite words.

When she climbed into bed later, she eyed her phone. She knew John's number by heart now. She wanted to hear his voice, but needed to come up with a reason to call....

Food. Food was always a safe topic. She would ask him if she should pick up something to eat tomorrow on her way to his place. He would have appetizers at the gallery, but not dinner, and she wasn't planning to stay for dinner at JoJo's, just to have a drink and show her face.

She dialed. The phone rang four times, then his answering machine picked up. She didn't wait for the beep, but hung up. She glanced at the clock—almost midnight—and tossed the phone out of reach.

Neither of them ever questioned what the other had done on nights when they weren't together, but this was the first time she'd called and not found him at home.

Jealousy reared up. She tamped it down. He'd said they didn't have an exclusive arrangement, but she didn't buy it. He wasn't a player. But she was curious about why he wasn't home yet.

Of course, she had no business calling him at midnight on a work night, when most people were sleeping, and especially to ask a question she could talk to him about the next day. He would see through her ploy. It didn't matter. She didn't care. Let him think what he would.

The phone rang. She leaped across the bed to grab it.

"Hey!" Summer said. "Where've you been all night? I've been calling for hours."

Scarlet settled into her pillows, the phone tucked between her shoulder and ear as she adjusted the bedding. Her disappointment that it wasn't John disappeared. "At the symphony with the Grands. What's up?"

"I just wanted to let you know that we're coming home a day early. The twenty-eighth instead of the twenty-ninth."

One less night. "How come?"

"I'm homesick."

"Really?"

Summer laughed. "No. Well, kind of. Zeke's got a meeting in New York on the twenty-ninth. This is not for public broadcast yet, but he's going to do the music and lyrics for a rock musical."

"Good for him!"

"We think so, too, especially since it means we'd get to live close to home."

"You're going to live together?" Scarlet had assumed they would, but having it confirmed—

"Well, yes. What did you think?"

"Are you coming back to work?" She recalled her grandfather assuming Summer wouldn't return to the job, and had wondered, herself.

"I don't know yet. I'm still figuring things out. Scar?"

"What?"

"You've seemed really distracted every time I've talked to you. This whole month. Longer than that, even. What's going on?"

"Nothing worth talking about."

Static crackled in the silence. "When I get home, we'll catch up. When I can see your face, I'll know whether there's something I should know."

She was right, of course. Nothing Scarlet could say or do would prevent Summer from seeing into her soul—her broken heart at that point, since her relationship with John would have ended.

"Are you planning your wedding yet?" Scarlet asked, changing the subject.

"Not yet. We don't feel we need to hurry. Maybe at Christmas."

"You'll want the fairy tale, I think. It takes time to plan."

"You'll design my dress, won't you?"

Scarlet smiled. "I already have."

Summer's voice softened. "I love you."

"I love you, too," Scarlet managed to say before her throat swelled shut.

"See you soon."

"Okay. 'Bye."

Scarlet could never do anything to alienate her sister. Watching Fin tonight with Gram and Granddad settled that in Scarlet's mind. Family came first. Always and forever.

There would be another man to love someday, she told herself as she turned off her bedside lamp.

Then she lay there in the dark, alone, denying herself the luxury of tears.

Eleven

As director of sales for *Snap,* the celebrity-watcher magazine of the EPH empire, Cullen Elliott had worked closely with John for several years. Almost the same age, they also had a friendship unrelated to the business, having known each other longer than John had known Summer and Scarlet. The men golfed together. Challenged each other. Wagered with each other, too. John liked Cullen and was glad the friendship hadn't been strained when the engagement ended.

"I can't believe you beat me by thirteen strokes," Cullen muttered as they rode the elevator to John's apartment late Saturday afternoon after a long day golfing. "*How* long has it been since you played?"

John smiled leisurely. "I told you. The last time you and I played. October, I think."

"You didn't squeeze in a round or two while you were in L.A. last month?"

"Nope. But conditions weren't the best today."

"Don't be condescending."

John grinned as they exited the elevator and walked down the hall. Usually a prankster, Cullen had seemed to be forcing jokes all day, so John hesitated before he spoke again, not knowing whether he should discuss what he'd observed.

"You did seem off your game," he said finally. "And distracted. Woman trouble?"

"Women," Cullen scoffed. "Sometimes I wonder if they're worth the effort."

"Amen."

"Although I don't ever question it when I'm in bed with one."

John laughed. As he opened the door, an incredible scent rushed at him. Garlic. Basil. Something Italian.

Cullen sniffed the air, making appreciative sounds. "I hope I'm staying for dinner."

Scarlet must be there.

"Sorry, Cullen," John said, upping his normal volume. "Private party."

He heard a soft scampering sound and talked over it, hoping Cullen hadn't noticed. "I'll get that book you wanted."

"Don't I get to meet the chef?"

"I'll check." He walked into the kitchen and looked around. A pot of red sauce simmered on the stove, the source of the mouthwatering aroma. A salad was half prepared. And a pair of spiky black heels lay jumbled on the floor.

He heard a noise from the pantry and headed there, opened the door—

"What are you doing with my cousin?" Scarlet asked in a fierce whisper.

She was wearing a French maid's costume.

John's shock instantly became laughter.

"It isn't funny," she said through clenched teeth.

"From my vantage point it is." He grabbed and kissed her. "I'll get rid of him. Cool your jets, sweetheart."

He shut the pantry door in her face.

"She left a note. Went to the store," John said to Cullen as he passed through the living room on his way to his office. He grabbed a book from his desk. "Here you go. No hurry getting it back to me."

"Feels like someone's shoving a boot against my ass," Cullen said with a grin, heading to the front door.

"What can I say?" The maid costume stayed emblazoned in his mind. The short, short skirt, revealing long, gorgeous legs in fishnet stockings. The low-cut, lace-edged top, exposing inviting mounds he wanted to bury his face in. He could untie her frilly white apron, strip her to whatever fancy lingerie she wore under—

"I'm glad to see you've moved on, you know, since Summer."

John came to attention. "I've become a fatalist."

"Everything happens for a reason?"

"Something like that."

Cullen stared out the window for a few seconds. "Have you stopped loving her?"

I don't think I ever did love her. He didn't say the words aloud, but their truth hit him like a thousand-watt lightbulb. "As you said, I've moved on."

"Mind over matter?"

The way Cullen pushed the conversation, John recognized there *was* something going on with him. "You need to talk, Cullen?" They couldn't now, not with Scarlet trapped in the pantry, but... "We could get together for drinks one day this week."

"Maybe. I'll give you a call." He left.

John returned to the kitchen and opened the pantry door. "Your master awaits."

She eyed him coolly. "My master?"

"If you're the maid, that makes me the master, right?" John admired her in full light. He'd never known a woman with so many dimensions. And he'd never known one so playful, so willing to get into a role just for the fun of it.

He was tempted now to untie the lacy cap on her head and let her hair down. He reached for the dangling ribbons—

"Why didn't you tell me you were golfing with Cullen?"

He lowered his arm, stuffed his hands into his pockets. Obviously she wasn't into her role yet. "I didn't want to wake you this morning. You looked so peaceful."

"You could've told me last night before we went to sleep."

"I could've."

"But?"

"My relationship with Cullen is separate. I don't relate him with your family, even though he is. Why didn't you tell me you were coming over early tonight?"

"I didn't know until after you left your message on my cell, saying to keep the night open for you." She shrugged. "And I wanted to surprise you."

"Which you did." He trailed his fingers down her face, gently, caressingly. "Can I go out and come back in? Start over?"

"First you have to put on your costume."

"Costume?" He hadn't minded the other games, but he'd never had to wear a costume before, either.

"It's on your bed."

"What exactly am I?"

"You're a nineteenth-century duke visiting my master."

"Did I time-travel forward or did you time-travel back?" he asked, pointing to her modern costume.

She ignored his question. "Do you know how men of your stature were treated in the merry old days?"

"With more respect than today?"

His comment earned him raised eyebrows instead of a laugh, then she hooked a finger behind his belt and pulled him toward her. "When a titled man visited, the lady of the house was often sent to assist him in bathing."

"I was born in the wrong century."

Her smile was slow and sultry. "When there wasn't a lady of the house, often a maid was sent."

No joke came to mind. "You're going to…bathe me?"

She dragged his shirt from his waistband and slid her hands up his chest. "I'm going to feed you, then undress you, then bathe you, then have my way with you. And you have to promise not to tell my master, or I could lose my position."

He closed his eyes and enjoyed the feathery touch of her fingers against his skin, although he was more than a little stunned that she had willingly assumed such a subservient role. Another layer of her. Another fascinating layer.

"I think you should go change now, your grace," she whispered. "You can wait in the parlor. I'll bring you some ale to sip while I finish supper."

He'd rather hang out in the kitchen with her, but he acknowledged that anticipation was an appealing part of the game. He expected to stay aroused until she chose to do something about it.

He just hoped his costume wasn't too dorky.

The following Friday, Cade McMann, *Charisma*'s executive editor, stepped into Scarlet's cubicle just as she was about to head to a meeting. Noting Cade's distant expression, she said nothing, especially since he'd come to her. Usually he summoned her to his office.

"You seem to have more influence with Fin than anyone," he said in a low, brusque voice.

"As her niece, not as her employee."

"I don't care which role you assume—whatever works, as far as I'm concerned—but she slept in her office again last night. Obviously I want her to win the contest as much as she does. I stand to win, too. But there's no reason for her to sacrifice everything to it. Someone has to convince her of that."

"If you can't settle her down, Cade, I don't think anyone can."

"I've tried. Short of sending an armed escort to her office to take her home each night, there's nothing I can do. She's the boss. But I'm worried about her."

"So am I." She tapped a finger to her lips. "Maybe I should talk to Uncle Shane."

"They may be twins, Scarlet, but they *are* in competition."

He was right. "Back to square one."

"Just talk to her, please. Better yet, kidnap her for the weekend. Take her to a spa."

This would be her last weekend with John. Summer would be home on Monday. "I can't this weekend, but I'll try to arrange it for the following one."

"Good. Thanks." He turned to leave and bumped into Jessie.

"I'm so sorry," she said, her eyes widening.

Cade frowned.

Looking a little flustered, she turned to Scarlet. "John Harlan is in the conference room."

"Thanks, Jessie."

She hurried away after muttering another "sorry" to Cade.

"She's always hovering," he said, watching her leave.

Scarlet picked up a file folder and stood. "What do you mean?"

"Just that. And she's too eager to please. She volunteers for everything."

"The way our internship program is set up, she's allowed to float from department to department if help is needed, or if she wants to be involved in a particular project. She just has to clear it through me."

"Is she good?"

"She's a natural. As if she's had years of experience instead of just having graduated."

"People said that about *you*."

"They did?" She smiled, pleased. She didn't want to tell the boss to get out of the way, but she did have a meeting to attend. She held up the file. "Is that all for now?"

"Yeah. Thanks."

She was the last to arrive at the conference room, which was populated by most of *Charisma*'s department heads. She was not in charge of the project, so the discussion was being led by the managing editor and the art director.

Scarlet slipped into a chair. John, flanked by members of his own staff, sat across the table. She met his gaze briefly, saw a smile flicker in his eyes, then she tried to focus on the meeting. An hour and a lot of discussion later, the meeting ended. She had no official reason to approach him, plus he wasn't alone, anyway.

She'd been waiting all day for him to call and make plans for their last weekend together. He'd had a lunch meeting, so they hadn't even met at his apartment as they often did. But Summer would be home on Monday. That fact had to be faced.

Scarlet lingered near the conference room in hopes of catching him for a second, but his employees were on his heels and he only got to say a quick goodbye, then he was gone.

Fin was in her office, hunched in front of her computer. Scarlet considered going in and talking to her about getting away next weekend, but decided it didn't matter when she did that, since Fin probably had no plans to interfere with anyway. Scarlet would need next weekend away even more than Fin. A time to mourn.

She returned to her cubicle. It was almost four o'clock. She and John were bad about making plans, but this was ridiculous. It was their last—

She spotted an envelope on her keyboard, her name printed on it. She opened it, unfolded a sheet of ivory-colored parchment. The note was handwritten:

Good afternoon, Ms. Elliott,

Your mission, should you choose to accept it, will begin at 6:00 p.m. You will be picked up from your home and taken to a secret location, where you will be wined, dined and sublimed until Sunday evening. Bring only the basics; no finery required. Lingerie optional but not preferred.

This paper is encoded with a special substance that can read your mind. If you decide not to accept this mission, this note will self-destruct in ten seconds.

10…9…8…7…6…5…4…3…2…1…

See you at 6:00.

Scarlet smiled. A weekend. A whole weekend…
To say goodbye.

Twelve

"I know it's unusual to come to the beach this time of year," John said, following Scarlet as she stepped onto a weathered porch. The surf pounded softly. Clouds hid the moon. Distant houses were the only points of light, like earthbound stars.

"It's perfect," she said, leaning her elbows on the rail. "How'd you find it?"

He rested a hand on either side of her, spooning their bodies, sheltering her from the breeze. "Belongs to a client. He's offered it a number of times."

It was late. They hadn't rushed to get there, had even indulged in a leisurely dinner at a roadside diner about an hour out of the city as they drove up the sound toward Rhode Island. They'd lingered in the small, homey restaurant—their first and probably only restaurant appearance as a couple—keeping watch on the parking lot, checking out the new arrivals, even as it seemed an unlikely concern.

After dinner they made the decision not to talk about anything serious while they were at the cottage. Maybe on the drive back, but not now.

Scarlet straightened, forcing him to, and leaned against him, nestling in his arms.

"I haven't been to the ocean in so long, except for The Tides," she said with a sigh.

Until now they'd always been in a hurry, as if someone or something would tear them apart at any moment. For two days, however, they could relax and enjoy each other's company. It was probably a big mistake to end their relationship with a trip to paradise, but he felt entitled to the grand finale. It had been about sex these past weeks—intense, driven sex, with a few quiet or playful moments now and then. That kind of intensity was good in the beginning, but now…?

Now he wasn't guessing anymore. He'd come to believe that Summer hadn't broken his heart at all. Maybe he'd assumed it went with the territory of broken engagements, that he should have been brokenhearted. He *had* been surprised, disappointed and a little humiliated when she called off the engagement, but he'd recovered too quickly for her to have been the love of his life.

But *this* Elliott woman—this one was the heartbreaker.

"Congratulations, John."

He pressed a kiss to her temple. Her hair blew against his skin. "On what?"

"On graduating from Woo U, with honors." She turned to face him and looped her arms around his neck.

He'd been inspired to do the weekend up right, just now realizing he'd been arranging a honeymoon.

And a farewell.

"I think it requires a valedictorian's speech," she said, her eyes sparkling.

He kissed her slowly, gently, thoroughly, savoring the warmth of her mouth, the softness of her lips, the searching brush of her tongue. It was a luxury not to rush, to know no one could arrive unexpectedly or recognize them out walking tomorrow. They could pretend they were a normal couple for once—except they would wear ball caps and sunglasses as a precaution.

"Ah, the ol' actions-speak-louder-than-words speech," she said, snuggling against him, shivering.

"A month in the making. Let's go inside."

The house was typical of seaside cottages, with a nautical theme and blue-and-white decor. Seashells decorated lamp bases and a mirror frame. Interesting glass containers held more, here in the living room, and everywhere, even the bathrooms. The master bedroom's French doors allowed a view of the ocean from the bed. The bathroom held a claw-footed tub with showerhead, and a wraparound curtain on a track.

"Would you like to take a bath?" he asked, still holding her hand.

"Sure."

"Go ahead. I have things to do."

She patted his chest, smiling. "I may have to change your grad status to magna cum laude."

"That would seem to require a more elevated speech."

"Oh, definitely. One that lasts for hours."

"I'll see what I can do."

She laid her hands against his face and kissed him. When she backed away, her eyes weren't smiling anymore but shimmering with something else he could only guess at….

That she didn't want to give up this relationship, either.

Scarlet had debated about what nightgown to bring. Although he'd said in his note that lingerie was optional but not preferable, she'd considered bringing none, then decided that she wanted to tease him with something red and lacy, a reminder. She'd chosen a long gown, which covered her, yet didn't. She'd never felt so voluptuous, her skin warm and damp from the bath, her breasts barely contained by the gown's deep neckline.

Silk brushed her body like a lover's caress as she returned to the living room. Candles were lit; the fire crackled. He'd plunged a bottle of champagne into a condensation-beaded silver bucket and draped a white towel around the neck. Two crystal flutes sat beside it, as well as bowls of strawberries and whipped cream. Quiet jazz played in the background. Pillows were piled on a quilt laid out in front of the sofa. A vase of yellow daisies topped the coffee table, which he'd moved aside. She recalled the white daisies in the master bedroom. He'd set a perfect scene.

How was she supposed to give him up after this? Maybe this last-hurrah weekend was a big mistake. Maybe they should've just kept everything simple. Focused only on the sex. Gotten that out of their systems.

Too late now.

"Did you do all this?" she asked as he came toward her.

He nodded. "I had the refrigerator stocked, too." He cupped her shoulders. "You've never looked more beautiful. And that's saying something."

"You're looking pretty good yourself." She admired his black silk pajama bottoms, and the flesh otherwise revealed. And the sexy mouth. And the gorgeous brown eyes.

Even though the house seemed relatively isolated, he'd drawn the curtains, and she was glad.

"What's wrong?" he asked.

She shook her head. She couldn't ask him if they were making a mistake. She didn't want anything to ruin their time together. "We agreed we wouldn't talk about anything serious."

"Then you need to wipe that serious look off your face."

He was right. She owed him that, anyway. He'd kept his part of the bargain. So she smiled and stepped close and kissed his chest. She felt him inhale, slow and deep.

Guilt settled on her shoulders. She'd started them on this path by going to him. Whatever pain they endured was *her* fault.

"This reminds me of the first time," he said quietly, breaking into her thoughts. "You wore red then, too."

She liked that he remembered. "And you wore black." She slipped a hand down his stomach, his abdomen....

He sucked in air, captured her hand. "I don't want to hurry tonight. Tonight's about romance."

"And memories."

He was quiet a few long seconds. "Let's sit by the fire."

They fed each other strawberries dipped in the whipped cream, and sipped champagne, and touched each other with feathery strokes as the fire provided heat and mood. Words swirled in Scarlet's head, but none she could utter out loud. They were too serious. Too full of what-ifs. Too sad. She had to let the thoughts go, let him fill her world, this world.

He didn't seem in the mood to talk, either. When they weren't kissing, they stared at the fire, hands clasped. But desperation finally seeped in. She toyed with the drawstring on his pajama bottoms, loosened the band and slipped her hand inside. He stretched out and closed his eyes.

She tugged on the fabric, dragged it down and off him, flattened her hands on his shins and kept moving, along his thighs, over his abdomen, up his chest then back down. He arched his hips. She held her champagne flute aloft and dripped the cold liquid over him. He lurched up. At the same time she took him in her mouth, warming him, tasting the champagne…and him. He lay back down, making sounds of need as her tongue sought and savored.

Every muscle was taut. Nothing about him was re-laxed. She loved that she made him that way, and that he let her take her time. He made her stop now and then, drew quick breaths for a few seconds, then gave her freedom again for a while. He was a wonder of taste and texture. Heat rose from him. Control slipped away min-ute by minute, touch by touch, breath by breath.

He stopped her. Moved out of range. Dragged him-self up and leaned against the couch. She wished she could sculpt. She would recreate that beautiful, chiseled body still full of need. His muscles were bunched, tendons visible.

She moved closer, laid a hand on his thigh. "Let me finish."

He smiled slightly and shook his head. "I like this feeling. I want it to last. C'mere."

He dove his hands into her hair, pulled her close and kissed her, but it was such a little word for what that kiss was, all open mouth and inquisitive tongue and nipping teeth and hot breath.

"Stand up," he said, low and fierce.

She rose.

"Strip for me."

She let the music guide her. Without hesitation or shyness she moved, turning in a circle, her hips swaying, then finally letting one strap fall down her arm, then the other. Gravity pulled the gown to the floor. She stepped out of it then over his outstretched legs. He grabbed her ankles, applied pressure until she moved her legs farther apart, found her with his mouth and fingers, taking long strokes with his tongue, his fingertips igniting fires, tickling, teasing, letting her need rise, pulling away to let it ebb, then returning again and again.

When her legs started shaking, he pulled her down. She took him inside her, clenched around him. She closed her eyes and arched her back as he drew one aching nipple in his mouth, then the other, cradling her breasts in his strong hands. He was fast losing control, though, she could tell. And so was she. She ended up on her back, somehow, in a maneuver she barely knew happened, and welcomed his thrusts, responded with her own, called out her pleasure, heard his rise above hers. The duet their bodies performed reached crescendo, stayed there, stayed there, stayed there, then slowly, slowly faded.

The beauty of it all made her throat burn and her eyes well up. She wrapped her arms around him, imprisoning him, and refused to let go. They had been well matched physically, sexually, from the beginning. But not like this. Nothing close to this. This was what came when everything was right.

I love you. She said the words to him over and over in her head.

"Fire's dying," he said after a while.

Not mine for you. "We could just go to bed," she said.

"You go ahead. I'll put out the candles and take care of the food."

"We can do it together."

Naked, they moved around the room, eyeing each other, flirting silently. She tried to picture him in fifty years, his hair silver, his smile still wicked. A father. A grandfather. The image came easily. Too easily.

They turned out the lights, walked hand in hand to the bedroom and climbed under a downy quilt. His hands roamed her body, warming her, exciting her when she should've been satisfied.

"Thank you for this weekend," she said, her lips brushing his neck.

"You took the words out of my mouth."

Later she felt him drift into sleep, his body heavy against hers. Only then did she allow herself the luxury of a few tears.

Even so, she had no regrets—except for how it all had to turn out.

* * *

"We have to talk about it," Scarlet said as they drove across the bridge into New York City on Sunday night.

She was right. John wasn't usually one to duck a situation, but he'd been diverting the conversation whenever she even hinted that they should discuss the future—or lack thereof—during the drive home.

They would make love one more time. That was all he knew for sure.

Last night they'd gone to bed and only slept, something a normal couple might do but they never had, because they hadn't had time for such a normalcy. He figured tonight would more than make up for it, sexually. Emotionally, last night couldn't be matched. It had felt good to just sleep together, to wake up in each other's arms and linger in bed.

"So, talk," he said now.

"Summer comes home tomorrow. We agreed to end the relationship when she returned."

"I'm trying to remember the reasons why."

"You know why."

"I know in the beginning we said it was about sex. We figured a month of sleeping together would take care of that." He gave her a quick glance. "It hasn't. Or at least not for me."

"Meaning?"

"I don't want to stop seeing you. Why can't we still meet at my place whenever we can manage it?"

"For sex?" Her voice was strained.

"Not just that." He reached over to wrap a hand around hers.

"It's hopeless, John. We can't ever go public, so why drag out the inevitable any longer?"

"Why not?"

"Because it's too risky. Every time we're together is a chance for exposure. And I'm tired of all the hiding. The sex has been great, but as long as we continue with it, I won't date anyone else. That's who I am. And I'm tired of going places alone. I want a partner. More than ever now, I want a partner."

She shifted toward him, her expression fierce. "Last week when I went with my grandparents to the symphony, Fin was there. They didn't speak to each other, except for Fin to tell Granddad off. It was horrible. My grandmother was so hurt. I've been an observer of their estrangement for years, but never like that. That total public snub. I won't do anything that hurts anyone in my family. I couldn't live with myself if I did."

"How would our relationship hurt your family?"

"It could hurt Summer deeply. Don't you think people might think I had something to do with your breakup if we're seen together this soon after? I'm the one with the reputation, after all. It could seem like I'm rubbing Summer's nose in her mistake—a reminder of how she hurt you. It would be embarrassing for her. I would never, ever hurt her like that, or betray her like that."

"Then maybe you shouldn't have slept with me in the first place."

A few long seconds passed. "I know you're upset, so I'm going to forgive the fact you just put the blame all on me. I was the instigator, I admit, but we both agreed to the terms," she said tightly. "I'm upset, too. But we've been lucky not to be caught. We need to end it before our luck turns bad."

She was right. He'd argued the point because he wanted her to come up with a way for things to be different. An impossible wish.

During the drive they'd agreed she should spend the night with him. It meant her getting up very early in the morning to go home and change clothes for work, but it seemed the best course of action, the path of least possibility of discovery.

He pulled into his parking garage. They got their suitcases from the trunk and headed to the elevator. They hardly took their eyes off each other. He saw in her everything he felt—expectation, need, gratitude and…desperation. In the elevator she went into his arms, pressed her face into his neck then leaned back to look right at him.

He kissed her without restraint, without hope. The doors whooshed open. He would've picked her up and carried her, except their luggage would've gone down in the elevator without them.

He opened his eyes, took a step back…and spotted Summer standing in the open doorway.

Thirteen

Scarlet's world took on a dizzying slant. Her sister stared in horror, in shock, in disbelief. The doors started to close. John slammed his arm against them, keeping them open, then grabbed both suitcases and set them in the hall as Scarlet forced herself out of the elevator.

"Summer," Scarlet pleaded, her hands outstretched. "I can explain."

Summer's face was ghostly pale. She looked back and forth between John and Scarlet. "Did you just spend the night together?" Her voice registered an octave higher than usual.

"Yes, but—"

"Let's go inside," John said, interrupting.

Summer shook her head, took several steps back. "This is the secret you've been keeping from me?

Him?" She looked around wildly. "Was he the reason you didn't come home that night? *The same day I gave him back his ring?*"

"Please let me explain."

Summer held up her hands, warding off the words, then punched the down button. The elevator doors opened immediately and she stepped inside. "And to think I came home a day early because I missed you so much," she said to Scarlet. "And I came here tonight to apologize to you," she said to John, "for treating you so badly."

The doors closed and Scarlet's heart shattered.

"Come inside," John said.

"No."

"She won't be going home. You know that. You won't find her tonight."

"I can't be with you," she said. "I have to go."

"All right." He spoke gently but firmly. "I'll put my suitcase in my apartment, then I'll drive you."

"I'll get a cab." She pressed the down button again and again. "C'mon, c'mon."

"I'll drive you."

"I can't talk to you right now."

"You're mad at *me* for this?"

"No. Yes." She closed her eyes, put a fist against her chest, over her heart. "Both of us. We were stupid to take such a chance just to satisfy physical needs. Stupid, stupid, stupid."

He grabbed her shoulders. "It wasn't just physical for me. Except in the beginning."

What could she say? She didn't want him to know she loved him. She'd kept it secret all this time. She could keep it secret until it died a natural death. She owed Summer that much. "It *was* for me."

"I don't believe you."

"That's *your* problem." She needed to find Summer. To explain. To beg forgiveness. When the elevator opened, she grabbed her suitcase. He followed with his.

"Go away."

"I'm taking you home."

She stopped talking to him. Didn't speak all the way home. Got out of his car and shut the door without saying a word. Words couldn't solve this disaster.

Her apartment seemed cavernous. She looked into Summer's room, saw her luggage still unpacked.

She sat on her sister's bed, brushed her hands back and forth over the spread, then dragged a pillow into her arms and squeezed.

Everything hurt—her head, her eyes, her throat. A cannonball had made a target of her stomach. Her heart pounded a painful rhythm that she could hear in her ears and feel everywhere else.

All these years—all these damned years—they'd never let a man come between them. Some had tried to play games with them, but they'd been open and honest with each other, had avoided misunderstandings and arguments because of that directness.

As soon as she'd realized John was interested in Summer, Scarlet had avoided him, so much so that Summer had asked if she even liked him. At least she had been able to answer honestly that she liked him just fine but that three was a crowd. Still, Scarlet had fallen in love even though she'd fought it every step of the way. Shoved it into a box until that night at his apartment—that amazing night that she'd never dared to hope would happen.

She pushed Summer's pillow against her face and screamed into it. Why had she gone to see him that night? Why had she let herself believe it would be okay to console him, to offer a friendly face? She'd known. In her heart, she'd known nothing good would come of her seeing him alone.

And then she'd convinced herself she only wanted some good memories. Instead she'd hurt the person she loved most in the world, the one who loved her the most, too. Her sister, her best friend.

And it all could've been avoided if she hadn't been so selfish.

Scarlet looked around the bedroom, decorated so differently from her own. Summer's stamp was here—more feminine than Scarlet's. More homey. Her love of antiques reflected their grandmother's.

Will you ever be back?

Will you ever forgive me?

She swiped her wet cheeks with her hands then picked up Summer's bedside phone and dialed her cell number, knowing her sister wouldn't answer it. She waited for the beep.

"Summer—" her throat closed up for a couple of seconds "—there's more to this situation than what you're thinking. I'm not trying to excuse what I did, only to tell you why it happened. Please, I beg of you. If you won't see me in person, at least call me. I...I love you."

She cradled the phone carefully, tossed back her hair and went to her own bedroom, closing the door on the empty room. She wouldn't sleep, she already knew that, so she grabbed her sketch pad and curled up in her armchair, but it was as if the creative forces in her body had imploded, leaving only rubble.

She tossed aside the pad, dragged her hands down her face and leaned her head against the back of her chair. The phone rang. She jumped up, answered it in the middle of the second ring.

"Summer?"

"No, it's me." John.

Scarlet sank onto her bed.

"I figured you'd still be up," he said. "Want to talk?"

"What is there to say?"

"You need to give her time to adjust to the idea."

"If the situation was reversed, I wouldn't adjust."

"Summer will."

"Meaning Summer is a better person than I am." Like she hadn't always known that.

"I didn't say that. You would adjust, too, but it might take you longer."

Scarlet thought she heard a smile in his voice. How could he be smiling?

"But she's in love and happy," he continued. "And she loves you. It's going to be fine. No one else knows, and she won't tell anyone. Except Zeke, probably. You'll get past it."

"How can you be so sure? Why are you so calm about this?" Tears sprang to her eyes.

"I don't think it's worth getting worked up about."

"Not worth—" Scarlet couldn't finish the sentence. "Well, that's easy for you to say, John." Not worth it? "I can't talk to you anymore."

She hung up then curled into a ball on the bed. She'd

regretted some of her actions before—small regrets, like immature choices she'd made or her constant attempts to annoy her grandfather.

But all of them together didn't add up to this.

"Are you in mourning?" Jessie asked Scarlet the next day at work. "I've never seen you wear all black to work before."

Without having slept, Scarlet had gone into the office early, straight into her cubicle, and hadn't emerged.

"Did you need something?" Scarlet asked.

"Touchy," Jessie said, her brows raised. "This came for you. You've sure made somebody happy, to get so many presents." She set a Tiffany's box on Scarlet's desk then strolled off.

Scarlet had no interest in opening a gift from John. She set the box in her desk drawer and went back to work, wishing the time would fly and the lunch hour would come.

At some point during the night she'd realized there *was* someone she could talk to—her cousin Bryan, the only person she was certain could take secrets to his grave. He'd had plenty of opportunities as they grew up to tell on her for things she'd done, misadventures he'd somehow ferreted out, but he never had.

She planned to head to Une Nuit at lunchtime and talk to him, had already called to make sure he would be there. Not only would he keep her confidences, she could count on him for good advice.

All morning long she reached for the desk-drawer handle then jerked her hand away and focused on work again. Every time footsteps approached her cubicle she hoped it was Summer. Scarlet had called her office, thinking maybe she'd come back to work today, but her voice-mail message still said she was out of town.

Finally it was time to leave for Une Nuit. Gray skies and a cool spring shower dampened her hair and matched her mood as she grabbed a cab. When she walked into the restaurant her cell phone rang. She didn't want to step back out into the rain to talk, but she didn't want to miss a call from Summer, either, so she answered it.

"Hey. I hope I caught you in time." Not Summer but Bryan. It could only be bad news.

"In time for what?" She looked around, saw Stash, who headed toward her. "I'm standing inside Une Nuit."

"Damn. I'm sorry, Scarlet. I had to leave. I'm on my way to the airport."

"Something that couldn't have waited until after you saw me?" She was on the verge of panic. She'd needed to talk to someone, and Bryan was her only hope. "What could be so important it can't wait for an hour?"

A few beats passed, then he said, "I got a good line on a saffron plantation in Turkey."

Scarlet sighed. "Okay, I got it. It's none of my business."

"I'll call as soon as I get home, I promise. Or talk to me now, while I'm driving."

Stash stood patiently in front of her.

"I can't. It's too complicated. And too personal."

"I'll make it up to you. I'll call you from the road, if I have time. In the meantime, have lunch on me."

Like she could eat. "Sure. Thanks."

"Later, Scar." He hung up.

She tucked the phone in her pocket, exchanged greetings with Stash, then looked around blindly, wondering what to do next.

"You do not look well," Stash said, concern in his eyes.

"I'm okay. Just not sure what to do, since Bryan's gone." Eating alone was not an option. *Eating* wasn't even an option this time.

"Your cousin Cullen is in the Elliott booth. You could join him." He touched her arm. "At least have some soup. Ginger carrot, one of your favorites."

She nodded, too tired to make conversation. She hoped Cullen was in a talkative mood. She wouldn't mind just listening, being distracted.

"Can I join you?" she asked Cullen, forcing a smile.

"Um." He looked past her, then at her again. "I'm expecting—"

"Me."

From behind her, Scarlet heard John's voice, even imagined that she could feel his body heat.

"So? Three for lunch, eh?" Stash asked cheerfully.

"No." Scarlet stumbled back a step, bumped into John.

Cullen's cell phone rang. He opened the phone then frowned at whatever number was displayed on the screen. He said hello tentatively.

"I...I won't interrupt your plans," she said over her shoulder, feeling John's hand on her back, keeping her steady. She just wanted to fall into his arms. She wanted to be held, and comforted and taken care of and soothed. She'd never wanted that before, never needed to be treated like such a...girl. She even forgot Summer for a moment. She wanted John.

"What?" Cullen asked, his voice rising. "How is she?"

Scarlet focused on Cullen, on the alarm in his voice.

"Where'd they take her?…I'll be there as soon as I can." He snapped his phone shut and stood. "I can't stay."

"What's wrong?" Scarlet asked. Cullen was always in a good mood. Nothing ever seemed to faze him—until now. "Who's hurt?"

"No one you know." He dropped his napkin onto the table. His gaze sought John. "Sorry. I appreciate you coming, but I need to get to Las Vegas."

"No problem. Anything I can do?"

"I'll let you know. Thanks."

He didn't even say goodbye.

John, Scarlet and Stash watched Cullen jog out of the restaurant.

"I wonder if he and Bryan will run into each other at the airport," Scarlet said, feeling sorry for Cullen without knowing why. She'd just never seen him as upset as that.

"Join me for lunch," John said to Scarlet.

She shook her head.

Stash made a quiet retreat.

"We need to talk," John said.

"I can't." She took a few steps, then returned, getting close enough so that others around them couldn't hear her. "And don't send me any more presents."

He looked surprised. "I didn't send you a present."

Then who had? Summer? Scarlet needed to get back to the office. Open the box.

"Goodbye, John," she said, hoping he heard the finality in her voice.

If he said anything, she didn't hear it. She made her way back to her office, pulled out the box, yanked off the ribbon, lifted the lid. Nestled inside was a hinged jeweler's box, which creaked a little as she opened it. Inside was a beautiful gold choker in a modern serpentine design with red enamel accents.

She scrambled to find the card, found it tucked underneath the necklace.

> Just a little something to show you how proud I am for what you're doing—with your life and your work.
> Love, Granddad

Scarlet put her head on her desk and cried.

Fourteen

Summer stood framed in the hotel doorway, looking only slightly more rested than Scarlet had two days ago at Une Nuit. John was prepared to prevent Summer from shutting the door in his face, but she crossed her arms instead and glared at him.

"How did you find me?" she asked, belligerence coating her words.

It was the first time John thought the sisters seemed alike, the first time he'd seen real fire in Summer.

"May I come in?" he said, not answering her question. He'd pulled strings and greased palms to track down Zeke's Waldorf-Astoria suite.

"I don't think we have anything to say to one another," she said.

"Yeah, we do. It's not like you to jump to conclusions."

"Oh? I have concluded that you and my sister slept together the night we broke our engagement, and have continued a relationship ever since. Is there some other conclusion?"

"The night *you* broke our engagement," he said quietly.

Her face flushed. She started to close the door.

He stopped it. "Look, Summer, I didn't come here to rehash the past—our past—but because I'm worried about Scarlet. I would prefer not to have this conversation in the hall, but if I need to yell it through your closed door, I will. I figure if there were security people in your suite, they would've been all over me by now, so let's just be civilized and talk in private."

After a few moments she stepped back in silent invitation. The enormous suite provided an unparalleled view. He waited for her to be seated, then sat across from her. "Where's Zeke?"

"Out."

"You know, you're acting pretty self-righteous for someone who slept with another man while you were engaged."

"It isn't anything I'm proud of, and you know it. And I also didn't carry on for two months in secret. I told you right away. I also tried to explain. As soon as I met Zeke... You know all this, John."

"You know why Scarlet couldn't tell you about us."

"And you're looking for what from me? Acceptance? Approval?"

"I don't give a damn how you feel about me. I don't want anything for myself." He leaned toward her. "But you need to talk to your sister. She's falling apart. She's not sleeping. She looks...haunted."

Summer pushed herself out of her chair and walked stiffly to the window, but not before he saw concern in her eyes.

"Do you plan to continue your relationship with her?" she asked.

"All I want is for you to reconcile with her."

"Do you love her or were you using her to get back at me?"

He came up beside her. What he felt for Scarlet was more real and powerful than what he'd felt for Summer, but he wouldn't tell her that. "I've learned a lot about myself recently," he said instead, "and I've come to understand what must have happened to you when you met Zeke. I now know I wasn't as engaged emotionally as I should have been or I probably wouldn't have been content with your insistence on abstinence before the wedding."

"And my sister more than made up for that. A good substitute, was she?"

"None of this had anything to do with you." It ticked him off that Summer wasn't seeing the whole picture, but he didn't rise to the bait, knowing it was the only way for her to understand what was happening—that Scarlet needed her. "You learned a few truths yourself when you met Zeke. Do you regret anything?"

She shook her head.

"You caused a small scandal," he reminded her. He didn't need to detail what happened, but it sat there between them, still a little raw. She'd not only ended their engagement in less than three weeks, she'd taken up with a rock star, publicly, happily. It had been a lot for John to swallow.

"You don't think this would be scandalous, John? For

you and my sister to be together? Don't you know how that would look?"

"I'm only interested in getting the two of you back on speaking terms. Nothing else."

"She has hurt our grandfather so many times with things she's done. Not big hurts, mind you, but things done just to irritate him. This would be huge. He might not ever forgive her. And just when they're finally starting to get along."

"There is no reason for Patrick to ever know."

She went completely still. "It's over between you?"

"Yes." Scarlet would never have anything to do with him again. He knew that without a doubt.

Summer was quiet for a long time. John had nothing more to say.

"Does she love you?" she asked. "Does she know what you're willing to sacrifice?"

He slipped his hand in his pocket and fingered his house key, which she'd returned to him by messenger that morning. In the box was a tiny piece of paper. She'd written on it, "Goodbye."

"There's no sacrifice," he said. "It's done. If I can look past what you did, surely you can look past what she did. We were going to end it that night, before you came home. You should've never found out. She was insistent, even though I wanted to continue. She was afraid that someone would catch us, and she would never do that to you."

"I'll think about it," she said after a little while.

But John knew she would go see Scarlet and they would make up. Maybe their relationship would change some, but it had been changing anyway since Summer's engagement to Zeke. John hadn't fully understood the bond between twins before, but he did now. That sibling relationship was like no other.

The distinctive sound of a key card preceded the hotel door opening. Zeke Woodlow came in, saw them together and headed toward them. He put his arm around Summer then extended a hand to John.

"I hope you had better luck than I did convincing her to see her sister," Zeke said.

Any small irritation he'd harbored for the man dissolved. John liked his directness, as well as his obvious love for Summer. "I tried."

"She can be stubborn."

John refrained from saying, "She can?" He'd never seen her stubborn, or pushy, or demanding—all those things he enjoyed about Scarlet. "Those Elliott women," John said instead.

Zeke smiled.

John focused on Summer. "I wish you only the best."

"Thank you," she replied. "That means a lot."

John walked out the door and went home to his empty apartment, where every nook and cranny held a memory of Scarlet Elliott.

Scarlet pushed her sewing machine foot pedal to full speed. She was making new drapes for her bedroom, something that would suit the house from the outside but blend with the contemporary interior. This was the fourth and final panel. In the past few days she'd worked at *Charisma* all day then sewed at night until she fell asleep with her head on the sewing machine table.

As for food—what was that? Toast and tea was about all she could stomach.

She came to the end of the eight-foot-long seam, shoved the pressure-foot lever into reverse, then stopped and snipped off the excess thread, the motion automatic, mindless.

The ensuing silence was horrific. Her CDs must have played out. She rolled her head, trying to relieve the ache in her shoulders, then stood, intending to start up the music again.

Summer was standing just inside the doorway.

Hope gathered strength inside Scarlet, a whirlwind of optimism, a powerful need.

"I came to hear what you have to say," Summer said. "But you have to tell me everything. Don't hold back because you might hurt my feelings." She turned around. "Let's go sit in the living room."

They sat at opposite ends of the sofa. Scarlet didn't know whether Summer was calm or detached, but there was definitely a wall between them, one they'd never had before.

Scarlet didn't know where to start, then finally started with the most critical fact. "I've loved John for about a year now."

A shocked silence blared in the room as if coming from a loudspeaker.

"You have?" Summer finally said.

Scarlet nodded. "I'm not proud of it or happy about it."

"No, I don't suppose you are. But it explains a lot."

"You thought I disliked—" Scarlet began at the same time her sister said, "I thought you disliked—"

They smiled a little at each other. "We haven't done

that in a long time," Summer said. "So, you love him. How did you feel when I told you I'd broken off the engagement?"

"Upset. And confused."

"Why?"

"I thought you were acting without thinking things through, and that you were hurting him unnecessarily."

"You didn't think that now he would be available for you?"

Scarlet shook her head vehemently. "It didn't occur to me. He was in love with you. I never, ever let myself think I had a chance to have him. And I also thought you were just infatuated with Zeke—and the newness of sex. Then when you said you'd never really felt any desire for John, I was angry, too, because you'd been cheating him of yourself, not giving him everything. And he deserved everything."

Summer retreated a little. "You're right. So, actually, you should've been relieved."

"I only knew that he must be hurting. I went to see him that night. To tell him I thought you'd made a huge mistake in ending the engagement, then suddenly we were kissing. And then more." She stopped, breathless, then continued more calmly. "It was my dream come true. I took advantage of it, knowing I would only have the one night. I knew we couldn't have a future."

"Yet it continued."

"Not right away. Not until after you left the country and he returned from L.A. It just grabbed hold of us, Summer. We didn't seem to have any control over it. Like you with Zeke."

"I understand that."

"We decided to take the month you would be gone. It…it was supposed to be a physical relationship only."

Summer's eyes widened. "You never told him you loved him?"

"No. And because we couldn't go out in public, the relationship was more…intense, I think. There were no diversions, no normal dates. We were going to end it the night you showed up."

She nodded. "Now what?"

"Now, nothing."

"You aren't going to see him anymore?"

"No."

Summer went to stand by the window. Scarlet waited.

"Why not?" Summer asked eventually.

"You know why. Because we still can't go public."

"Why not?"

"Because there will be a scandal when that happens, and another scandal when it ends. I'm not putting the family through that." *Granddad just told me how proud he was.*

"Why do you think it would end?"

She'd returned his key. He hadn't called her or come to her to try to give it back. If he loved her, he would fight for her. "I just know."

"You know, Scar, if you'd just been honest with me from the beginning, we could've avoided all this."

"That's not true. You know it's not true. You would've been just as hurt and angry—maybe even more so. You would've hated both of us, John *and* me."

"I meant way back, when you first fell in love."

Scarlet joined her sister at the window. "How could I tell you? What was I supposed to say? He preferred you."

Summer pressed her fingers to her eyelids. "Maybe you're right. And maybe you're right about not telling me after the first night you shared. I certainly would have thought that John was using you to exact revenge on me."

"He wasn't."

"I realize that now." Summer stared at the street. A long time passed, more than a minute. "I think you should go after what you want," she said at last, her voice wavering just a little.

Scarlet felt her jaw drop. "You're kidding."

"No."

"How can I do that? What would everyone say? The Grands—"

"They always liked John."

"How do I explain it? People will talk. I'll need to have answers."

"The four of us will go out together. Be seen. Let them talk. Who cares?" Summer's whole attitude changed, from her posture to her voice. She exuded strength and certainty.

Hope returned to Scarlet with a vengeance, but practicalities still got in the way. "I can't do the public thing unless John and I have a future together. A long future."

"So find that out first and go from there."

"I can't believe how generous you're being. If the situation were reversed—"

"You would do the same thing."

Scarlet put a tentative hand on her sister's shoulder. "It was so hard keeping this a secret from you."

"Don't do it again." Summer's eyes welled. "I know a lot has changed for us, but nothing can destroy our bond unless we let it. Regardless, Zeke is a part of my life now."

"I know that, Summer. I do. I think I felt left behind. Maybe a little jealous. You were so in love and so happy. And I envied you leaving your job, even if it was only for a month. It was only for a month, right?"

"I don't know yet. I doubt it, though. I'm finally going to do it, Scar. I'm going to make a career as a photographer."

There were no more questions, no more revelations. They went into each other's arms and held tight.

"I love you so—"

"I love you more than—"

They laughed shakily.

"So, why don't you show me your design for my wedding dress," Summer said after wiping Scarlet's tears away.

"Have you set a date?"

"We're talking about one. But I'm willing to wait until it can be a double wedding."

More hope wove its way through Scarlet. A different kind of hope. One with John as the focus. "You'll want the big, splashy wedding, Summer. I won't."

"Yes, you will." Summer's smile was all-knowing.

"It's never been my dream."

"Until you fell in love." She hugged Scarlet. "Show me my dress. And yours."

She found the sketch of Summer's dress and brought it out to her. Scarlet didn't want to jinx anything by pulling out the sketch of her own dress—the wadded-up paper she'd rescued from her trash can at work with her impetuous design. She hadn't redrawn it on clean paper. Nothing was certain yet.

"Oh!" Summer traced the lines of the gown with her

fingertips as if the fabric were in her hands. "It's exquisite. And exactly what I want."

"I know."

Summer shoved her, and they laughed.

"I'll hire someone to sew on the beads and crystals, but I want to make it for you," Scarlet said.

Summer nodded, tears in her eyes. She grabbed Scarlet in another big hug.

"Can you stay tonight?" Scarlet asked.

"Don't you want to go see John?"

"Not tonight. Tonight I want to be with you." She stepped back and smiled. "And sleep."

"I'll call Zeke and let him know."

Scarlet wondered if they would ever have another night like this, just the two of them. Probably not.

The thought colored the rest of the evening, giving everything they said and did a bittersweet edge. Who could have predicted they would undergo so many changes in just a couple of months?

Where would they be a year from now? Would they even be in the same country? When Summer and Zeke decided to have children, would Scarlet even get to know them or would they always be on the road?

She pictured her sister pregnant, smiling serenely. Summer would take motherhood in stride.

As for herself, Scarlet couldn't bring up the picture as readily. Maybe because her future wasn't as settled as Summer's.

But that was all about to change.

Fifteen

The Elliott helicopter swooped over The Tides, preparing to land. Scarlet took in the vista from above—the enormous turn-of-the-century home rising near a bluff overlooking the ever-changing Atlantic. The elegant circular drive, so often filled with cars. Her grandmother's glorious rose garden and perfectly manicured lawn, fragrant and inviting. Many a game of hide-and-go-seek had been played in that garden and countless touch football games on the lawn.

Hand-carved stone stairs led down the bluff to a private beach where Scarlet and Summer had whiled away warm July days and hot August nights as they talked about boys and life and their parents, desperately trying to keep them alive as their memories threatened to fade.

Scarlet's relationship with The Tides was complicated. A haven but occasionally a jail. Gram the peace-keeper; Granddad the warden. Summer the diplomat, and Scarlet the rebel…until this past year, when she'd stopped waging war with her grandfather. It had felt good, too. Incredibly good.

She gathered her courage as the helicopter set down gently, then she thanked the pilot and battled the wind generated by the blades as she ducked to race across the helipad.

For the first time ever Scarlet had ditched work.

She ran into the breezeway and entered the house from the side entrance. Heading straight into a powder room tucked under the staircase, she brushed her hair, straightened her clothes then went in search of her grandparents, who were expecting her and had surely heard the helicopter arrive.

Her stomach hurt from stress and anticipation as she walked through the house, expecting to find them in the solarium enjoying the morning sun. They sat on a love seat, heads close together, speaking quietly. Maeve touched Patrick's face lovingly. He laid a hand over hers. Their tenderness after fifty-seven years of marriage was enviable.

Scarlet closed her eyes; drew a slow, deep breath; let it out just as slowly then walked into the room. "Good morning," she said, bending to kiss each of them. "Thank you for sending the chopper," she said to her grandfather.

"It sounded urgent."

"Have you not slept in a month, then?" her grandmother asked, concern creasing her face.

"I'm okay." Scarlet thrust a box at Patrick. "I can't keep this. It's beautiful, Granddad, and exactly the kind of necklace I would wear, but I don't deserve it. I don't deserve what it represents, what you said in your note. You won't be proud of me once you hear what I came to tell you."

He frowned. "You've caused no gossip since that hoodlum a year ago. And I've been assured that you've become invaluable to *Charisma*."

"Just because he rode a motorcycle doesn't make him a hood—" Scarlet stopped the automatic argument. She couldn't lose her temper now. "It doesn't have anything to do with my job," she continued, forcing herself into control, then remembering he had a snitch in place at the magazine. "Who's your source there, anyway? Fin hates being checked up on."

"Fin's paranoid."

"Patrick," Maeve chided.

"Well, she is. I don't check up on her. I've no need to. I can see the numbers any time I choose. I asked Cade how Scarlet was doing. At least he speaks to me. Finola chooses not to."

With good reason, Scarlet thought.

"Sit down, missy. Tell us what's on your mind."

She pulled up a chair, grateful to sit. "I've been seeing John Harlan."

Her grandmother's eyes opened wider, but that was her only outward reaction. Her grandfather's expression darkened, the calm before the storm.

"Seeing him? What does that mean?" he asked coolly.

"Dating him."

"Sleeping with him?"

"Yes." Okay. The worst was out now.

"For how long?"

"A month." She decided they didn't need to know

about the stolen night, the first night a month earlier. That could only hurt all those involved.

"Does your sister know?"

Scarlet nodded. "She wouldn't have, but she came home a day early and saw us together. We were going to end it that night."

Her grandfather shoved himself up. Scarlet stood, an ingrained response. She wasn't wearing heels this time, so she couldn't meet him eye to eye. He seemed to tower over her.

"I thought you'd grown up finally. How could you do that to your sister? Betray her like that?"

He'd used the word before—betray. Even though Summer had forgiven her, it still stung, especially since she'd worked so hard to change. *Had* changed.

"I couldn't help myself," she said quietly. "It's no excuse. I know there'll be penance to pay."

"Couldn't help yourself?" he roared. "Animals can't help themselves. The weak can't help themselves. You're a strong woman who knows the difference between right and wrong. This is wrong, missy."

"I know."

He walked away.

"I'm sorry," Scarlet said. "I know I've disappointed you. Both of you." She dared a look at her grandmother. "I didn't mean to hurt Summer. She's the last person on earth I'd ever hurt."

"But you did, *colleen*," her grandmother said.

She could bear being a disappointment to her grandfather—that was nothing new—but not Gram. Scarlet wanted to stare at the floor. Instead she kept her head up.

"Why are you telling us?" he asked.

Scarlet hated that she'd put that tone in his voice that said she'd failed him, had fallen short of his expectations. "Because I'm in love with him."

"You mean you have every intention of going public with this? Humiliating your sister?"

"Summer is fine with it. As for going public, I don't know for sure. I just wanted you to know, in case."

"Does he love you?" Gram asked.

"He hasn't said so."

"Are you looking for my blessing?" Granddad asked, as if dumbfounded. "You think I would—"

"Quit prowling," Maeve said, interrupting. "Sit yourself down. You're not helping."

"I should help this?" he queried righteously, but he sat anyway. "I should make her comfortable?"

"Yes, I do believe you should, dearie."

Scarlet was grateful to sit again. "I didn't have anything to do with their breakup."

"Of course you didn't," her grandmother said, patting her hand.

Scarlet grabbed it as an anchor. "I do want your blessing, Granddad. I don't know what will happen. Maybe all this would have been unnecessary. But I can't even begin to hope things can work out with John unless I know you accept it."

"Give my blessing, you mean."

She nodded.

"And if I won't?"

She met his gaze directly. "I won't see him anymore."

He sat back, his brows raised. "You would give him up?"

"I'm not the girl I was. I've grown up. I appreciate

all you did for Summer and me after Mom and Dad died. I'm sorry it took so long for me to show you."

The room held no clock to tick during the long silence that followed, but the sound seemed to reverberate inside Scarlet's head, anyway, a time bomb determining her future—she hoped. John still had to have his say.

"You have our blessing," he said at last.

As if a nuclear blast hit her, she fell into her grandmother's waiting arms, wishing she could control the relief that spilled out in huge, gulping sobs, but finally just giving in to the overwhelming emotions. She felt her grandfather pat her back a few times.

"You'll make yourself sick," he said, obviously uncomfortable with Scarlet's tears when he was accustomed to arguments.

He stuck a handkerchief in her hand. She grabbed hold of his hand, too, then shifted from her grandmother's arms into his. "Thank you," she whispered shakily. "Thank you so much. I'll try to handle it in a way you can be proud of."

"I am proud, missy. I've always been proud. You've got a good bit of myself in you. It's why we butt heads. I expect you'll go far in the company, maybe even run it someday."

Scarlet used his handkerchief to dry her cheeks and blow her nose, stalling. She tried to smile. They had, after all, taken Summer's request for a leave of absence well. "About that…"

He raised his brows.

"No matter what happens with John, my plan is to stay on at *Charisma* until the end of the year—when Fin wins the contest," she added pointedly. "And then I'm going to try my hand at designing full-time."

"You couldn't have saved that bit of news for another time?"

"Might as well put everything on the table at one time. Deal with it and move on."

"That sounds suspiciously like a motto of your own," Maeve said to him.

He smiled, then shrugged.

"You'll be wanting to take the helicopter back right away, *colleen*."

"Yes, Gram. Thank you." She stood.

Patrick stood as well, and passed the jewelry box back to her. "I haven't been more proud of you than now, Scarlet. Wear it with pride. My pride. You've become your own person. It needs recognition. No more tears," he added in mock horror.

She laughed. Then she left to find the man she loved.

Sixteen

Late that afternoon John closed his office door, shutting out the normal workplace noise, which seemed suddenly chaotic. He'd been sure he would hear from Scarlet as soon as Summer forgave her—or whatever they did to make things right again. He'd certainly expected their reconciliation by now. He didn't know what to make of Scarlet's silence.

He checked the time. She would still be at work, but just barely. He dialed her number, got her voice mail, waited for the beep. "It's John." Did he really have to identify himself? "Give me a call when you have a minute. Thanks."

If she didn't call back before he left the office he'd try her home phone, then her cell. He needed to know what was going on with her, wanted to tell her a few things, too.

His private line rang. He let it ring twice, his hand on the receiver. "John Harlan."

"Hi, it's me."

Scarlet. Message received. He dragged a hand down his face and relaxed into the chair.

"Thanks for calling." He held back from bombarding her with questions because he wanted to see her in person, to know for himself how she felt. He needed to talk her into meeting him somewhere. "Did you and Summer settle things?"

"Yes."

He waited, but she didn't add anything. "Well… good."

"John? We need to talk."

"I agree. That's why I called you."

"You—" A pause, then, "When?"

"Just now. Isn't that why you're calling?" he asked.

"No. I wanted to let you know I'm sending you an envelope by messenger. You can read what's inside and think it over and get back to me."

"Why don't we just meet?" he asked.

"Everything will be clear when you get the message."

At this point in their relationship she'd decided to play a game? Why wouldn't she just talk to him? "All right, Scarlet. I'll get back to you."

"One way or the other, please?"

He wasn't sure what she meant but figured it would work itself out. "Okay."

"See you later," she said, almost turning it into a question, but not waiting for an answer before she hung up.

He called the doorman in his apartment building to

say he was expecting a delivery and to call him as soon as it arrived. Someone rapped sharply on his office door, then opened it without waiting to be invited.

"Got a minute, son? We need to talk."

John stood to greet his father, aware of how ominous those words sounded, echoing his own to Scarlet. It was not the best day in his life.

Scarlet shook out her hands to help calm her nerves then strode lightly across the sumptuous hotel suite to the door. She viewed the room from the entry. The small fortune she'd paid for one night in the two-room suite at the Ritz-Carlton was worth it. A table for two was already set by a window overlooking Central Park. She'd arranged for a memorable meal from the hotel's award-winning restaurant, Atelier, everything from beluga caviar, to bluefin-tuna-and-artichoke salad, to herb-crusted rack of lamb with spinach-and-ricotta gnocchi, to the decadent final touch—warm molten chocolate cake with caramel ice cream.

It was a meal meant for a celebration. She'd even met with the master sommelier to choose wines for each course.

Now all she needed was John.

She paced the room, caught a glimpse of her reflection in a window in her fitted black sheath, black-satin-and-rhinestone high heels and her mother's pearl-and-diamond necklace and matching earrings. She'd never worn them before, had saved them for a special occasion. She couldn't imagine an occasion more special.

The mantel clock struck six. Any moment now, he would arrive.

She was scared and anxious and exhilarated.

She wandered around the room, moved dinner plates half an inch then back again, straightened perfectly aligned silverware, picked up a wineglass, held it to the light then set it down again in precisely the same spot.

She walked some more, stopped at a window. A siren blared, an everyday sound that pierced the quiet hotel room then stopped nearby.

In the sudden silence the clock chimed the quarter hour.

She went into the bedroom to find her watch, double-checking that the clock was right. It was.

Six-thirty came. Anxiety played hide-and-seek in her head.

Six forty-five. Worry joined the game.

The phone rang. She almost came out of her skin. He was delayed, that was all, and calling to say so.

"Hello?" She heard herself, breathless and hopeful.

"Miss Elliott?"

Not John. "Yes."

"Were you ready for room service?"

"I need a little more time." She'd arranged to call them when she was ready but had told them it would probably be about 6:15 p.m. "I'll get back to you as soon as I can."

"Of course, ma'am. Good evening."

Scarlet blew out a breath. Where was John? She had left nothing to chance, had even called to alert him about the envelope. Yet now she was left staring at the hotel door, willing him to knock on it, but only silence echoed back.

Seven o'clock came. Eight. She dimmed the lights and curled up on the sofa.

He wasn't coming. Apparently he'd thought about what she said in the note and made his decision. Except that he'd told her he would call, one way or the other, and he hadn't, and he was usually a man of his word. Maybe she had been too pushy, her expectations too high.

But he'd called her, too, wanting to talk. He'd said so. What did it all mean?

At 9:35 p.m. she cancelled room service and turned a chair to the window. Headlights dotted the nightscape as a steady stream of traffic passed below her. They blurred into ribbons of light, red one direction, white the other. Horns honked. Life went on.

But not hers.

Why didn't he want her? Was she too much trouble? Maybe she'd been too bold, undermining him as a man. Maybe he thought she was high maintenance, someone who brought too much drama into a life.

Okay, perhaps she'd stirred his life up a bit, but she wasn't exactly a drama queen. She hadn't changed him. He was still the cool, calm person he'd always been.

Maybe that was the crux of the problem. She was too intense. He was too calm.

Fire and ice. Good for a sexual relationship, but not for life.

She looked blindly around the room, aching disappointment drifting around her. How could he just blow her off like that? Okay, so she hadn't exactly encouraged him since Summer had discovered them, had actually discouraged him. But he was big on courtesy. He should have at least let her know he wasn't coming. He'd said he would. He was a promise keeper.

Unless he was hurt?

She laughed at the idea, the sound brittle, and wished she'd ordered the champagne to be delivered anyway, so she could toast her fertile imagination. She'd seen *An Affair to Remember* too many times, that was all. And she'd heard the siren earlier. It had stopped right in front of the hotel, hadn't it? Had it been an ambulance?

"Right, Scarlet. He was looking up at the hotel and was hit by a car on his way to meet you."

Frustrated, she walked to the window again and looked out, resting her forehead against the cold pane. She just wanted—needed—a reason for why he wasn't there, that was all. Because her imagination put him in an ER somewhere, bleeding, barely conscious, calling her name, since in some way it was preferable to him ignoring her.

And that was her wake-up call. She grabbed her things, then left for home, wanting nothing more than to curl up in her own bed, and never see the Ritz-Carlton again.

In her car she rolled down her car window, felt the chilly air against her cheeks as she drove, trying to erase the memory of the night. The short drive seemed infinite yet instantaneous.

She reached the town house, hit the garage door opener and saw the spot where she usually parked her car, gaping and empty—a glaring reminder of the state of her life.

Some welcome home.

John clutched a Glenfiddich on the rocks in one hand, his first of the night, and a ring in the other, not missing the irony of the déjà vu moment and wishing he was as close to drunk as the other time.

A small scraping sound made him turn toward the

front door. Something flat and white lay there. He slipped the ring into his pocket, walked over, picked up the envelope. Finally, Scarlet's envelope had arrived. Instinct made him open the door, because the doorman would've called first.

A woman stood at the elevator, her back to him. There was no mistaking her this time.

"Scarlet?"

She spun around. "I thought—" She hesitated, looking confused. "Your car is gone."

"It's in the shop." He waited for her to approach, but she didn't, which confused him.

The elevator door opened. She looked into the empty cavern then didn't step inside. The doors closed quietly.

He opened the envelope and pulled out a piece of paper. "Obviously we don't want the same things," she'd written. "Goodbye."

That was it? The big mystery in the envelope? She'd already said goodbye, when she'd returned his apartment key. So what did this goodbye mean? She'd changed her mind, but had changed it again now?

"Come in," he said.

"I'm comfortable here."

Leave it to Scarlet to make everything a challenge. She kept him on his toes, and fascinated.

John held up the paper. "I don't understand. What do you want that I don't?"

She pushed back her shoulders as if gearing for a fight. "I had *wanted* to continue our relationship."

"Continue in what way?"

"As we had. Just spending time together."

As they had? "In private?" he asked, bewildered.

"Snatches of time during the week when we can find it? Maybe an overnight on Saturdays? An occasional week-end away?"

"Yes."

He studied her. It wasn't what he'd expected. He'd thought she would either cut him off altogether as a sac-rifice to her relationship with Summer or demand more of him. At the least he'd figured she wanted the one last time in bed they'd missed out on when Summer had sur-prised them.

"Nooners?" he asked, stepping into the hall.

She flinched. "Everything the same as it was the past month," she said. "Except this time with everyone's blessings, which they gave."

"Even Patrick?"

"I think he's mellowing."

John didn't have time to consider the implications of that. "No," he said.

Silence stretched out for days, it seemed.

Finally, she jabbed the down button.

A door across the hallway opened, and his neighbor looked out, eyeing the both of them.

"Sorry, Keith," John said to the man, taking quick strides to get to Scarlet before the elevator arrived and she was swallowed up by it. His neighbor shut his door.

In a low voice he told Scarlet, "I'm not interested in that proposition, tempting as it sounds on a base level."

"I figured that out already. *No* has no alternate mean-ing. This conversation is over."

"Not even close. But unless you want my neighbors to hear the rest of it, I suggest you come inside." He put his hand on her arm, urging her toward his apartment.

"There's nothing more to say."

"There's a helluva lot more to say."

After a moment she went along, although jerking free of his grasp. She walked directly to his couch then didn't sit.

"May I take your coat?"

"I won't be here long." She crossed her arms.

"I'm missing a piece of the communication puzzle, Scarlet. You act as if I should've known what you wanted."

"If you'd shown up at the hotel, you *would* know."

"What hotel?"

She looked at him as if he'd lost his mind. "The Ritz-Carlton, of course."

"Of course," he repeated without any understanding. "I was supposed to be there, I gather."

She narrowed her gaze. "It was in the envelope."

He glanced at her note. Had she lost her mind?

"Not that envelope," she said. "The other one."

"This is the only one I've received."

"But…it was delivered five minutes after we talked. The courier confirmed it."

He stared at her, baffled. "At my office?"

"I told you it was coming." Frustration coated her words and stiffened her body.

"My father dropped by. He needed to talk to me about some family business, so we went to the bar next door. I called my doorman and told him to contact me when—" He paused. "I assumed you would send it *here*."

"I didn't."

He'd gone crazy sitting at the bar with his father, waiting for a call. "Sit down, please. Can I get you something to drink?"

She shook her head then perched on the sofa, her hands clenched on her knees. John sat in a chair opposite from her. He wasn't alone in his loss for words. A comedy of errors, he thought, but not funny at all.

"You're wearing one of your new suits," she said after a moment. "It looks nice."

Avoidance. She was trying to regroup. What was in that envelope, anyway? "You were right. I got compliments."

"Why are you still dressed up?"

He ignored her question. "What was in the other envelope, Scarlet?"

"A key card for a room at the Ritz."

"And when I didn't show up, you thought I'd left you high and dry? Do you know me at all?"

She looked out the window. "I didn't know what to think," she said into the quiet.

"Why didn't you call?"

"Because if you were intentionally ignoring me, I didn't want the humiliation."

"So you came in person instead?" He smiled at her, not quite following her logic but appreciating how much her emotions were involved.

She stood abruptly. "This isn't going anywhere. Let's just call it a day. A month. Goodbye, John." She headed toward the door.

"When I said *no* earlier," he said, following her, "I meant I wasn't interested in keeping the status quo."

She continued toward the door.

"What I *am* interested in," he said, "is a full-time, publicly acknowledged relationship."

Her steps slowed.

"I love you, Scarlet."

She stopped and turned around, her gaze meeting his, her expression one of guarded surprise. He caught up with her and slipped his arms around her, but still she didn't speak.

"This is the part where you say you love me, too." His heart thudded. He was taking a leap of faith, based on everything he'd seen in her eyes this past month, heard in her voice, felt in her touch. Still, he wouldn't know until she said—

"I fell in love with you a year ago," she said, her voice just a whisper, as if she were afraid to admit it.

"A year ago? But—"

She put a hand over his mouth. "As it turns out, you're not the man I thought I fell in love with."

A year ago. She fell in love with me a year ago. The unbelievable words kept repeating in his head. Then it hit him that she was speaking in the past tense. "Meaning what?" he asked.

She toyed with his lapels. "You were an ideal, and I loved the ideal without really knowing the man. I hadn't seen below the surface until this month. Now you're real. And now my love is real, too."

The world righted itself. He pulled her closer, needing to hold her, needing her arms around him, squeezing tight. She pressed her face against his neck.

"Do you want to know when I started falling in love with you?" he asked, loving the feel of her breath against his skin, warm and unsteady, hinting at intense emotions. "At the country club. In the conference room. When you stopped me from making love with you on the table. That hadn't been my goal when I got you in there. All I wanted was a kiss, but things escalated. You do that to me."

He stroked her hair, enjoying the soft sound of plea-sure she made as she snuggled closer. "There is much more to you than I'd guessed, and I want to know it all. I want *you*."

He kissed her, long and lingeringly, putting every-thing into the kiss that he felt, feeling everything back from her. Then he framed her face with his hands, keeping her close.

"I want you to marry me, Scarlet. Will you marry me?"

She smiled; her eyes welled. "Yes," she said, then repeated it in a stronger voice. "Although one little problem does stand in the way. Summer wants to have a big, splashy wedding. Those take a while to arrange."

"What do Summer's plans have to do with us?"

"She'd like to have a double wedding."

It didn't surprise him. The twin bond was a powerful force. It did surprise him that they'd discussed it already. "And you? What would you like?"

"I want to marry you, period."

"But you'd like to do the spectacle with your sister. The Cinderella thing."

"I promise it won't be a three-ring circus. It'll be tasteful and classy and—"

He kissed her, this time without restraint and with the intent of getting her to think about something else—him. Them. Now.

He lifted her into his arms and carried her to his bedroom, as he'd done the first night she'd knocked on his door. In his pocket was the ring, nothing as simple as a diamond. She was a complex woman who needed a different kind of engagement ring, something untradi-tional, something with flair.

He'd chosen it yesterday, had tried not to think about what he would do if she said no. He would've fought for her, though. Fought hard.

He wouldn't give her the ring tonight. Tonight he would give her himself, and let himself just enjoy her. Tomorrow, though, he would find a creative way to present the ring to her. His magna cum laude graduation from Woo U wouldn't go to waste.

"I love you," she said, reaching for him.

There was so much yet to say and do and discover. But it started and ended with one truth. "I love you, too," he said. "Forever."

* * * * *

MILLS & BOON®

*Super*ROMANCE™

MORE TO TEXAS THAN COWBOYS
by Roz Denny Fox
Home To Stay

Greer Bell is returning to Texas for the first time since she left as a pregnant teenager. She and her young daughter are determined to make a success of their new ranch – and the last thing Greer needs is a romantic entanglement, even with the helpful and handsome Reverend Noah Kelley.

PARTY OF THREE by Joan Kilby
Single Father

Ben Gillard finally has a chance to build a relationship with his son, instead of being a weekend dad. But he and Danny can't seem to find any common ground. Ben is surprised to find that it is the straitlaced Ally Cummings who can make them a family.

THE MUMMY QUEST by Lori Handeland
The Luchetti Brothers

Now that Tim Luchetti has found himself the best dad in the world, he needs a mum! Only, picking a wife for Dean is proving harder than he thought. But when Tim ends up in his headteacher's office, he decides Ms O'Connell might just be perfect.

ALMOST A FAMILY by Roxanne Rustand
Blackberry Hill Memorial

Erin can't believe she has to work with Dr Connor Reynolds – the man her family blames for what happened to her cousin. As well as that, she has to contend with her recent divorce and three children who don't understand why Daddy left. If only she could act as if Connor was simply another colleague…

On sale from 16th March 2007

Available at WHSmith, Tesco, ASDA, and all good bookshops
www.millsandboon.co.uk

MILLS & BOON®

Blaze™

ROOM SERVICE by *Jill Shalvis*

Do Not Disturb

TV producer Em Harris has to convince chef Jacob Hill to sign
up to her new show. But when she sets foot in Hush, the sex-
themed hotel where Jacob works, she develops an insatiable
craving for the sinfully delicious chef...

WHY NOT TONIGHT? *by Jacquie D'Alessandro*

24 Hours: Blackout

When Adam Clayton fills in at his friend's photography
studio, he never dreamed he'd be taking *boudoir* photos –
of his old flame! Mallory is just recently single, but luckily
for Adam, a blackout gives him a chance to make her forget
anyone but him...

HER BODY OF WORK by *Marie Donovan*

Undercover agent Marco Flores had ended up working as
a model. A nude model. He'd taken the job to protect his
brother, but he soon discovered the perks. Like having his
sculptress, sexy Rey Martinson, end up as uncovered as him...

BASIC TRAINING by *Julie Miller*

Marine captain Travis McCormick can't believe it when Tess
Bartlett – his best friend and new physiotherapist – asks for
basic training in sex. Tess has been working on her battle plan
for years, and its time to put it to work. She'll heal him...if he
makes her feel good!

On sale 6th April 2007

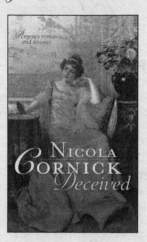

FREE!

2 Books
and a surprise gift!

We would like to take this opportunity to thank you for reading this Mills & Boon® book by offering you the chance to take TWO more specially selected titles from the Desire™ series absolutely FREE! We're also making this offer to introduce you to the benefits of the Mills & Boon® Reader Service™—

- ★ **FREE home delivery**
- ★ **FREE gifts and competitions**
- ★ **FREE monthly Newsletter**
- ★ **Exclusive Reader Service offers**
- ★ **Books available before they're in the shops**

Accepting these FREE books and gift places you under no obligation to buy, you may cancel at any time, even after receiving your free shipment. Simply complete your details below and return the entire page to the address below. You don't even need a stamp!

YES! Please send me 2 free Desire books and a surprise gift. I understand that unless you hear from me, I will receive 3 superb new titles every month for just £4.99 each, postage and packing free. I am under no obligation to purchase any books and may cancel my subscription at any time. The free books and gift will be mine to keep in any case.

D7ZEF

Ms/Mrs/Miss/Mr ....Initials ....
BLOCK CAPITALS PLEASE
Surname ....
Address...

....

....Postcode ....

Send this whole page to:
UK: FREEPOST CN81, Croydon, CR9 3WZ